THE MAN
WITH TWO
NAMES

Thirteenth Press
901 West Elk Ave
P.O. 611
Elizabethton, TN 37643
www.thirteenthpress.com

Ordering Information:
Quantity sales. Special discounts are available on quantity purchases by
corporations, associations, and others. For details, contact the publisher at
the address above.

Printed in the United States of America

THE SERTORIUS SCROLLS:
BOOK 1

VINCENT B. DAVIS II

The Roman Republic

The City of Rome

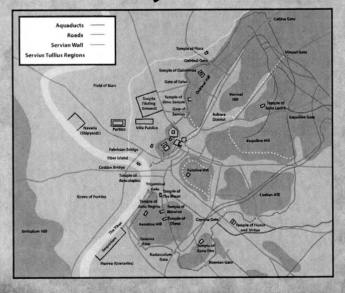

For Buddy Rowlette, Donald Davis, and Jimmie Hutchison

THIS STORY IS BASED ON A
REAL MAN AND REAL EVENTS

I am not sure I will live long enough to finish this account. My enemy surrounds me, and the time has almost come for another battle. But the gods have protected me thus far, and so with haste I will write my story to the best ability of a man whose fingers have clutched the hilt of a *gladius* far more than the wood of a stylus.

My name is Quintus Sertorius, and this is my account of the life and death of the Roman Republic.

I have devoted my life to serving Rome. I've spent years on the battlefield under the silver eagle, and I've given speeches and worn the spotless white toga in the Senate House. But for these last twelve years, I have been forced to fight against the only country I've ever loved.

I am now considered a rebel, an enemy of the state. Citizens are duty-bound to kill me on sight if able, and the heads of those who once called me friend are rotting on pikes in the Forum. The corrupt oligarchy that now calls itself "Rome" has destroyed every bust of me in Italy. They have burned my writings and slandered my name and those of the people I love.

I write this so you may understand how the Republic died, and I along with it. I am not so naïve as to believe that this account will undo any of the damage done to my reputation, but I feel obliged to tell this story as it truly occurred. History belongs to the victors, and I am not guaranteed victory.

Yet I want you to know, Reader, that I do not simply write this to tell you the heroism of dusty old men—least of all myself—but to inspire heroism in you. Because Rome needs heroes; the world needs heroes. I hope that upon reading this, at least one brave patriot will work to restore the Republic to what she once was.

I don't want anyone to believe this is simply the "memoir of Quintus Sertorius" or a vain attempt at restoring my legacy. For what is one man in the end? I am simply a fading shadow along the Forum of the great nation that was Rome. Instead, consider my work a eulogy for Rome and all that she could have been.

I swear to be honest with you about my own shortcomings and failures, if you in return allow me the opportunity to gain your respect despite them. I have entered the fray both with and against patriots, warriors, sycophants, murderers, and dictators. I will share their accounts where they are honest.

I must go. The horn is sounding in the distance. It's time for battle. Another battle. Whether on the front line or on the marble floors of the Senate House, I can hardly remember a life without bloodshed.

But it was all worth it—every ounce of sweat and blood willingly poured from this body and every grudging tear wrenched from this soul. I would do it all again, because there is no sacrifice too costly for the people and the country that I love.

Quintus Sertorius
678 ab urbe condita

PART ONE:

Tirocinium Fori, 647–648 ab urbe condita

"If history is deprived of the Truth, we are left with nothing but an idle, unprofitable tale." —Polybius

SCROLL I

By my count, I was born 628 years after Rome's founding—384 years after the establishment of the Republic. The gods blessed me with a strong father and a loving mother. My brother, Titus, was six years my elder, and though we were hardly the best of friends, we each made the other stronger and our problems always worked themselves out.

The gods were no less gracious in birthing me into a good homeland.

Have you ever heard of Nursia, Reader? Most haven't. Little of note has come from it. If you have ever heard anything of Nursia, you would likely know of its harsh winters, the snowfall that comes down in blankets from the Apennine Mountains, or the quality of our turnips (the only crops our hard, frozen soil can grow). Nursia, dull as it was, was my birthplace and my home, and I've always cherished it.

My first memory is of drowning, five years after my birth.

When I close my eyes, I can feel the freezing water enveloping me, the undertow pulling me further from the light. Sometimes the breath catches in my lungs as I remember how my body went numb and how I lost all control of my senses.

It was a small river that lay just outside Nursia. I went to it often for bathing, but I was forbidden to go there without my mother or my father's supervision. Yet, careless sort that I was, I decided I would go to cool off after playing with my friend Lucius. It took only moments for my feet to sink into the mud and for me to slip below the rapid current.

My thoughts were clear at the time. I remember them well. I didn't think of life or death, only that my father would be disappointed. *He will kill me if I make it out alive*, I thought. But, as it turned out, he nearly killed himself trying to rescue me. Lucius had run back to warn my father, and he bolted faster than the god of wind Zephyr to my rescue. The rapids nearly took him too, but he fought like a warrior until I was on dry land once more and the water pumped from my lungs.

The event had a lasting effect on me. I developed a stutter, which keeps the memory always at the forefront of my mind. Though I have remained afraid of water, the near-death experience forged in me a deep gratitude for life and the ability to draw breath that had been so difficult at the time. My father never mentioned it again. He could have punished me, but he knew that the shame I felt was greater punishment than the whip could ever be.

My father often taught through lessons rather than punishments. He was a man of strong character, often quiet and contemplative and direct in his dealings with others. Nursia had no real local government to speak of, but people often looked to my father as the governor of our little village. In all my years with him, I never saw him turn away a man in need. He devoted endless hours to supporting other villagers—usually in the way of offering a warm bed or a plate of food.

His devotion to Nursia and its poor never detracted from his dedication in raising Titus and me. He was deeply invested in our education and procured for us a Greek tutor for formal instruction. Whenever he could, he would insert lessons into our daily lives, teaching us history, languages, and most importantly how to be a man of character in a world where such men were sorely lacking.

It often amazes me that he taught us so much without saying a word. We learned more from him while out hunting than we ever did from that tutor.

All Nursians hunted, both for sustenance and trade. The mountain passes that surrounded us were swarmed with roe deer, red deer, and wild boar. Every chance he could, Father took us to those passes, where he taught us how to use a bow and how to defend ourselves in case we ran into a pack of wolves or the infamous Marsican brown bear. But most importantly, he taught us virtue.

I remember one such lesson in particular. On this particular occasion, the sun was beginning to set and the clouds were beginning to conquer the sky. All was made gray. In the distance I saw a deer, huddled and sleeping on the precipice of a mountain. I scaled the side of the cliff as swiftly as I could manage, leaving Father and Titus in the dust and hoping to impress them with my feat of daring. When I was within range, I notched an arrow and pulled the string taut. As I focused in, I noticed that the deer was a mother, feeding her fawn. I hesitated for a moment, but when I considered the admiration I would receive, I pulled the string tighter.

Before I could let loose the arrow, my father's hand dropped on my shoulder. I turned in consternation, but he only shook his head.

"I thought you would think I was brave!" I cried after him, following as he descended the cliff.

"You were brave to climb that mountain. But you were not courageous, son."

"Are they not the same?" I was frustrated, to say the least.

"No. It does not take courage to be cruel in a cruel world, Quintus. That doe will rear bucks that will feed your children, and your children's children. Sometimes you must sacrifice gain now for what is right and what is beneficial for others." Suddenly, I realized this was about more than deer hunting, and I said no more, even as we returned home with nothing at all to show for our adventure.

I know I have many contradictory qualities. My father introduced me to Zeno and the other Stoic philosophers, and ever since, I have tried to live by their creed. That being said, I have many shortcomings. I value sobriety but have been known to drink more than my fair share of wine—especially in my younger years. I value restraint but have always had a weakness for women. I value self-control but haven't always succeeded in restraining my anger. What good qualities I do have, I attribute to my parents.

———

By trade, my family bred horses and had done so for as far back as we could trace our lineage. Growing up, it was the greatest honor in the world to work on the farm with our horses. My father, mother, brother, and I all worked with the sun, without any off-season. When we weren't training a new stallion, we would scour the hills for packs of wild horses. I remember the joy that welled in me whenever father would take the rope from his satchel and, trying to contain his excitement, give us instructions for securing the animal. Afterward, we would often return home with a snorting, rearing stallion that would soon become another member of our family.

Perhaps these aren't the beginnings you would expect from the infamous traitor Quintus Sertorius. But I cannot imagine any other childhood. We hunted for our food, made our clothing from the pelts of deer and river otters, and traded with the other villagers. Life was simple.

Only my father's political connections made my upbringing unique. The Sertorii are an ancient family, and hundreds of years before my birth, when our people were assimilated into Rome, my ancestors developed relationships with the leading Roman families. Those relationships passed down to my father—a responsibility he took very seriously. His patrons in Rome single-handedly supplied Nursia with our grain, our olives, our grapes. By my time, most of the grain actually came from Egypt or Spain, but everything was circulated through Rome before it reached provincial villages like Nursia. Without someone important lending an ear, Nursia would go hungry.

In return for their patronage, my father served as these families' spokesman to the Sabine tribes. He was considered an elder in the Stellatina Tribe and therefore held a great deal of sway in how we voted. My first experience of Rome—all its power and glory—was of accompanying him and Titus to vote in the elections.

It was more than I could have imagined.

The temples and state buildings of the Forum were as tall as ancient beeches and seemed to my seven-year-old self to extend all the way to the heavens.

There were all sorts of new sounds and sights: lute players and dancers, important men in togas whiter than Nursian snow, and ancient columns even whiter than that. Rome was brimming with people. There were more people there than in a thousand villages like Nursia.

On every corner, merchants offered fresh, succulent vegetables and fruit. The streets were wide enough for chariot-like wagons to pass through. The rich were carried about in litters, and I craned my head until my neck hurt to see if I could recognize in any of them the famous generals or senatorial heroes I knew from stories.

There was also a foreign element that I'd never before encountered. People of all different nationalities lined the streets, some praying rhythmically in strange languages, others shouting at their companions. Scarlet rose petals lined the stone roads to celebrate the coming of another year.

Rome was simply alive. It was all moving; it was fluid. It operated faster and more vibrantly than Nursia ever had or ever would.

However, one thing impressed me more than anything else: the aqueducts.

"Look, Papa!" I pointed to the aqueducts, pulling him away from his conversation with an old friend.

"What of it?" Titus laughed at me. "So they have clean water. We have wells." But the convenience of having water close to hand, rather than having to carry it from far away, wasn't what amazed me.

"Yes, Quintus. They bring in that water directly from the Tiber.

It gives these people all the water they need." My father returned to his conversation, but only after giving me a smile that suggested to me he understood. The Romans had conquered the one thing I was most afraid of: water. They had tamed it, controlled it, bent it to their will. I had been astounded at Rome's sheer size and might, but this impressed upon me the belief that Rome was all-powerful. Rome could do things Nursia could never accomplish. Part of me believes this is why my father brought me with him, so that I could gain this knowledge.

So this was my youth. It was all I had ever experienced, known, loved. It was hard but peaceful, rough but nurturing, frigid outside but warm indoors. And it remained this way until my father fell ill.

Just before my seventeenth birthday, my father took ill. He was robust, tough, full of strength and endurance. But something violent took hold of him, and in a matter of days he lost control of most of his major faculties. He was confined to his bed, his hands so weak he could barely pull up his blankets to warm himself.

It shocked us more than anything. To me, my father seemed stronger than a thousand bulls, tougher than any gladiator. But the sight of him lying there did not worry me as it ought to have; the idea that he could die was preposterous. I knew he would recover.

My mother and Titus both felt the same way. Perhaps they had discerned the situation better than I, but nevertheless they too were shocked.

The only one who didn't seem surprised was my father. It was as if the gods had whispered in his ear beforehand to prepare himself. He seemed resigned to whatever fate demanded.

I realized how serious the situation was when my mother pulled me aside and said,

"Quintus, Father wants to talk with you—alone." Tears welled in her eyes. Love for my father alone caused me to walk into his sick-room; everything else within me begged me to run away.

"Come close, son." My father's voice was strained and weak. He'd grown thin and his cheeks were gaunt.

"Papa," I said, reaching for his hand.

"I have a question for you, my boy."

"Anything."

"Where is a ship safest?" he asked.

I thought about it for a moment. "The Mediterranean? No, the Tyrrhenian." My answer caught him off guard, and he struggled to laugh.

"No, no. The ship is always safest at shore." Well, that seemed rather obvious, I thought. "The ship is always safest at shore. But never forget, my son, that the ship is made for the sea. To explore, to discover, to protect, to provide. Every ship must sometimes leave the safety of its dock to serve its purpose in the world, to do as its nature bids."

"Yes, Father." He waited for a moment and then nodded his head.

"Come here." He pulled me down, and I touched my forehead to his. "Take care of your mother first, always. And when you marry, provide for your wife and protect her at all costs. When you have little ones, raise them to be honorable, sacrificing, resilient. Be a better father than I and my father."

"I could never—"

"Yes, you can. There is so much good in you." He released me and patted my cheek. He smiled for a moment and then became very serious. "When I am gone, I will leave this village to your care. You know this, don't you?"

My voice caught in my chest. I felt such a deep sorrow that it resonated as physical pain. How could he talk about leaving me?

"What about Titus?" I asked.

"Titus has a role to fill, and he will fill it well. But he is not you. You are not him. You have your own life to live, and I hope you will live it well." He rested his head and breathed heavily. "You must look after this village in all that you do. Empower it, serve its people. In this, I believe you will do even more than I."

I looked down and fidgeted, feeling like a child again. "You don't know that you are going to die, Papa." When I looked up, he was wearing a sad smile, and he waved me forward to kiss him.

"I love you, son." Such affections were rare and cherished in our home, and I understood how real his illness was. "Will you go and get your brother? I'd like to speak with him as well." I gave him one last nod as I left the room and went and did as he asked.

He died in his sleep that night. The gods took him while he still had his dignity and his honor, and for that I know he was happy.

Sometimes when I am alone and nature sways around me, I sit and reflect on my father. He told me I had a role to play. I sometimes wonder: if he could see me now, would he believe I have played my part well? With all my heart I hope so.

Everything changed.

Before I could even shave my mourning beard, our farm began to struggle. We had less success training our horses. We were all hard workers and knew how to handle our steeds, but Father had a special way with them.

In the months following Father's burial, Gaia evidently deemed that Nursia should face even colder conditions than before, and because of this, the village had a hard time producing anything for trade.

Titus married the daughter of a successful drover; her name was Volesa, and the dowry helped bandage our losses for a time. But it wasn't long before the strain began to wear on us once more.

Before I could even see what was happening, we began selling some of our furniture, some of the decor my father had collected during the military campaigns of his youth. The house seemed bare and cold—but then again, so it had ever since his passing.

It wasn't long until we faced other consequences as well. Suddenly our grain imports began to slow, and eventually they disappeared altogether. Because me father's friends in Rome hadn't heard from him in some time, so the imports had ceased to arrive. As a result, Nursia's economy struggled. There was little to trade in the markets, and so they stayed closed most days.

Slowly, we began to see more people living on the streets. Families huddling under wool blankets and asking for small jobs in exchange for money for food. My mother, Titus, and I all considered it our responsibility to serve the community—as Father had instructed— and so our atrium and guest bedrooms were often filled with our unfortunate neighbors. If we ever had anything left over, Mother and Volesa would take it to the other villagers who most needed it. We would often walk through the silent Sabine streets and offer condolences to those who had become impoverished. More than once we found someone dead from the cold or from a sickness borne of exposure. It was hard to forget those images, those sights, those feelings.

At this time, it was determined that Titus should leave for Rome. There is a process known as the tirocinium fori, wherein a young Roman client lives under the tutelage of his patrons. Generally, the process is intended to teach the ways of the Forum and so begin the young man's career. Titus feigned that this was his desire, but I believe he simply wanted to secure patronage and ensure that aid would be available to us all.

So, just after his wife gave birth to their first child—a son named Gavius—Titus packed his things and left for Rome. He shook my hand and told me to look after the homestead while he was gone.

Within six months we received a letter from Titus.

Beloved Family,

I write in haste, with news that I am sure you are not expecting. I have left the care of our patrons in Rome. I have proven unable to continue that path. I have failed you, and I am sorry. I am not fit for that life. Instead, I have made the decision to pursue a career in the legions. I have begun my training and sworn my oath. I'll earn respect through the ranks and begin a political career with the backing of my men.

Brother Quintus, I leave the care of my wife and child to you. Please look after them. Do all that you must to ensure their safety and provision while I am gone, as I know you will. If all goes well, I will visit at the beginning of this year when my legion settles in for winter quarters.

Your devoted son, brother, husband, and father.

Of course, we were all devastated. We couldn't understand it. We wanted to support his decision, his desire to serve Rome as Father had, but with Nursia crumbling, our fear overwhelmed our pride.

At first, I was so startled I did not understand the implications of his letter, and so my mother came to speak with me.

To my surprise she said, "I think you need to go to Rome, my boy."

"What? I cannot leave you. What about Gavius? How can he be raised with neither a father nor an uncle present?"

"We will be fine, Quintus. The gods will provide, as they always have."

"And what about Nursia?" I gestured to the doorway and beyond, where so many people were starving. "These people need me."

"And that is precisely why you must go." Even as she spoke I saw the life I had imagined for myself evaporating before my eyes. The life of a rural farmer, raising horses, hunting, establishing a family, and serving my village.

"But Titus ... if he couldn't do it, what makes you think I can?" I searched for other excuses. *Titus's path is not yours.* I recalled my father's words, and a chill shot down my spine.

"You are a leader, Quintus," my mother said. "You inspire others. You love Nursia. I know this, but by staying here you would be sacrificing the gifts the gods have given you. You would hurt Nursia if you stayed. You were made for something greater." She reached forward and grabbed both of my hands between her own. "I know it."

"I ... I ... I want to be like father. I want a quiet life!" I pleaded, as much with myself as with her. As much as a young man dreams of doing important things with his life—like seeking office or holding a command in the army—I had never wanted to make the sacrifices necessary to achieve such heights.

"I know you do. But sometimes men have to sacrifice their own peace to ensure that of others. And if you stay here, will you not be discontented? Knowing that you were destined for something greater by the gods and yet declined to answer fate's call?" She began to weep.

I knew she was even more conflicted than I was, and I knew her heart broke to ask this of me. I couldn't imagine her without either of her sons around the farm. But I could think of no other protests. I knew she was right. She always was.

"I will go," I said in a voice as frail as a whisper.

"You cannot simply go to earn their grain. Because one day you will die and your patrons will die, and we will be left in this situation again. You must change everything, Quintus. You must take the sword into your own hands." She kissed my forehead and I held her as she wept.

Two weeks later, I packed my belongings. In the meantime, I bade farewell to my neighbors and friends and told them to hold on to hope, for help would soon be coming. As I made my rounds, a change began in me: I realized that I could truly do something for Nursia.

I embraced Volesa and told her to be strong. I held Gavius and wept as I rocked him gently in my arms, thinking it a grave injustice that this boy would have no father or uncle to help him learn to walk.

My last farewell was to my mother. This was perhaps one of the hardest moments of my life, yet without it, I believe I would never have been able to handle the challenges I later faced.

"I love you so much, my son. You are so brave." She wept, and I understood this was as difficult for her as it was for me—especially since I was leaving at her bidding. She was making a sacrifice just as surely as I. I held her hands in my own. They were soft as silk but tough as leather; they were callused from grinding our grain, but they had helped birth our cousins.

I was nineteen—a man by all accounts—but before my mother I was still a child.

"Goodbye, Mother." I kissed her head, then turned for the door.

SCROLL II

As difficult as it was to leave my mother all alone, I had one solace: my dear friend Lucius Hirtuleius accompanied me to Rome. He had been a fixture in my life for as long as I could remember, and along with his twin cousins, Spurius and Aulus Insteius, we'd plundered our fair share of orchards and drained enough wine for all of Nursia. Now, Lucius's company was the only thing keeping my nerves relatively still.

As we began our three-day journey, a crowd gathered outside our homes to see us off. For the first time, people called me by my family name, Sertorius, rather than Quintus, my given name. Lucius, too, was forever after known as Hirtuleius, except by some of his closest friends.

We took the Via Salaria—typically used for the salt trade— straight for Rome, neither of us daring to look back. This was the same way my father and I had come years ago, but this journey felt so very different. The air heated up as we went, and our downcast spirits slowly warmed with it. Our destinies lay ahead and there could be no better future than to serve our country.

Each night we would find a safe spot along the side of the road and set up camp. I showed Lucius a few things, like how to start a fire.

"I wish my father had been around to teach me things like this," he muttered to himself. His father had given his life for Rome in a battle against northern invaders. Lucius had been too young at the time to be left with any memories of the man.

"At least you have a friend who can show you." I patted him on the shoulder.

"And I thank the gods for it."

In recent years, we'd grown even closer due to our mutual hardships. We had both been bereaved of our fathers, and we shared this common wound together. Unlike myself, however, Lucius had also lost his mother when he was no more than a toddler; she'd died giving birth to his brother Aius. When his father died, both Lucius and Aius had been taken into the household of their elderly grandfather Manius.

The pain he had endured—and endured with the resolve of Troy's golden walls—kept me moving forward when I faltered. Though I was his elder and often the leader of our merry little band, I looked up to him for how bravely he'd withstood such suffering.

That night beside the campfire, he asked, for what felt like the hundredth time, "Are you excited to get to Rome?"

"In some ways. I'm nervous though." I split a few strands of grass and idly threw them into the fire.

"I've always wanted to be a soldier. Remember when we were kids and we'd play legionnaires? You always wanted to be the general, and I always wanted to be the rank and file, like my father."

"I remember clearly." We both chuckled. "I believe that with all the experience we've gained from stick-swords, they ought to give you a promotion immediately."

Lucius smiled and looked up at the stars. "I will miss my brother though, quite a bit." He took a long pull of water from his wineskin.

"I know you will. But before you know it, you'll be back home. Either that or he'll join you on campaign."

"Eh, I hope not. He's smart, my brother. He should be a poet or a philosopher … something like that. Leave the swordplay to fools like me."

"*Bona Dea*," I punched his arm, and we fell silent, enjoying the insect orchestra. "Lucius?"

"Yes, *amicus*?"

"You know how I said I was nervous?"

"Yes."

"That's not really it. I'm just plain scared." I continued to pick at the grass and avoided meeting his eye.

He waited for me to look at him before he asked, "What are you scared of?"

"I'm scared that I don't have what it takes to make it in Rome."

"What? Quintus, how can you say that? Ever since I have known you—"

"Lucius … I know. I've heard it all before. I don't need to hear how successful I'll be. I just need someone to be scared with me right now." We looked back up at the Italian sky, before he reached over and patted my arm.

"I'm terrified," he said.

"Liar," I jested, ready to lighten the mood.

"Do you think I'll be able to join the army in the north? And fight the Cimbri?" he asked as he lay back against his bags. The barbarian hordes of the Cimbri and their allies had taken the life of Lucius's father as well as grotesque numbers of other Romans. Every soldier dreamed of defeating them, but dreaded an actual encounter with those hordes.

"I'm not really sure, amicus. You could be sent anywhere," I replied.

"I think I'd like to go to Gaul. All the mountains and trees and snow might feel a little bit like home … don't you think? Or maybe Spain would. You think I might be sent to Spain?" Lucius always had a habit of chattering when nervous, whereas I often clammed up. "I'd like that. But I don't really care where I am sent, as long as I have a sword in my hand. Manius says he'll disown me if I'm not campaigning by the *kalends* of March!" We laughed, knowing that the first of the month would be fast upon us. But Manius was a hard, unbending man and probably meant it. Given to illness and anger in his later years, he had once been an honored centurion for well over sixteen campaigns. As a result, he often treated his kin much as he had the soldiers he'd once commanded. At the time of Lucius's father's death, Manius was Lucius's only surviving relative—all the rest of their male family had given their lives for Rome in battle. So it made sense that Manius demanded so much of his eldest grandchild.

When finally we arrived in Rome, we knew we would soon have to part ways. And so we held off for as long as we could, roaming instead around the streets and reacquainting ourselves with the sights and smells of the eternal city. After all the time that had passed since I had last seen Rome, it made me dizzy to look up at the tops of those massive temples and state buildings.

Eventually, we knew we had to say goodbye. Hirtuleius was going to the Esquiline Hill where he was to find housing in a small *insula,* and he needed to get there before sundown. I, on the other hand, continued fumbling my way around those busy streets I would come to love until I found the palatine, where Gnaeus Caepio and the fortunate rich resided. I remember seeing people of all ethnicities moving busily like an army of ants, executing the tasks before them. Rome was pregnant with energy and vitality.

I arrived at the large *domus* only after receiving directions from a few busy passersby. I paused in front of a door painted scarlet and bearing two gilt wolf heads with iron rings in their snouts. My fist trembled as I reached up and beat against the door, knowing that once I crossed that threshold I would be stepping into my people's hopes and dreams.

An old slave answered and eyed me curiously for a long moment before speaking. "You're an *equestrian,* are you?" he said, looking at the thin purple stripe on my toga that designated my class. "And you don't look like a city boy. No, you're a farmin' lad, aren't you? What does an Italian equestrian want from my *dominus* on a Wednesday afternoon in August? We have three months until the elections, if that's why you're here." He shielded his eyes from the sun.

"Uh, no. I am a client of your dominus. This is the home of Gnaeus Caepio, is it not?" I stammered.

"Right you are! Certainly! Indeed! Come on in, lad. My name is Crito, and I am the doorkeeper of this house," the slave said, opening the doors wider and stepping aside. "Dominus doesn't typically see his clients after midday, but given that you've come here all the way from … where did you say you are from?" He cocked his head and gave me a discerning glance.

"Nursia," I replied, struggling to take off my muddy sandals.

"Nursia, ah? So you're a Sabine? I've heard many stories about your kind—hardy folk! I've heard it's mighty cold there, too. So are you a turnip farmer? Dominus often buys turnips in droves from that very city. Something about the soil there, I suppose," Crito rambled.

I'll admit I was shocked at how chipper this slave was. Later, I would become very fond of him, and even now I smile as I think back to his peculiar speech and amicable disposition.

As I followed Crito inside, the atrium stole my attention. Awestruck, I gazed around at the beauty of the bright frescos that lined the walls. Luscious azures, greens, yellows, and ochres danced across the walls and even up to the ceiling, telling the story of an aquatic adventure. In the center of the rectangular room was a small pool of water below an opening in the ceiling, and a thick stream of sunlight reflected off the shimmering water onto the walls, making the frescos come alive.

"Is it different than your Italian villa?" Crito grinned, as if he was very proud of the domus.

"It is more … colorful."

The slave let out a raspy laugh. "Very good! Yes, yes, the domina is quite particular about the way her home is decorated. She refuses anything less than the best. Even though the ground floor is the men's floor, she makes the entire house as elegant as any eastern palace. If you'll follow me, I'll take you to Caepio straight away."

I snapped out of my trance and followed him closely. We passed through the halls, the death masks of Caepio's ancestors looking on without emotion. Several slaves peered curiously at me from other rooms, and the big Gallic slave guarding the silver and expensive trinkets in the atrium flexed his muscles.

"Do watch out for the dogs—any suspicious movement or the command of the dominus and you'll be gnawed to pieces quick as Pan. Here we are." The slave halted. "Give me just a moment to address the master. If he is busy, he certainly will not appreciate the interruption." I wiped my damp palms on my toga and bounced anxiously on my toes as the old slave opened a folding wooden door and disappeared.

It seemed an eternity before Crito returned. "He's ready to see you, lad!" He leaned in and whispered, "He's a bit ornery when you first meet him, but that's just due to his weariness. His charms don't shine through right at the offset, but you'll come to admire him, I'm sure. I'll be at the door if you need me!"

Here it was, the beginning of my destiny—and the last hope for my mother and my people. Needless to say, I was anxious—still would be, I think.

When I entered, Gnaeus Caepio continued scribbling on an old piece of parchment. He sat slumped in an ivory chair much like the consular chair I knew he had been voted into thirty-one years earlier. He was old—older than I'd expected, even though I knew he was well weathered in politics, his accomplishments dating back to before my father had even donned his *toga virilus*. Still, though, I figured a man of his reputation and vitality would be imposing. But Caepio was wrinkled and drastically overweight, his hair desperately attempting to cover the crown of his head. It wasn't until he looked up that I noticed it: ice-blue eyes beneath two bushy white eyebrows, revealing a fixed desire, almost a hunger.

"What is it?" he sighed.

"I-I am a c-client of yours, Quintus Sertorius." In that moment, my childhood stutter returned uncontrollably.

"I receive my clients in the morning, as is custom. You can return to me tomorrow," he said, turning back to his writing.

"He is Proculus's son, Gnaeus," said a voice behind me. Though sound was soft, it nearly startled me to death. I turned to see the wife of Gnaeus Caepio, who then and always stood with an elegance and grace that remains unmatched by any Roman matron I've ever had the pleasure to meet. Her hair was dark and streaked with gray, her nose beaked, and her cheeks prominent. Though her face wasn't particularly attractive, she made up for this with an excessive amount of makeup and bright-red lip coloring. Her frame was thin. "Greetings, Sertorius. I am Caecilia Metella, wife of Gnaeus." She smiled and held out her small hand gingerly. I was unused to such formalities in Nursia and was confused for a moment before hastening to kiss it.

"Good d-day, ma'am."

"Gnaeus, you remember Proculus, don't you?"

"Yes ... yes I do." He leaned back in his chair and squinted, starting to put the pieces together. "What can we do for you, Quintus?"

"Call him Sertorius, Gnaeus. He is the leader of his family now, after all—not a boy." She placed a gentle hand on his shoulder. "Excuse me. I must go. It has been a pleasure, Sertorius." She left the room, the scent of her perfume wafting behind her.

"Very well, what can I do for you, Sertorius?" He rubbed his weary eyes.

"I'm here to learn the ways of the Forum, sir, and to offer whatever support I may to your cause."

"Ah yes ..." He stood and lowered his eyes, balancing two fingers on his desk. "Was it not your brother Titus who showed up at my door less than two years ago with the same proposition?" Suddenly he looked up, his blue eyes piercing mine.

"It was, sir." Really, I could say no more than that.

"For that insult alone, I should refuse you. But your father was a good and loyal client for many years, and for that, I will have you." My mouth opened, but I could find nothing to say. "Your brother developed a great many misconceptions about Rome and her politics. I hope you will not do the same?"

"No, sir. I have no conceptions *at all* about Roman politics. I hope to learn them from you and your family," I said.

"Good." He returned to his seat. "You've already proven to be superior to your brother, then, specifically in your demeanor. He had a way of … not understanding his place." I balked inwardly at the thought of being my brave and noble brother's superior in any way, but offered no retort. After all, my silence may have been the quality that impressed him. "I want to ask you now, young man, what do you know of me? Of my family?"

"I know that you rule Rome. You are in a close network with the Metelli, the Scaevolae, and the Aurelii Cottae, as well as other leading consular families in Rome. I know that you and your brother were consuls consecutively thirty-one years ago." With more agility than I presumed he had, he leaped from his chair and approached me.

"You mention my brother and I. Two old, dusty men. One of which is barely sane. Yet you do not mention my son. What do you know of *him*?" He locked eyes with me.

"I know that we share the name Quintus." I fumbled through my memories but could find little else.

"By the gods, you're right! And you had better remember that name, too. My son is going to be consul soon, and he will take Rome back to the days we only dream of now. Let me give you your first piece of advice, boy; stop worrying about old dates and old men. Those things mean nothing now. Focus on the future. That is what you must prepare for."

"Yes, sir, I can do that."

"Tonight, however, you will show respect to those dusty old men and play the sycophant to the best of your ability. My wife and I are hosting a dinner party for the families you mentioned, which means you will have the rare opportunity to dine with the most elite men in Rome. You will not be eating our food, though, of course." I had presumed as much, but his reminding me made me uncomfortable. "My slaves will see to it that you are properly bathed…. You look like a farmer and you smell like horse shit. I will not be embarrassed by any client of mine when the Father of the Senate is here, do you understand?"

"Understood, sir."

"Good." He waddled back to his ivory chair and returned to whatever he was working on. "You're dismissed." I bowed and lowered my head, my heart still beating in my throat.

To say the least, the bath I was given then was unlike any other I had taken previously. When the water in our home was frozen, the only bathing available was in the stream in the north corner of the city. Those youthful cleanings were the coldest and fastest I've ever endured. Caepio's baths, however, were so hot that I felt Vulcan himself must live beneath the home.

Silent slaves lathered me in oil and lavender, taking away my toga (I assumed the provincial stink of it was just too much for Caepio's honored guests) and presented me with a heavily scented one. They styled my hair, ensuring that every strand was perfectly delineated. I was uncomfortable and felt like an imposter. It was not long before I realized that this practice is very much the status quo in Roman high society.

As the slaves escorted me back through the long, torch-lit corridors to the *tablinum*, a shrill laugh greeted me. Caecilia was welcoming the first of the honored guests, and it was he who spotted me, causing Caecilia also to notice me. She'd painted her face more heavily even than before, and her plain black-and-white hair was now covered in a fire-red wig piled magnificently high.

"Oh, Sertorius, how wonderful! Cincinnatus in the flesh! Please, come—allow me to introduce you. This is the former consul, Lucius Aurelius Cotta, our in-law. Cotta, this is Quintus Sertorius, a provincial client of ours who has come to us to learn the ways of the Forum! What a marvelous meeting this is, to see a robust Italian greeting a magistrate of Rome! It's symbolic." She tapped the tips of her fingers together delicately.

"Greetings, sir. It is an honor. The first time I came to Rome for the elections, I voted for you," I said honestly, as he halfheartedly accepted my proffered hand.

"R-really? I feel quite honored. Well, I th-thank you for your help, young man," he stammered as the slaves perfumed and dried his feet. Cotta's legs seemed awkwardly thin, though his arms were flabby and his face was round like his nose. He did appear noble and seemed to belong in the toga he wore, but altogether he looked fragile and waning. His limbs shook slightly and his eyes blinked often. Cotta was different than I'd imagined him, but I admired his meek demeanor and his stutter, which reminded me of my own.

Caecilia led the two of us back to the center of the atrium where lanterns burned brightly on candelabra, shining on the water in the *impluvium* and sending shadows of flower petals across the walls. All the while, Caecilia continued talking pleasantly. But it was only moments before new guests arrived in the entryway amidst a cortege of slaves. When she saw who'd arrived, Caecilia dashed back to the entryway, her arms thrown wide.

"My baby boy! My baby boy!" she exclaimed as she embraced the grown man entering the room.

"Hello, Mama," he said as he squeezed her like a child would. I stifled a grimace. What an awkward display. I would have been ashamed if my mother ever made such a public spectacle of me— even though we'd always been very close. But rather than displaying embarrassment, Caecilia's son clearly basked in her attentions.

"How was your ride, Quintus? Do tell!" she said, completely ignoring her daughter-in-law, whose name I later learned was Junia. Entering behind her husband, Junia stood in plain clothes and with slumped shoulders. Still, it was clear even to a provincial like me that she was extraordinarily beautiful. Yet for some reason, she didn't seem to fit in.

"It was marvelous, Mama. It's only about a two-day journey, but Puteoli sure is stunning this time of year, don't you think, Junia?" He turned to his wife.

"Certainly, husband," her voice was soft, expressionless.

"Well, I am glad the villa is still in decent shape. Your father takes less and less interest in it. He never wants to take his eyes away from his precious documents. The man is consumed with politics. But enough of that—enough of that. Gnaeus!"

After a long pause, Caepio waddled into the room. "Oh, son, what a pleasure. How was your little holiday, eh? I hope you enjoyed it. While you were playing in the ocean, I was molding you into a powerful man." Even to my untrained ears, displeasure mingled with the humor in his voice.

"I did enjoy it, Father. Thank you for allowing me the use of the villa, and thank you for your aid." He glanced uneasily at his mother, and I spotted his fingers tightening on Junia's hands.

"Gnaeus, did you see our other guest?" Caecilia said, evidently supposing her husband must not have spotted Aurelius Cotta, or perhaps he wouldn't have spoken so openly.

"Dear Cotta, what a pleasure it is to see you here tonight! What a pleasure," Caepio said, shaking Cotta's hand and nodding fervently.

"Oh, you t-too, dear Caepio. Thank you for such a kind invitation. I usually don't come out this late in the evening, but how could I ref-refuse such a kind offer? Where is my sister?" Cotta asked, looking about the atrium.

"She and my brother haven't arrived yet. And you know how sick he has grown … in his mind. It's likely she may come alone," Caepio said.

"Caecilia," Cotta began. "I know the guests aren't all here yet, but I am v-very much in need of rest. I would like to recline for but a moment, if you would allow me to be so rude."

"The *triclinium* is right this way. We'll all go—come along!" she replied, and I followed the procession to the dining room until I felt a hand on my shoulder. It was that of Gnaeus's son, Quintus Caepio.

"*Ave*, Sertorius."

"*Salve*, Patron. You are Gnaeus's son?" I asked. I had never met him before and was stunned he already knew my name.

"Yes, I am. I apologize that I was not present at your arrival; I was off on a little adventure with my wife and my son, Marcus. But clients of ours are always welcome in our home, and we will help you in any way we can—so long as you will help us." He stood rather awkwardly for a man of increasing power.

"Are you planning to run for office, sir?"

"As a matter of fact I am, although the public doesn't know this yet. I'll be running for consul, and with the support of my family, I have no doubt my campaign will be successful. Even still, I desire your support."

"Of course, sir. I've always dreamed of seeking public office myself," I replied, doing all I could to maintain eye contact. He stood awfully close when he spoke—a habit that, I remember now, made myself and others slightly uncomfortable.

"A good dream for a Roman. And with our help, there is no doubt you can achieve it. Well ... don't expect to be consul or anything... . I mean to say, don't get your hopes too high ... the consulship is reserved for the elite, after all ..." He droned on, while I tried to keep my expression blank. Eventually, he looked away uncomfortably and with an, "Excuse me," he moved on without further ado.

In the dining area, we were ushered to our couches by designated slaves as other guests began to join us. First came Marcus Scaurus preceded by a *lictor,* who shouted, "Make way! *Princeps senatus,* Marcus Aemilianus Scaurus has arrived! The Father of the Senate, Scaurus, has arrived!" Scaurus entered, his arm linked with that of his wife, Dalmatica. Well into his fifties, Scaurus was an impressive man. Though of average height, he was in great physical shape; his skin was tanned and his teeth white as doves, and though his black hair was sprinkled with gray, he had lost none of his youthful vitality. His face, too, was totally and utterly masculine.

Scaurus smiled suavely. He offered everyone in the room an equal amount of time and attention. To my surprise, he even addressed me, and rather than asking for my name, he seemed to assume that we'd met before and shook my hand without any introduction. When

Gnaeus mentioned that I was his client and had come to learn the ways of the Forum, Scaurus turned to me and said, "Well, I salute you for doing your duty as a Roman citizen." Over time, I came to learn that Scaurus—perhaps more so than any of the others—rarely spoke without such words as "duty," "glory," and "Republic" pouring from his lips.

More calls rose from the entrance. "*Pontifex Maximus* Lucius Caecilius Metellus Dalmaticus and his brother, former consul Quintus Caecilius Metellus Numidicus!" Though the two men walked in together, they carried themselves with very different postures. The former was heavyset and far older, and he slouched. He had a jolly red face with a protruding chin, dull eyes, and a balding head that he made no attempt to hide. He didn't appear to be much of a patrician, but rather looked as rough as any pleb in the street. His smile was wide and he had laughter in his eyes, like he was preparing to tell a good joke. Numidicus, however, was very differently composed. Although not as naturally attractive as Scaurus, he had a presence one couldn't help gravitating toward. Upon entering, he did not smile but raised his hand with a small flourish like a triumphant general—as, of course, he was, having returned earlier that year from war in Numidia, where he received his *agnomen*.

"Greetings," Numidicus said in a serious tone, while Dalmaticus laughed heartily as he embraced his sister Caecilia and his daughter Dalmatica, both of whom rose from their couches to greet him.

"Who's ready for some food, eh?" Dalmaticus's voice boomed. The brothers were ushered to their places as Caecilia praised them both. Numidicus remained indifferent to the compliments, but Dalmaticus seemed almost irritated. "All right, all right!" he cried. "We can talk more when I have some wine in my gullet and meat in my belly!"

Finally, a great many slaves entered the room carrying trays full of delicacies I had never seen before: oysters, flamingo, dormouse,

I later learned. I, of course, was given lesser foods than these. My bounty was the figs leftover from the first course.

It quickly became apparent to me that patricians dine together not for the food, but for the gossip and conversation. They picked from their delicacies abstemiously—save Dalmaticus, who gorged himself rather crudely and blurted only infrequent comments. While the women were present, the conversation remained civil—primarily city gossip and witty banter. After several hours, however, the women were ushered away to their litters and taken home, while the men stayed behind. And then the purpose of the dinner became clear.

Gnaeus got to his feet. He said, "My good men, I thank you all for joining me at my abode. It has been a pleasant evening, but now it is time to discuss weightier matters. I know you understand why you are here."

"By the gods, he's got that right. This meeting has been a long time coming," Numidicus said, almost to himself.

"At this time last year, we were sluggish in planning for the elections—and look at what has been the result," said Gnaeus.

"We need look no further than our current consuls. Gaius Marius, who parades himself through Africa like a King—" Scaurus began scornfully.

Numidicus cut him off. "You need not mention his name."

"Fair enough. The Man with Two Names, then. His colleague, Cassius, is a damned fool and has long since dug himself a massive hole of debt. An indebted man is a desperate man, and a desperate man is a dangerous man," Scaurus went on. Dalmaticus exclaimed angrily how much he disliked Cassius's father, who had gone out of his way to oppose them years earlier.

"You're all correct, gentleman. And that is why this year must be different. Gods, Rome is now in the hands of madmen, with not a drop of good blood between them," Quintus Caepio added.

"Don't forget that the Father of the Senate is still a man of nobility," Scaurus reminded them, holding his chin high.

"We can never forget, nor can we forget that the high priesthood is still in my noble brother's hands and will be for the remainder of his life. But the people look to their consuls, and we can no longer afford to allow that noble seat to be defiled by ruffians. Are we all in agreement on this?" Gnaeus asked, looking around. Everyone nodded.

"But what do you propose we do?" Quintus Caepio asked, but one could surmise from his posture that he already knew the answer.

"We sweep the elections, my son. This will be the year of the *boni*. And once we take our hold, we cannot let go. Rome has remained unsecured since the Gracchi waged their rabble-rousing wars in the streets. We must rid the Senate of the inept, incompetent fools that claim to run 'for the people.' They do not wish to help the people, or the state. No, they serve their own interests. And as you all know, their interests are crippling Rome and our families. Numidicus, you were consul two years ago, and look what happened to you—deposed from your rightful place as imperator in Africa by the Man with Two Names!"

Scaurus rubbed his chin thoughtfully. "Sweep the elections.… . Explain."

"Place a name on every ballot. If we cannot secure a magistracy, we must ensure that the man who does is either an ally, neutral to us, or else can have his loyalty bought," Gnaeus said confidently.

"Easier said than done." Dalmaticus looked down and dug his finger into his teeth.

"Doubtless, but who do you think we are? The Metelli own Rome! Scaurus owns the Senate. The Cottae have their fists ready to strike if the *publicani* get in our way," Gnaeus continued.

"And I have stone quarries all throughout Spain, so we can fund all necessary expenses," Quintus added.

"Gaius Marius also has stone quarries in Spain. Some say that after his time as praetor and consul he now is the richest man in Rome," Dalmaticus objected, violating the rule to not mention Gaius Marius by name.

"Yes, but he has only two names. He is a nobody who has surpassed the limits of his birthright tenfold, and now it is time that he and his lot are returned to their proper place." No one made any response to Gnaeus's statement, and it took me a moment to understand what they meant by "two names"—and that it was an insult. Having three names was a simple way of showing your aristocracy; therefore, men like Gaius Marius—men like myself—were provincial nonentities. To the patricians, two-named men were of little consequence.

Gnaeus continued, "The alternative, of course, is to allow the tide of the times to continue washing away all that our ancestors worked to build. We can allow our family names to become obscure and meaningless in an age controlled by the power-thirsty, money-hungry proletariat." Again, there was no reply. "Gentlemen, I am dying. I feel it in my bones. I am old, and I can hear Pluto whispering my name. I have never been afraid of death—a true Roman cannot fear death—but I hate to believe my name will not live on after me. And so I refuse to allow that to happen. I refuse to allow *my* Rome to crumble while an imposter rises to take its place."

"Exactly how do you propose we d-do this?" Aurelius Cotta spoke up for the first time. "What must we do first, next, and s-so forth?"

"This is why we are here," said Gnaeus.

"Father." Quintus made his way to the center of the room and looked around at all the boni, as they called themselves. "I've talked about it for years, and now it is time for me to realize my greatest ambition: I will follow in all of your footsteps and run for the office of consul, with your blessing."

"You are well suited, nephew. It's high time you ran for consul," Numidicus said.

After a brief silence, Scaurus spoke up. "I must do my duty as the Father of the Senate and run for censor. It's only fitting."

"I had no idea you were planning to run for the censorship! A grand idea," Dalmaticus exclaimed, before pointing to a chalice of wine and asking for more.

"I'll not be running this year—for anything," Numidicus said, a statement that raised eyebrows all across the room. "But I believe it is time for my son to run. I believe he should run alongside Quintus for consul." There was an awkward pause.

"He must be forty to run for consul, brother," Dalmaticus spoke up cautiously.

"I know the protocol, brother," Numidicus sneered, "but if a lowly provincial can be elected consul, then why not my son in his mid-thirties? I told that two-named pleb that he should wait to run for consul with my son and he didn't, so my son must be elected following him. Honor demands it." Numidicus was a dutiful father— perhaps even a little too dutiful. His son was given the name Pius because of his loyalty to his father, although I never really knew if this was meant as a compliment or an insult. "Why can't we get him elected? We're the boni, after all. We *own* Rome." Numidicus's voice seemed to verge on mockery, but I wasn't certain.

"We certainly can!" Gnaeus exclaimed, and no one voiced an objection.

And so the evening continued. The boni decided on position after position and seemed to have no shortage of names. Cotta's distant cousin Orestes would run for praetor (the man was proposed without his knowledge, as I understood it), Claudius Pulcher, the son of one of Gnaeus's old friends would run for quaestor, and a priest heavily indebted to Dalmaticus would run for tribune of plebs.

There was some debate about this last man. Dalmaticus described him as a gambler, drinker, and degenerate but claimed he had no love for the people, which apparently meant he was perfect for the job.

"Really? Scaevola?" Gnaeus asked, sounding suspicious. "I haven't had my eyes opened wide enough apparently. He seems quite the boring man to me. Is he not the one who wrote a book on regulating boundaries?"

"Certainly! Hah! Your eyes *are* open, that's for certain—it's your mind that isn't perceiving," Dalmaticus rejoined. "Have you seen me out there in the Forum? Just as formal and polite as a Roman can be. But here, behind closed curtains, I realize I have reached the tip of my political career, and I aspire no further. Hah! The only reason I even try is to continue lending my aid to you fine noblemen. But I digress. Trust me, Scaevola will be our man."

And that was it.

That night, I tried to analyze the men in the room. I attempted to copy their movements and posture as they reclined easily on their left elbows. I meticulously matched my movements to theirs, blending in as best I could. In my inmost thoughts, of course, I wished to make an impression, to be noticed and appreciated and not dismissed as only an ignorant provincial.

I know now that I was naïve, for there was a part of me that believed my name might be mentioned for a junior magistracy, one where I could support their cause and learn all about Rome at the same time. But that was not to be.

That night has stayed always in my memory. Those dusty old men and their conspiring would result in a tidal wave of change in Rome. I now find it extraordinary that this meeting took place on my first night in Rome, and I can't help but attribute it to the beneficence of the gods. But it was the next politician I'd meet who would have the most profound impact on both me and the Republic.

SCROLL III

What follows is an account by my old friend Lucius Hirtuleius. This was not only a monumental chapter in his life, but it proved to be life-altering for me as well, though it would be some time before I knew it:

Lucius Hirtuleius—October 648 ab urbe condita; three months until election.

I will apologize in advance for my crude writing. I know about as many words as Sertorius does languages (although I have double his knowledge of profanity). Regardless, he has asked me to write about one of my final days training for the Roman army. Before I can get to that point, though, I suppose I should provide some preliminary information about joining the legions.

When I arrived in Rome, I used what little money I had to make a down payment on an insula apartment in the Subura. I went to the military registrar on the Field of Mars toward the end of August and was as nervous as a young man can be approaching that large scarlet tent. It is no easy task to swear away your life.

The man inside was a young quaestor, working diligently on some parchment before him. He only acknowledged me after some time had passed.

"What is it?" he asked.

"I am here to join the legions, sir."

He laughed harshly. "Whatever for?"

I wasn't sure how to reply. "Because I want to serve Rome, sir."

"Of course, of course! But what is your *real* reason?"

The words caught in my throat.

"Never mind that." He tried to stop laughing. "We have a rotation beginning three days hence, if you're ready to join now. We've been instructed to have the legions ready to march by the kalends of January, so you'd be training quickly."

"I am ready, sir."

"Fine then. Are you a citizen?"

"Yes."

"Are you from Rome?"

"No, sir. I am a Sabine."

"What's your occupation?"

I hesitated. "I work on my grandfather's farm."

He brandished a wax tablet and began carving some notes in it.

"I thought you said you were a citizen? You sound more like a slave." I didn't respond. "Well, at least you've a manly occupation. You'd be surprised how many poets, pastry cooks, weavers, and cloth makers try to join the legion. We don't want their damn kind. A man with soft hands is no use to Rome as a soldier. Do you have any letters of recommendation?"

"No, sir." My heart sank. I'd not known I would need anything like that.

He rolled his eyes. "It'll be much harder to find you a path, then. But with Consul Marius's reforms, we're taking damn near anyone. Do you have any special skills?"

I must have looked blank.

"You know, good with money, numbers, supply … anything?" I could think of nothing. He grunted and made more notes. "To the front lines with you, then."

"I'll do whatever is asked of me, sir."

"Then take off your tunic." When I hesitated, he continued, "Oh come on, boy. I've got better places to get my jollies than from a twenty-year-old farmhand. I have to check you for scars and deformities. I used to check to make sure recruits were tall enough, in good shape, and all that ... but now, if you can breathe and carry a weapon, we'll take you."

He put me through a series of tests, making me run in place, throw a *pilum*, lift a large stone outside the tent; however, he paid very little attention to my efforts. As I replaced the stone, he announced, "You'll be entering an auxiliary unit. As soon as your training is finished, your unit is expected to move north to reinforce the legions in Gaul. Any questions?"

"Sir, I thought the auxiliaries were for noncitizens. I thought I would be joining as a *hastatus*." The hastati were young infantry soldiers, the front line. But they were citizens. My grandfather Manius had begun as a hastatus and worked his way up to centurion. I was unsure if auxiliaries would have such opportunities.

He glared at me. "Have *you* come to tell *me* how the army works? Please continue, I obviously have much to learn!" When I remained silent, he said, "The hastati are being phased out. We don't use them anymore. Another of Marius's glorious changes. Everyone is just a legionary. But you—you will be an auxiliary. Why? Because you might be a citizen, but you're a Sabine and I have a quota to meet. Unless you'd like to argue?" I shook my head. "Good. They're all the same really, except you'll be paid less and your life will generally be less valued. Come back in three days at first light. And I would advise you to have that stubble of a beard shaved and your back straighter."

I nodded and left. That quaestor was my first impression of military culture. It wasn't an easy transition, being talked down to like that, but in the end, that man proved to be a gentle soul compared to our training instructors.

We began with marching drills. We were to move in perfect unison, with no one appearing out of step. The worst insult was to be called a "damned individual." Day after day, the training grew harder and harder, as we were eventually issued combat gear and drilled on how to use it. We sparred against lifeless six-foot posts, threw pila so often we learned to bury their iron tips in trees from one hundred paces, and rolled logs and earth into embankments in ever shorter periods of time. Perhaps the most difficult challenge was the forced march, during which we had to move in quickstep for twenty-four miles in five hours. This was known as the "victory run," because those who finished were considered "soldier material"; those who limped in after the vanguard were sent home in disgrace. We finished our training with battle simulations, and it is here that I begin the story Sertorius has requested of me.

Although the blood of soldiers ran in my veins, being one didn't come naturally to me. I found discipline easy enough due to my grandfather's strict instructions, but being a soldier is about far more than discipline and swordplay. For whatever reason, after only a few days of training, I was given the position of squad leader. My instructors must have seen something in me they liked, and although they offered me no compliments, they gave me this small position of authority and didn't revoke it. During these training exercises, therefore, I played the role of a centurion, giving orders and controlling the formation of my century.

I believe the day of which I speak was October 12, if my old letters are correct. We moved through the field in a typical formation, and I remember struggling to balance the wooden gladius, wicker *scutum*, and the armor we'd been issued. We ran to our next objective with the instructors shouting all around us. Our "enemies" were role-players dressed as Germanic tribes, similar to the ones my father had fought. As we neared the checkpoint, they launched a volley of sticks and stones behind staged shrubbery.

"*Testudo* formation!" My shout came hoarse from all the earlier drills. The trainees obediently bunched even closer together and raised their shields up like a tortoise shell to protect the group from the missiles. I fell in with them and waited for the volley to cease. *"Tecombre!"* I cried, and my men reverted to their former position, a few of the slower ones struggling to get back in formation. Suddenly, warriors in Germanic garb rushed from behind the vegetation, wooden spears in hand. And although it was only a training exercise, I could feel the fear radiating from my men. "Hold! Hold the line!" My throat ached as I continued to shout over the tumult, waiting what felt like an entire life span. "Throw pila!" The men threw their wooden pila at the oncoming enemy. I'm sure our execution wasn't as smooth as it would later become, but I'll admit I was very proud of our performance .

"Contendite vestra sponte!" I yelled—a command for the troops to assume an aggressive stance and prepare for pursuit. I gave the command to march and we began to move.

My feet were sweaty and blistered, but I continued to push forward and match the impetus of my men. My heart pounded against my ribs and my breathing became erratic. The commands I'd been learning continued to form in my mouth, although I was not consciously trying to recall them. I have shed much blood in sacrifice to the gods for this grace that has followed me through many battles since that day.

The enemy turned to form a solid line of defense before us, taunting us and flexing their muscles with anticipation. As they awaited us, I gave the command to form a wedge, surprising myself and apparently even the enemy. It wasn't a formation we'd practiced much, but it was being prioritized in Marius's reform. Now seemed like the time to try it out.

My men fell into place just before they met the enemy. The enemy's wooden swords thrashed against the shields of the men in front and the battle began. It was as real to me as any I've experienced since.

I rushed to my position, keeping my shield (which felt smaller than ever before) directly in front of me with the tip of my gladius right behind it, ready to strike. The first German role-player pounced on me like a lion, waving his spear wildly. I ducked quickly behind my shield, struggling to keep my unfitted helmet from falling off. I absorbed his blows with the scutum before me, and at the first opportunity, I lunged forward with my gladius, poking the man in the chest. He flopped to the ground as if the wound had been mortal, and several more role-players gathered around me.

"Publius, stab, don't slash!" I shouted to the man on my right, noticing his error out of the corner of my eye. It was easy to forget the little things we'd been learning, so I did not blame him for the mistake.

Masses of the enemy role-players fell over, and the others wavered. They turned and began to scatter, regrouping only to hurl whatever they could grab at us. I fumbled to bring the centurion's whistle to my lips and signaled to reform the wedge and advance forward. The "Germans'" morale was broken and they scrambled into a full retreat. We were victorious—for whatever it was worth, in the scenario.

Suddenly a drum roll burst three times in the distance, the echo encircling the battlefield and calming our hearts. "Reform!" The instructors shouted as we turned and marched back to drill formation. I was unsure how my performance would be received. Still, I was relieved that the exercise was over and felt that I had done well enough. As we formed our line, I remembered the tongue-lashings I'd received in the past for breathing heavily or shaking, and tried to maintain the most stoic composure I could.

"Adequate work, men. You're beginning to look like soldiers," one of the instructors, Septimius, said. This was by far the highest compliment we'd received yet. "You are about to be greeted by a very important man. You will appear disciplined and noble, or I will know the reason why," he announced, holding our attention with a fixed gaze. As soon as Septimius turned his back, whispers began to circulate as to whom the visitor might be. We hadn't spoken to a civilian or outsider of any kind since donning the colors, and we'd barely seen a soul outside of our comrades and instructors. There was a great sense of excitement.

"Quiet, men!" I ordered in a low voice that I hoped would carry to the ranks behind me.

After a long moment, a man on horseback galloped toward us, followed by a long line of important-looking men, some in togas, some in the red tunics of soldiers. The rider came to a halt before us and squinted at us appraisingly through the sun. He leaped swiftly from his steed, ignoring the aide running forward to give him a stool.

"You should be very proud of yourselves," the man said as he removed his plumed helmet and placed it under a thick arm. He was built like a bull, short, stout, and with limbs the size of tree trunks. His face was hard, his jaw wide, and his skin etched with years of difficulty. There was an old, yet deep, scar on his right cheek and his voice was as low and rough as any I'd ever heard. He didn't appear noble, but his presence demanded respect. "I know that none of you has marched under the standard before, but you have conducted yourselves as soldiers and have learned the ways of the warrior very quickly. Whether you know it or not, you are entering into a very different military than the one your ancestors served in. These past years, I have labored to reform our military and to use the strength of Roman arms to the best of our ability. Many said it couldn't be done. A great deal of naysayers in the Senate House still balk at the idea of altering the ancient methods of fighting, yet they know nothing of the battlefield. I do." He paused to cough into his arm. "You have proven my convictions by assimilating quickly, and I have no doubt that you will one day stand as the greatest Roman force the world has ever known." I remember my heart swelling with pride in that moment. In the back of my mind, I thought of my father and grand-father and how they would have clapped me on the shoulder and congratulated me. I could feel every back in the ranks straighten.

"Many of you are wondering who I am, but you have doubtless heard my name. I am your consul ... General Gaius Marius." There were audible gasps from our ranks. This man was a legend in Rome. He'd been away defeating the rebel-king Jugurtha, yet his name was whispered with hope and praise everywhere throughout Italy. Now

I recognized him as the one whose powerful image was drawn in graffiti on every wall in Rome. He'd been rumored to be returning after war season ended, particularly for the festival of the October Horse, yet none of us had imagined he would come to see us. "I have been fighting in foreign lands for years and have had to entrust your training and development to my colleagues. That has been mentally taxing for me, because there is nothing I take more pride in than commanding fine young soldiers. Yet I am relieved to see you are where you need to be.

"You may be disappointed that the war in Africa is nearly over; however, you will not have to wait long to wet your swords with blood. There will be hard fighting ahead—that much I promise. Continue to prepare yourself for what lies ahead and do not ever doubt that what you are learning will be put to the test. Your work today will predict whether you and your comrades will live or die tomorrow." A sudden smile on his lips, he turned to Septimius. "Do you mind if I lead it?"

"By all means, Consul." Our instructor bowed; he was far more cordial today than we had ever seen him.

"Jupiter!" The consul's voice erupted like Vulcan's flame.

"Optimus!" We replied as we had done since day one, praising the God of War for preparing our swords.

"Jupiter!"

"Maximus!"

"*Jupiter!*"

"*Optimus!*" We hoisted our swords in the air as Marius held his fist aloft. As he dropped his arm, we began to beat our gladii against our shields violently, letting out a chorus of shouts that would have sown fear into the hearts of the fiercest of enemies. I truly believe that this moment of passion has lasted my entire life. The flame that was lit that day has never died; for good or bad, Marius made good on his promise. My blade hasn't dried since.

I stepped away with the rest of my century, wiping the sweat from my brow and congratulating some of my men, when I felt a hand on my shoulder. I turned to find my instructor Septimius behind me. My heart began to race again, although his face was calm.

"Sir," I snapped to attention and waited to be addressed.

"It's your lucky day, soldier. General Gaius Marius would have a word with you. You are to report to him at once." He pointed to a tent at the far end of the Field of Mars, the sacred grounds where Roman soldiers had trained since the founding. Two lictors were posted in front of it.

"Right away, sir." I gave a proper salute and turned on my heels, not knowing what could have caused Marius to wish to speak with me. My knees felt weak.

I hurried across the open field, ignoring the catcalls of my men and trying to prepare what I might say. When I arrived, the lictors stood aside, and one of them opened up the leather tent flap with the back of his arm. They both eyed me curiously as I stepped through, keeping my eyes fixed and my resolve firm.

Before being addressed or even scanning the faces in the room, I snapped to attention and gave the most powerful salute I could muster.

"Sir—Lucius Hirtuleius reporting, sir."

"At ease, soldier," Marius replied from the table before me. I allowed my eyes to lower to meet his, then looked around the room at the men gathered. I suddenly became aware of how sweaty I was and of the mud streaking my legs.

"I will introduce you. This is my brother-in-law Gaius Julius Caesar."

"Call me Julius," the handsome man said. Fair-skinned and with golden hair, he appeared in every way a noble. "My brother will be joining us shortly. He might be my elder but you can call him by his first name, too. Sextus—he's not much for tradition."

"This is Gaius Norbanus," Marius continued.

"And you can call me Norbanus." He bowed sarcastically. "I'm not much for tradition either, but about half the men in Rome are named Gaius, so let's just keep it simple, eh?"

"And this is Gnaeus Mallius Maximus." The man stood and shook my hand, looking me in the eye.

"I am happy to make your acquaintance, Lucius." Maximus was a handsome man and the tallest in the room. I could tell by the way he addressed me that he didn't have the impressive lineage of the others, but still there was a silent nobility to him.

"And finally, this is my good friend Publius Rutilius Rufus, who has served with me for what feels like a lifetime. It was Rufus here who brought you to my attention. While I've been in Africa fighting with Norbanus and Julius, he's been here ensuring that the military reforms move forward and that our new soldiers are strong and prepared."

"You caught my eye a while ago, initiate. You have made yourself known through your discipline and attitude, not to mention your performance," said Rufus, raising an eyebrow slightly.

"I am honored, sir. I hadn't realized I'd done anything out of the ordinary. I simply wish to serve my country." I stumbled over the words. I never was much of a talker—especially compared to Sertorius—and I was sure my inadequacies were evident to all.

"That desire is extraordinary in today's day and age, initiate, and don't let the politicians tell you otherwise. So few men truly care about the state." Rufus's voice was heavy and held little expression. In fact, he exuded stoicism.

"Take a seat." Marius gestured to the single chair before his desk. The stool had no back, so I found myself sitting at attention, with my shoulders back, chest out, and chin up. This seemed to amuse the general's friends—or else something did, because they exchanged glances and chuckled quietly.

"I am not one to give compliments so quickly, soldier, as these men can attest." Marius says to more laughter. "But I will admit that I am very impressed by you and your class of recruits. You handled yourself well out there. I have half a mind to ask you where you served previously, but your instructor tells me you've never wielded a sword before."

"No, sir, I haven't. But I plan on doing so until fate takes me."

"You and I are of one mind. I have no doubt, then, that we will share the same fate. But I must ask—why did you form a wedge before continuing the final assault on the 'Germans'?" He cocked his head and rubbed at the stubble on his chin.

"I looked at their equipment, sir. With mostly ranged weapons and without durable shields I didn't believe they would be able to withstand the wedge if it was coupled with shock tactics." The reply came as I'd intended, despite my nerves. The general looked to his friends with raised eyebrows. I couldn't really discern what this meant.

"I like that. What is your training routine for the rest of the evening?"

"I believe we are set to continue our work with marching drills in full kit."

"And how do you march?"

"Well enough, I believe, sir."

"Good. I'll let Septimius know you'll be with me this evening. These gentlemen and I are going to Ostia for a drink. We'd have you join us." He stood.

"With you, sir?" I'm afraid I wasn't able to hide my astonishment. "Certainly, sir."

He made his way to me and gave something of a grunt of laugh. "That's an order." He clapped me on the back and led the way out of the tent.

I still remember how cold the air was that October evening. I have a natural affinity for the cold due to my upbringing in Nursia, and my recent training had exposed me even further to the elements, but there was a nip in the air that hurt my lungs when I breathed.

As we left the Field of Mars, I tried to walk behind the men as a sign of my immense appreciation for the invitation and that I understood my place, but the general continually slowed his pace to walk at my side.

"So, how does that helmet feel on your head?" He put his arm around my shoulders and directed his lictors to clear the way before us.

"Well enough, sir." It was a lie, which I'm ashamed to admit. That oversized hunk of metal chafed my forehead awfully.

"*Cac!* You look like a natural, but I remember the first time I donned one. I was serving in Spain under Scipio Aemilianus. I'd always wanted to be a soldier, but the first time I tried on that gear I was quick to change my mind."

I remember that as we walked I could see the breath of every member of Marius's cortege. Most of them were wrapped in woolen cloaks, but I had only my soldier's cape and Marius wore little more. I assumed it was a display of his toughness and endurance.

"Consul, where are we going exactly?" one of them asked.

"Damned if I know the taverns in Ostia! Maximus, you're from Ostia—do you have any ideas?"

"I can't say that I do. I'm not a drinking man, Marius."

"I'm not from Ostia by any means, but I know every damned drinking establishment within thirty miles of Rome. I'll set us up right," said Gaius Norbanus.

Marius returned to his pleasant memories of his first days as a soldier and the time he was a trainee like me. I listened as best I could, but I'll admit I wondered what this was all about and why I was even there.

"And Rome?" he asked, catching me off guard.

"What, sir?"

"What of Rome? How do you like it? As a provincial, I'm sure it has been an adjustment. I found this city absurd when I first came here after being raised in Arpinum." How he knew my background was beyond me.

"I can't say that I've experienced it much yet, sir. I moved into a villa in the Subura, but I kept mostly to myself until I joined up with the Colors. I haven't been back since." When we reached the town walls of Ostia, we were stopped by two sentries.

"Sorry, Consul, no soldier's capes or helmets in Ostia, even for you," one of the guards said nervously, trying to ignore the intimidating looks the lictors were giving him. Marius removed his plumed helmet, revealing a sweaty head with little hair. I followed his example, feeling the cold air strike my arms as I removed my cape.

"I'm sure no harm will come to our gear under your command—right, soldier? Keep in mind that that helmet outranks you, so don't touch it," Marius said as he entered the gate.

"If we head down this road here, there is a fine establishment run by some Egyptian. It has the cheapest wine and most exotic whores from here to Capua," Norbanus said as we neared the Ostian Forum.

"We won't be taking whores, you dog, and money isn't a problem. But lead on," Marius said, grinning coyly as he pushed Norbanus forward.

The group halted as the chief lictor approached the wooden doors of the tavern.

"Clear out! Clear out, I say! Make way for Consul Gaius Marius!" he shouted as he slammed the butt of his *fasces* into the ground. There were quiet gasps from those inside and some anxious whispers before they all piled out. The bawdy crew that passed us by looked at us with wild eyes and toothless grins—some of them shouting out praise to Marius, who simply responded with a nod and a wave.

"Consul! I am honored to have you here." The Egyptian proprietor gave an exaggerated bow.

"Leave off it, man. Just bring us some wine," Norbanus replied impatiently. He waved to the tables before us, as if *he* were the host. The lictors pushed the abandoned plates of food and cups of wine—full or empty—onto the floor to make a place for the consul.

"All right, all right. Now go wait outside," Marius ordered. The lictors shrugged and left.

"Take your whores elsewhere, Egyptian. They are a disgrace

before the consul," Maximus growled with displeasure. The Egyptian shooed the girls away as Norbanus shot Maximus a look of ire.

"A disgrace? They are the Consul's people, too," Norbanus said, eying the girls as they passed.

"Sit, all of you. Sit," Marius said, taking his place first. "You sit here." He directed me to the seat beside him.

The Egyptian arrived at the table with a large amphora of wine.

"I hope it's unwatered. That's how I want it tonight," said Marius, raising his voice above the noise.

"One of *those* conversations, eh?" Julius said, raising an eyebrow mischievously. "You'll receive no complaints from me."

"I'd have it no other way. I need a few real drops to warm me up," Norbanus said.

Maximus waved off the Egyptian reaching for his cup. "None for me, thank you."

"What? Come on, man. We've just arrived back in Rome from a prosperous war season. Make time to celebrate!" Norbanus put his arm around him. "Not to mention it makes me uncomfortable to partake while another man sits dry."

"You know I don't drink, Norbanus. You should have seen what wine did to my father. So I'll not, thank you. But you'll receive no judgment from me," said Maximus in return, and he placed his arm around Norbanus, too.

"Perhaps you'd like to order some goat's milk?" Marius grinned, as the table erupted in laughter. I joined in, but I wasn't keen to offend the man. Luckily, Maximus smiled and shrugged it off.

"I'll take a willow-water instead, thank you."

"But in all seriousness, this conversation does need strong drink, and I wanted to set up my friend here with a nice drop." Marius patted my arm. His hands were heavy like mallets and as rough as old leather.

"Did I hear someone say strong drink?" came a loud voice behind us. We turned to see another man walking in with a long gait and his arms outstretched. He moved with so much bounce that it seemed his legs were made of liquid rather than flesh and sinew.

"Sextus! How good of you to meet us," his brother Julius said, rising to embrace him.

"To see you buggers? Bah! I had no idea you would be here. I was just coming to get drunk and penetrate something." Guffaws erupted as Sextus took his seat. He wore a mischievous smile as he scanned the table, his eyes locking on me. "And who is this, then?"

"This is Lucius Hirtuleius, Rome's newest legionnaire."

"What an honor, eh? For an initiate to dine with the Republic's finest men," he said before I could murmur the proper acknowledgments. He was grinning slyly, and the way he looked at me was unnerving—as if he knew a great deal that I did not. And perhaps he did.

"This is neither an honor nor a favor," Marius said sternly. "I have brought Hirtuleius here today with orders." My heart dropped into my stomach, and I felt my face color like a soldier's cloak. What kind of soldier receives his orders in a tavern in Ostia? "Gentlemen, things are about to change. Rome is in a period of transition." Marius got to his feet and began pacing back and forth before the table, his arms moving passionately as if he were preparing his men before a battle. "The Senate and Rome's fat nobility are gorging themselves on the blood of the Republic, and I'm not so sure this great state will survive many more attacks from the likes of Jugurtha."

"Marius!" Sextus began to say before pausing to laugh. "All due respect, your highness, but you cannot possibly believe an African scoundrel like Jugurtha could ever truly harm Rome? Not to mention that Rome desired this war and did everything but cause it."

Marius thought for a moment. "What you say, my friend, is correct. There will always be power-hungry renegades that seek what Rome has, but that is not my point. The *optimates*, the old families, are a greater danger to Rome than any outside threat. It isn't Jugurtha or those like him that threaten Rome, but the bribes they offer the greedy, incompetent leadership, who sell their city and their very souls for a few gold coins. The Cimbri and Teutones are frightening too, but they hold not a tenth of the power to harm Rome that the Senate has." This time, no laughter followed.

"So it's revolution you advocate? You want to join the bloated corpses of the Gracchi in the Tiber River?" Julius said, taking a long pull of purple wine.

"Revolution. What messy business." Norbanus winked at Marius.

"Call it what you like. But that's not that word I would use. I'll bring no swords to the Senate House. I'm saying that we pursue our legal rights as Romans, of procuring power in the legal way, to lead this Republic in the legal way. If someone tries to stop us from doing that, we will resist and continue our mission—just as we are doing in Africa." Marius resumed his seat and looked into the eyes of each man.

"You think the nobles will try to retaliate if we run for office?" Rufus said, his eyes containing disbelief.

"Perhaps."

"People run for office every year, Marius, from all parties and alliances. The results might vary, but we haven't seen bloodshed in Rome for fifty years," Rufus added.

Marius lifted to his hands and eyes to the heavens. "And I sacrifice to Jupiter Capitolinus that we won't see it for another fifty years. But unfortunately, the universe is a commonwealth of which both men and gods are inhabitants, both wielding free will. The gods cannot stay the hand of the man with a crooked heart." He stood up again; it seemed he was unable to control the intensity of his feelings. "Gentleman, our brother Maximus is standing for the consulship this year. As my future son-in-law, he can continue to enact the measures that I've begun during my term of office. But, as my future son-in-law, the nobles will despise him and do whatever they can to bar his entry. They will see it as my second term, and the optimates won't stand for it. Julius, you mentioned the Gracchi, and that is what they think I am. They think we're all monsters."

"Perhaps we are," Sextus said, shrugging his shoulders. The corners of his grin were apparent even behind his clay cup.

"Monsters who seek to save this Republic," Marius replied. He swallowed the last of his unwatered wine and slammed the cup down on the table. "Bring me more wine, Numidian." His voice was almost a growl. The look in his eyes ensured there would be no more jokes.

"What would you have us do, Consul?" Maximus asked seriously, his voice calm and soothing, but Marius seemed to not hear him. The general stared off as if something in the wood of the tavern was speaking to him. His breath seemed to quicken, and we all stared at him with apprehension, waiting for his reply.

"I know there was a great deal of jesting about my superstitions while we were in Africa. I am unashamed of it. Yet in my time, I have seen the gods. I have seen what they do and how they interfere in this world. You should have seen it … in Spain." He paused and exhaled deeply. He coughed into his arm and sat down. "What I say next is not to leave this table." He waited to receive a nod from every man present. "I was visited by a priestess in Numidia. She came to me late one night, with tears in her eyes. She said the gods had visited her and had left her a vivid image of the future. She told me there will be bloodshed in Rome—that friends will kill friends, sons will kill fathers, and brothers will kill brothers." He nodded at our dubious, fearful looks. "Trust me, I didn't believe her at first either. I asked what she wanted for this revelation—was she there for coin, for favor, what did she want? She replied that she sought nothing. She said she came to me personally because I was destined—I was chosen—to be the savior of this Republic. Her only request was to visit Rome—after I save it. She said that I must ready myself, for I will be called on to defend this state against both the enemies abroad and the enemies within. And she said … she said …" He looked down at the table.

"Said what, Marius?" Norbanus asked in a low voice. It was the first time I had seen him serious.

"I cannot say." He looked up again. "I will be consul again … and perhaps again after that. The Republic needs me, and I need you. All of you. From this point forward, I must regard those who aren't with me as against me." The dull flickering of the torchlight across our rapt faces added power to his words.

"We are with you, Marius," Maximus said, as the others nodded.

"All this talk of saving republics is making me weary." Rufus got to his feet. "I must retire for the night." He bowed deeply to the consul, then snapped to attention and saluted. Marius duplicated the gesture as Rufus turned on his heels and left. By the furrowed brows of Norbanus and Julius, I could see they were worried about Rufus's sudden departure, but Marius appeared unconcerned.

"Hirtuleius, this is why you have been called. I need an initiate, someone untainted by service to others in the Republic. I am asking you to pledge undying loyalty to *me*." My face felt hot, though I had only taken a few careful sips of wine. Though I did not yet know this man, I had already come to admire his soldierly ways. My hands shook beneath the table, and I tried to calm my voice before replying.

"What will be required of me, Consul?"

"Whatever I ask of you." His voice was so low that I had to lean close to hear him. "You are to go where I go and do as I do."

"With all due respect, Consul, why me? Do you not have lictors for your protection?" My voice quavered more than I would have liked.

"That's where you are wrong, initiate," Maximus said from across the table. "I was a lictor for a few years when I was young and doing whatever I could to earn a living. There is a very lucrative trade among the lictors; they trade secrets. They may protect Marius, but they are not *for* him. They will share information with the lictors of other magistrates if offered the right amount. They cannot be trusted."

"And trust is what I will need, Hirtuleius. Can I trust you?" I felt all eyes on me. I was awed by their solemnity and by my own ignorance of politics, rivals, schemes, and wars.

"Yes, Consul." Though I spoke honestly, I knew I had no idea just what that promise would entail.

SCROLL IV

From August to October, Gnaeus and his son Quintus prepared for the election while I watched. I helped Gnaeus with the paperwork involved in his morning client visits and took dictation from Quintus when he returned from the Senate each morning. Gnaeus had instructed Quintus to wait until October to announce his bid for consul, when it was sure to cause quite a stir and garner fresh support in the lead-up to the elections at the end of December. So until October, their goal was threefold: to win general affection by avoiding political outcasts and rigid stances on political issues, to form relationships with the heads of all the *collegia*, and to defend others in court in order to grow his clientele. Quintus was particularly active when it came to this last task. Gnaeus said of his son, "He is a middling lawyer, but his name assures acquittal and that gives us votes."

Despite this political need to be in the public eye, Quintus had a difficult time leaving the domus. Perhaps this is why I found him to be such a strange candidate for greatness. He did not love going out and playing the sycophant to the populous, and instead much preferred to recline in the *peristylum* and read poetry with his effeminate friend Lucius Reginus. I recall Gnaeus saying, when a few cups deep into his evening wine, "I love that boy, but sometimes I look at him and have no idea where he came from. Caecilia is shrewd and vastly intelligent, and I have always been ambitious and industrious ... but Quintus, he ... he likes poetry and friendship. Where on Gaia's earth did that come from?" Gnaeus seemed to find it very amusing, but I wondered if there was more to it than that.

I learned so much in those few months and was beginning to understand that life in the public arena came with many nuances. Although still in the midst of the awkward transition from farm boy to assistant to the most powerful men in Rome, I was beginning to come into my own.

October 648 ab urbe condita; three months until election.

Three months later arriving, I was still having difficulties adjusting to life in the city. My body was attuned to waking up at sunrise, and whereas back home I would have been preparing the field where we would train the horses, here I had nothing to do but silently pass through the halls and admire the ancient lore covering the walls. Occasionally, Gnaeus would wake up early too and bark at the slaves to prepare for the morning levy, but he wasn't prone to making pleasant morning conversation. I developed a liking for the peristylum, where I sat every morning at the same bench, usually reading Socrates, Thucydides, or my personal favorite, Zeno.

I would also use this time to write letters home. I told Mother of all the men I had met, and how amazing the Caepio domus was. Perhaps I embellished a little bit about how well I was adjusting, but the last thing I wanted was for my mother to worry.

I enjoyed being in the peristylum with its greenery and flowers and the soft birdsong, the slaves bending gracefully to tend the garden. The only sound was that of trickling water coming from a large pool in the center of the garden, where the statue of a naked goddess let water fall continuously from the basin on her shoulder.

My keenest sense has always been that of smell, and the peristylum had a sweet aroma. These many years later, I can't attribute it to any one flower in particular, but I always felt a profound sense of peace when I sat among the flowers in the gardens of Gnaeus Caepio's home, closing my eyes and taking in whatever sounds or smells greeted me.

I was resting here one morning when Crito interrupted my reverie.

"Morning to you, Master Sertorius! You've had a letter this morning—from your mother, looks like." He handed me the scroll, and I smiled as I saw the seal of my house on the scarlet wax.

"Thank you, Crito," I said, as I hastily broke the seal and began poring over my mother's penmanship.

My dear son,

How delighted I am to hear from you! Seldom has a moment passed by that I haven't wondered where you are or what you are doing. The only peace I have is the knowledge that the protection of the gods rests upon you. I know that you are doing your part to ensure we receive the help we need, but if there is anything you can do to expedite the process, I beg you to do it. If we have ever been in need of help from our friends in Rome, it is now.

I know I write in haste, and for that I apologize. I wish I had more time to write of all that is occurring here at home, as I'm sure you are missing our farm. But today there is a great deal of work to be done, and I must get to it. When I have time, I will update you on the progress of your horses. Volesa and Gavius send their love. I'm sure Titus will write you soon.

I am with you wherever you go.

When I reached the bottom of the letter, I was overcome by a powerful, bittersweet homesickness. I sat back and thought of Nursia and stroked the tips of my fingers over the soft parchment, stopping to admire the scribbles at the bottom of the page; these, I knew, came from my baby nephew, sending his greetings as well. I let my hands fall into my lap, and I sat back. How could Nursia be any worse than when I'd left it? How could there be any semblance of normality with even *more* people starving in the streets?

"What are you thinking of, Sertorius?" The soft voice caught me off guard. It was Junia, Quintus's wife.

"Ah, sorry, I hadn't noticed you." Speaking of fragrances, Junia wore a haunting, subtle perfume that seemed to greet a man and gently engulf him. I felt it slow the beating of my heart. "I was thinking of the past—and the future," I said, my answer less direct than I'd intended.

"Careful, Sertorius," she said, holding a few crumbs of bread to the beak of one of the garden birds. "The man who thinks only of the past is already dead. And the one who lives only in the future will never really live at all." I was surprised by this response.

"I've been known to do both. I'll have to work on that." I replied. She looked at me. For such a meek soul she could make eye contact far longer than most, which I decided meant that she had an inner strength that didn't shine through upon first introductions.

She took a few steps closer to me. "Your hands." To my confusion, she pointed to them. "You know, you can tell a lot about a man by his hands."

"Is that so? Are you a prophetess?" I tried to jest, but she took my left hand between both of her own. She rubbed her silky-smooth fingertips over my palm's every callus, stopping to analyze each one.

"You have an important future. You will be a great man and do great things. But there will be turmoil." She stopped to look at me. "The gods would not have given you so much hard work in your youth if it were not so. But the same childhood that will make you great may also be your downfall." She stopped suddenly and let go of my hand.

"*Are* you a prophetess?" By now I was completely perplexed.

"No," she said definitively. "Perhaps I've had too much wine." Any wine before sunrise would be too much wine, I thought, but nevertheless I found myself returning her smile. Just as seamlessly, I felt myself gravitating toward her. I seemed to have come nearer than before, and we stared at each other for a long moment.

Both of us jumped when we heard Gnaeus waddle into the

peristylum. He paused for a moment to look at us and then shuffled his way on out.

"Have you enjoyed your stay in Rome thus far?" she asked, tilting her head sideways.

"I have. I feel very honored to be here in this house, to be able to learn from Gnaeus and your husband." She didn't respond but looked down with a gentle smile.

"What an honor you've received." She seemed to roll her eyes.

"Sertorius, it's time to receive our clients. I want you present," Gnaeus called.

"Certainly, sir." I sprang to my feet and nodded at Junia, who turned and continued to feed the birds.

I was standing behind Gnaeus in his tablinum when Quintus entered. Clearly he was in a good mood—he bounced into the room, smiling. Gnaeus looked up, as if he resented the young man's enthusiasm.

"You sleep too late, Quintus," he said, returning to his documents.

"Sorry about that, Father. I stayed so late at Reginus's that I was most tired." He didn't seem to mind his father's bad mood.

"You're going to be the greatest man in Rome someday, son. So start acting like it," Gnaeus said. It appeared Gnaeus was trying to convince himself as much as anyone else that his son was going to be the next leader of Rome.

"I'm getting there, Father. Are you ready to see your clients? They're lined up all the way to the Crassi house this morning. I presume it's to do with the drought. Some of them probably need money," Quintus said. His father sighed and hung his head.

"Yes, yes … fine. Go tell your mother to come stand by me as is proper, and then let them in. Have Crito rank them by importance." Quintus nodded dutifully and began to do as ordered. "And, Quintus, you come back, too. Stand by me the way you have been taught. You will need to address them, and you will take care of their needs. I will only sanction. I'll be dead soon enough and then these

will be your clients, so you need to learn how to take care of them."
He stared at Quintus through his eyelashes.

Quintus Caepio took a deep breath and tried, poorly, to restrain
his irritation. He likely had clients of his own and had probably aided
his father since he was a child. But nevertheless, he nodded and left
the room.

"My boy, he's always been a people pleaser," Caepio said. "Have
you noticed? When he was a child, he worked harder than any of the
other students, just to get a few congratulations from his tutor or his
mother. I always got the impression he didn't care about learning—
he only wanted to make people admire him. It makes me wonder if
he even wants all this for himself. A politician without drive is a poor
one, I say. What do you think, eh?" he asked, but as he didn't turn
around to me, I decided he must have been talking to himself. But:
"Are you not going to say anything, Sertorius?"

"I don't know, sir. Quintus seems to want to further his career as
much as the next man."

Gnaeus chuckled. "It's as if you think you are a better judge of
Quintus's character than his own father. Not likely." I bit my tongue.
"And don't think I'm too hard on the boy, either. He is my son and
I can see him for what he is. His best interests are my priority. I am
this way to toughen him up. I'll appear as sweet as Aphrodite once
there are three hundred senators yelling at him and demanding to be
heard." He shook his head. "But never fear, I'll make a man of him
yet." He returned his attention to the scroll before him.

Caecilia entered the room, looking as if she had been up and
working for hours. I supposed she had been.

"Good morning, all." She smiled as she positioned herself at
Gnaeus's right shoulder.

Junia entered as well. She shot me a quick smile and batted her
eyelashes. "Still enjoying your stay, Sertorius?"

"Quite pleasant, ma'am."

"Really? I am happy to hear it."

"Father," Quintus said, peering into the room. "Gaius Mucius is here to see you first. Is that fine by you?" Gnaeus nodded, and after a pause, Quintus departed.

"Is he your son or your errand boy?" Caecilia said, looking at her husband. "We have slaves for these things, Gnaeus."

"Yes we do, and we also have a son who needs to learn what I do. He has to be involved, Caecilia," he said firmly.

Quintus Caepio strode into the room and took his place to the left of his father.

"Sertorius, come stand by Quintus's side," Caecilia said to me, adding in a whisper, "You will appear as his aid—or his bodyguard, even, if you like. The people want to be ruled by the nobility, but they also like for the nobility to show a little affection for them too. Having a strong, rustic commoner like yourself will boost us in the people's esteem." It surprised me that Caecilia gave this order rather than Gnaeus, but I obeyed without hesitation. "Actually, Gnaeus, why don't you give the chair to Quintus? It would look better for the consul-elect to receive our clients—at least until the elections."

Gnaeus turned to his wife, visibly flabbergasted. She met his gaze without emotion, and he pushed his chair out, the sound like thunder against the floor. He stormed from the room, muttering expletives under his breath. From the atrium, he shouted, "Sertorius, I have need of you!" I stood, my mouth fallen open, and looked to Caecilia and Quintus.

"He's the head of the family ..."

"Go." Caecilia pointed to the door and I hurried away. The entire situation was making me uncomfortable.

It soon became apparent that Gnaeus didn't have anything for me to do. He simply didn't want to storm out of the room alone.

"Sometimes I worry about the two of them," he said as he plopped down on a bench beside the impluvium. "She coddles him. Makes him weak. Sometimes I wonder if she even cares about me anymore, now that I can't provide security for her future the way Quintus can." He looked up and remembered himself. His posture straightened, and he tried to reclaim the dignity his voice had lost.

"I've sent one of the slaves to replenish the wine cellars, but I need to get some fresh foods for tonight's dinner. We'll be entertaining Numidicus again. I expect you would like to explore the city, so I'm sending you on this errand."

I didn't desire this, actually. "Certainly, sir," I answered.

"It's unnatural for a young man to stay cooped up in a house like this. How will you know what city you're serving if you don't enjoy it?"

"May I go, too?" Young Marcus ran in from his bedroom. He must have been thirteen or fourteen by this time, but in my mind I remember him as far younger. He seemed to me more like eight or nine, perhaps because of his short stature or, more likely, his child-like mannerisms.

"No, grandson, your tutor has prepared lessons for you today." Gnaeus patted him on the head and turned back to me.

"But I need to buy new sandals! The leather of mine tore while I was playing with Crito yesterday."

"No, Marcus."

"Father, he really does need new sandals. The tutor will still be here when he gets back," Quintus shouted from the tablinum. He'd evidently overheard.

"Fine." Gnaeus shrugged and shuffled off. "Have Crito give you some coin … for the food and for a new pair of damned sandals. Be back no later than the seventh hour."

"Come then, Marcus," I said with a smile, not unhappy to have a companion. He raced me to the door.

Naturally, Marcus led the way. He moved with the energy common to his age, and I'll admit I had a hard time keeping up with him through all the hustle and bustle of the busy streets. Marcus was completely unconcerned about everything going on around him. Having been raised in Rome, the sights and smells were utterly familiar to him, but to me, everything was new and caught my attention. I remember by the end of that journey my neck was sore from jerking this way and that to glimpse all the important men and women being carried past in litters.

Marcus believed that taking the main *via* to the Borarium Forum would be much too hectic and filled with traffic at that time of day. So, touting himself as an expert, he led us off the road and onto the *semitae*—the little back roads that were far steeper than the main streets, or any path in Nursia for that matter.

"It's easy to get lost back here if you don't know the way, but I know every path in Rome by now," Marcus said, grinning proudly as he moved on, his arms swinging energetically to propel him up the hills. A recent rainfall had turned the dirt into mud, and the cold air had hardened it, making it difficult to move without slipping.

Rome was remarkable to me. As I sit here now in Spain, it moves me deeply to consider the intricacies of that city, and I'm reminded of all I felt on that day. Marcus and I crossed through the crowded courtyards of insulae, ducking under clotheslines filled with wet laundry, and doing all we could to ensure we didn't step into piles of animal dung. I remember narrowly dodging the waterfall of a pisspot some citizen dumped from a window three stories above us.

Soon we exited the maze of insulae into an open courtyard, and I was glad for this, as my blood had been chilled by all the shade— even though we'd moved swiftly enough to break a sweat. Here, the sun greeted us with warmth, even if it was accompanied by a haze in the air, presumably from all the hearth fires that had been lit to ward off the growing cold.

"If we cut through there we'll be just a few paces away from the Bronze Bull," Marcus said, pointing toward another back road.

"Lead on, my friend," I replied as he took off with youthful energy. We passed by a group of children heckling their tutor; he pretended not to notice their taunts and continued on with the lesson.

We approached a large marble building covered in chipped scarlet paint. Though my eyes were untrained, it was apparent that this was a temple. A large number of people loitered in front of it, and from the Tiber that flowed behind the temple, came a chorus of vulgar one-lined jokes. I was ashamed for Marcus to hear it, but he didn't seem to mind.

As we passed the building, Marcus stopped.

"Have we any spare money?" he asked, looking serious.

"I assume we could spare some. Why? What is it?"

"To give to that man," he replied, pointing to a beggar sitting on the temple steps. He was a rough-looking man, to my recollection, and I considered dissuading Marcus from approaching such a person. But I'll admit it warmed me that a noble-born Roman like Marcus would want to approach a forgotten man such as this. In his innocence the boy seemed not to notice class distinctions.

"Of course. The gods will look kindly upon such a charitable gesture." I fished through Gnaeus's coin purse for a few *sesterces*, careful to ensure we still had enough to purchase the food and sandals. Marcus took the coins happily and ran toward the beggar, leaving me behind.

"Ave!" Marcus said as he approached. The beggar looked up with furrowed brows. Unlike the other beggars, he wasn't holding out a plate or calling for alms. Instead, he sat quietly with an old helmet before him, a few *denarii* in it.

"Morning to you, young master," he said, bowing his head. Marcus dropped the coins into the helmet but lingered for a moment.

"What is your name?" As I looked at the beggar, the wetness of his eyes, his unkempt beard and sunburned, wind-bitten face, I understood there was a story behind this man. The helmet proved that.

"Rabirius." He bowed again.

"Were you a soldier?" Marcus asked, presumably referring to Rabirius's helmet. Even without it, though, the question would have been a natural one; this Rabirius had a distinctly military aura. Rabirius smiled and looked boldly into Marcus's face.

"I was. And I'm very proud of it."

"Where did you serve?" I asked, wondering if he was ever in Gaul with my relatives or Lucius's.

"I've been on a lot of tours, lad. Seen more countries than I care to remember. I think only of the experience. The chill of the Gaelic breeze, the warmth of a Spanish sunset, the marble cities in Greece that seemed to rise and rise ... to the heavens," he fixed his gaze on the ground and seemed to lose himself. "Of course, the best thing about the military has very little to do with the scenery. It is the brotherhood, the devotion that arises from serving and suffering together. Nothing in civilian life can rival it, in my experience."

"Then, how did you get here? To be a beggar?" Marcus asked. There was genuine concern in his voice, and Rabirius chuckled sadly.

"Oh, I am not a beggar. I am simply an old soldier who lives off the welfare of the state ... and by that I mean the goodwill of Rome's citizens. If you're asking why I haven't taken up some other trade, I don't really have an adequate answer for you. I spent the best years of my life being a soldier, and I learned nothing from the legion except to salute an officer, to march in cadence, to obey orders ... and to kill. None of these things are valued much in civilian life, unless I take up a less-than-honorable job as some henchman or bandit, and that I will not do."

"But why don't your old soldier friends help you, if you were so close?" Marcus asked.

Rabirius paused and then said simply, "Look around you, young master. They're all just like me." Marcus and I scanned the area, and I saw that most of the beggars wore army crests on their tunics, or sat beside a shield or helmet. Many of them were covered with old wounds or were missing extremities. I felt ashamed that I had not noticed them, that I'd been too fascinated by all the other sights and overwhelmed by the effort of keeping up with my young charge.

"Rabirius, I'm sorry for your lot ..." I searched for more words but none came. Instead, I opened my own coin purse and took out a few denarii. Rather than drop them into the helmet, I shook his hand and left them there. "Is this where you stay?" I asked.

"Yes, it is. Right here on the doorstep of this Temple of Asclepius. I vowed my life to the god of healing if he cured me of an infection from a battle wound. He did, and here I sit before you. You don't need to be sorry for my lot, young man; I'm lucky to have come home alive."

"Well, perhaps we will visit you here again sometime." I met his gaze and nodded, before stepping off with little Marcus, feeling a weight on my heart. That could have been my father. It could be Titus, a few years down the line. Something ought to be done. Something. Anything. And someone would have to step up to do it.

We purchased everything we'd been sent to get and hastened back. Marcus was clearly perplexed and didn't stop asking questions the entire journey home. I'll admit, my own mind was swimming too. I wanted to do something, just like I wanted to do something about Nursia, but looking around the Forum as we went—seeing the high temples and the great statues to both god and man alike, I felt utterly powerless. What could a farm boy like myself do in the face of all this? I felt like a pawn of fate, the same as Rabirius.

As we entered Caepio's home, we found the place in as much chaos as the roads had been. Slaves were moving every which way preparing for the meal, Quintus stood in the tablinum rehearsing a speech in a bronze mirror, and Gnaeus was rubbing his eyes with his forefinger and thumb, complaining of all the "blasted noise."

"We've gathered everything you sent us for, sir," I said, interrupting his complaints.

"Take it to the *cocina* and let the cooks have at it. Tell them to be quick about it, too." His eyes were weary as he looked at me. I assume he'd been working hard all the while we'd been gone, his red eyes a result of poring over too much small print.

As I moved off toward the cocina, there was a clatter from the atrium.

"Gnaeus! Gnaeus!" a familiar voice shouted, accompanied by a pair of heavy, hurried footsteps. I could tell from the expressions of the slaves that this wasn't a routine occurrence. My heart started racing and I ran back to Gnaeus, worried there might be a confrontation.

To my relief, it was only Numidicus approaching, along with a young man I supposed to be his son, Pius. These were our expected guests, but I was certain this wasn't the usual method of arrival.

"Brother, what's wrong?" Gnaeus asked, deep concern writ upon his features.

"Look! Look at this!" Numidicus spluttered, holding out a torn document. Gnaeus strained to read the words.

"A bid for consul?"

"Yes, but look who's running!" Numidicus paced back and forth, his hands on his hips, his lips a snarl.

"Gnaeus Mallius Maximus? You'll have to forgive me, comrade, but I cannot place the name," Gnaeus said, looking both relieved and perhaps annoyed that this disturbance wasn't of greater importance.

"He is engaged to the illegitimate daughter of Gaius Marius," Pius explained from behind his father. His lips were pursed and his nose was scrunched as if he smelled something revolting.

"You cannot possibly believe this man poses a threat to us. He's a nobody!" Gnaeus shook his head.

"That is where you're wrong, friend," Numidicus seethed, doing all he could to keep still. It seemed very unlike this haughty man to reveal so much emotion.

"My father is right, Caepio. This man was seldom seen anywhere but at Marius's ankles the entire time we were in Africa. He is a thorn in our side, just the same as Marius," Pius asserted.

"You are correct that he is a nobody. But it would be very much the same as a second term for the Man with Two Names. One term was enough." Though Numidicus breathed heavily, he seemed to be calming.

"We often said 'cave canem' when the man approached, because he was very much a dog at Marius's side. He did everything Marius asked of him and followed the fool's directions more than his own commander's when my father was still imperator there. Marius is the deity he pays homage to." Pius spat.

"All right, all right, gentlemen, I'm beginning to understand. Lets have some wine in the triclinium. The food should be prepared short—"

"I will do no such thing!" Numidicus's fury returned, his hands clenched into fists.

"What do you propose we do then, brother?" Gnaeus's eyes flashed with irritation.

"We go into your tablinum and do not come out until we have devised a plan to ensure his victory cannot happen."

"We must ensure it, Gnaeus," Pius added, as if his father had not spoken forcefully enough.

"Quintus!" Gnaeus called. "We have work to do." The three men joined Quintus in the tablinum and closed the folding door, leaving me alone in the atrium.

This would have been a fair time to retire, but instead I waited outside the door, hoping to be called in and assigned a task. I refused entreaties to dine in the triclinium, wanting to be close to hand if my name happened to be called.

Time crept on and it wasn't until long after my usual bedtime that the doors of the triclinium opened. Numidicus and his son left without any formal farewells, but the confidence on their faces was clearly evident. Gnaeus exited behind them, but he looked more grave than confident.

"Sertorius," he said as he approached me, "are you ready to perform your first service for Rome?"

"Yes," I said. I didn't need time to reflect. In fact, I was nearly overcome with excitement. Hazy visions of grandeur danced in my head; I was eager for whatever fate the gods had prepared for me.

"Good. Then come to me at first light." He rested his hand on my shoulder and gave me a light squeeze, conveying an air of seriousness and trust. Then Gnaeus waddled off to bed, leaving me in the dusty atrium to collect my thoughts. I found it nearly impossible to do.

SCROLL V

October 648 ab urbe condita; three months until election.

Sleep eluded me that night. I lay on my back and stared at the ceiling. I tossed. I turned. My mind wouldn't stop wandering. When I closed my eyes, I pictured Nursia with no people starving in the streets, only smiling faces of neighbors. Everyone was fed and everyone was happy. I thought of Rabirius and the look of joy on his face when land was given to old vets. I imagined the streets of Rome clean and the people prosperous.

I woke at the same time as usual, before the sun. I dressed quickly, holding my shoulders particularly straight. Not only was I excited, but I felt a confidence that I'd never before known.

I left my room with a tablet of parchment and my pen; I had a mind to write home again. As I made my way to the peristylum, I saw out of the corner of my eye movement in the atrium. I halted and craned my neck, finding Gnaeus standing there, staring quietly at the masks on his wall.

"Good morning, sir," I murmured as I approached.

"Oh, good morning, Sertorius." He seemed surprised by my arrival. "I like that you rise so early. It's a rare quality in a man your age." He turned back to the masks and a silence followed.

"You asked for me to come to you this morning?" I interjected into the quietude.

He disregarded my question. "Do you like history, Sertorius?" he asked, pausing before one of the masks and moving his fingers gently over its features.

"The only thing I like better than language is history," I replied. "Sir."

"What do you remember of the Gracchi?"

I searched my brain but couldn't find much. "I'm embarrassed. Most of my interest has been for early Rome, rather than modern times, I'm afraid. I know the Gracchi were tribunes of the people, and they were killed. That's about it."

"Ah. That's good...." He inhaled deeply before continuing. "I guess they died just a few years before you were born. Those old enough to have been there try our damnedest to forget it. You've been afforded the luxury of not having to." Gnaeus fell silent again. The emptiness stretched for so long that I wondered if he'd forgotten my presence. I considered moving away and giving him this quiet moment, but then he spoke again. "About your mission. I need you to go to the Aventine Hill and visit a tavern. You're to give a man some coin in exchange for votes." He finally turned to me. My face must have shown the extent of my disappointment.

"You want me to bribe someone?"

"It's not really you doing the bribery, so much as I am, but I need someone not directly connected with me to deliver the sum."

"I see." I couldn't continue to meet his gaze. I was repulsed. And angry.

"Sertorius, you said to me when you first arrived that you did not have any particular opinions on politics and that you came here to learn. That is a very good thing, to an extent—but you are so young that you do not understand the impending danger the state is facing. Marius is a very dangerous man. He has proved time and again that he is a threat to everyone but himself, and he continuously threatens violence in the Senate House, just the same as he does on the battlefield."

"From everything I've heard, I agree with you. He must be stopped from securing this consulship for his son-in-law, but is there no other way than to *buy* votes? I thought you and your allies owned Rome?"

"I wish it were so, young Sertorius, but unfortunately this republic has always belonged to the highest bidders. We can ensure the votes of the tribes aligned with our families and friends, but those local to the Aventine will only vote for the man who buys their loyalty. And after Gaius Marius has spent the year in Numidia, raiding treasuries and sacking strongholds, he is monstrously rich and can afford to buy himself the whole of Rome if he so desires. Which I assure you he does. We must strike first or his reign will continue."

"Why is this man *so* dangerous?" I asked, exasperated.

"If only you'd been around a little longer. This is why I mentioned the Gracchi. It began with the elder brother, Tiberius, who set all of Rome ablaze with his land reforms. The people loved him. To this day, there are those who sacrifice to him on the anniversary of his death. Yet they did not know that he was damaging them—he was crippling Rome for his own interests. He used legal means to achieve illegal ends. He had men, respectable men, thrown into irons and taken away in the middle of Senate debates if they disagreed with him. He cried out from the *rostra* for a tribune—elected just the same as he was, under the auspices of Jupiter Optimus Maximus—to be removed from office, so that he could continue his measures. He snubbed his nose at all the reasonable advice from his fellow magistrates and the august Senate body."

"And what was so dangerous about all this? He was a rascal, a rabble-rouser, sure. But what danger lies in that?"

"Sertorius!" Gnaeus was beginning to lose his patience, but he didn't seem angry. He grabbed my shoulders and looked me in the eye, as if pleading for me to understand. "Those kinds of actions are forbidden in Rome! Don't you see that? Rome became great four hundred years ago, when we threw out King Tarquin and all Romans swore to never be enslaved to one man again. We crafted this thing, this image, of a state run *by* the people, *for* the people! And they called it *Res Publica* ... a republic, Sertorius! One man cannot have ultimate authority. And Tiberius Gracchus was not voted into ultimate authority, but rather achieved it by clever political maneuvering, distracting the people from the fact that their freedoms were dissolving! Do you know how the Gracchi did this, Sertorius?"

"How, sir?"

"They enact the measures the people desire. So the plebs in the street clamor that their freedom isn't being stolen—nay they are gaining it because of his measures! And Tiberius and his lot fanned this flame, so that he became the only elected official who protected the rights of the people, while the mean old Senate was condemning them. But that is how they lull people into a slumber! Then, once power is seized, they will do whatever is necessary to ensure that it is secured! They no longer need the approval of mere proletariats— they use violence to ensure their victory."

A knot grew in my stomach. "I understand."

"That is what he did, Sertorius. Or was beginning to do." He turned back to the mask he had been pondering for so long. "This was my father. He was a senior member of the Senate at the time, and was one of the men who put down that rebellion—gods protect him. But unfortunately you can kill a man, but you cannot kill an ideology. Tiberius set the precedent, and others have employed it after him. His brother quickly followed suit and was put down the same way. And for years we have been rid of this criminal, infectious ..." He paused and took a deep breath. "But now we have another. Marius is using the very methods that the Gracchi employed. He even had my brother Dalmaticus—the chief priest and a senior member of this state—thrown into shackles and led from the Senate House like a common criminal! He has no boundaries, no ends to his desires, and like the Gracchi he will stop at nothing to gain power. Unlike his predecessors, however, Marius is rich and powerful. He is brilliant militarily, and he looks at the Senate House in much the same way he does the battlefield. He is a dangerous, dangerous man, Sertorius."

"Sir, I understand," I said firmly. "Excuse me, but I must spend some time on this before I accept. Apart from my family, nothing is more important to me than my honor." Gnaeus laughed, which perplexed me.

"I appreciate your virtue, Sertorius. It is part of the reason I brought you on. But if you want to be an honorable, clean-handed man then you are attempting to enter the wrong profession. The idea of an innocent statesman is more myth than the Minotaur. You might as well return home." He placed a hand on my shoulder. "You speak of history. Do you know of Viriathus?"

"The Lusitanian revolutionary?"

"Yes, that is the one. I'm impressed you know him. His revolt was some time before you were born. You'll have to forgive an old man his stories, but this is relevant, I assure you. Lusitania had been under Roman control since the Punic Wars, and for the most part we had peaceful, if not friendly, relations. Then the rebel began his war-mongering and his revolution. They took up arms and took the fight to us before the Romans there had a chance to defend themselves. The men were butchered, young ladies were gathered up in hordes and raped before they too were killed. Women like Caecilia and Junia, like your mother …" I shuddered at the thought. "And then the children were enslaved. By the time a Roman force arrived to fight him, Viriathus had fled to the hills, like the coward he was. He refused to meet the Romans in open combat and relied on ambushing scouting parties and conducting night raids to continue his fight, all while killing innocent Romans across the country. We were at a loss for how to stop him. I remember clearly how frightening those Senate meetings became, as we went through all our options and came up empty. We felt defeated—and not by a great warrior like Hannibal, but by a snake who hides until he sees a chance to strike at your heels.

"We were almost ready to relent and let this treacherous criminal go free, because we saw no other option. But my brother Quintus could not stand that thought. He applied himself vehemently to get command of the province. When he was finally successful, he decided something had to be done. He bribed three men to kill Viriathus in his sleep." I assume I winced at this, for he said, "I know, believe me. It seems dishonorable, right? My brother, if he were still sane, would agree that there was nothing honorable about this. But he sacrificed his honor for the good of his soldiers, for justice, and for his people. To my thinking, skewed though it may be, my brother is the noblest Roman I've ever known.

"There comes a time, Sertorius, when a man must decide: does he want to be an honorable man and do nothing, or be a bad man and do good things?" I remember the feeling of the heartbeat in my chest, the creeping silence that followed, and the flickering of the candle-light. The audience of masks watched us blankly, seeming to attest to the truth of Gnaeus's words. This question has never left me. I've pondered it every day sense, and there is no easy answer, I'm afraid. Because in many ways he was right—I was under Rome's shadow, I believed the mythology about what she was—but the shroud was beginning to be pulled back. I was beginning to understand.

"That is a hard question to answer ..." I finally said, my words barely audible.

"I know that, son." He seemed to offer condolences, as if he remembered the time when he himself learned of Rome's true nature. "Jupiter Capitolinus runs this republic, but he must have both a left and right hand to accomplish his will here. His right hand stands before the crowd, leads, enacts measures ... but there must also be a left hand—men who work tirelessly in the dark to ensure that the right hand, men like my son, can keep their freshly laundered togas clean and white, while we take care of the dirty work to ensure that this state runs properly. Do I make sense?"

"Yes, sir." I had to struggle to summon the words.

"I have had my chance as the right hand, and it is my hope that you will one day have your time there as well, because you have the stuff about you that makes for a leader, I can see that. But now Rome needs you to help my boy get elected. Rome needs you to stop a madman." He locked eyes with me and conveyed such a feeling of importance that I was unable to refuse.

"I'll do it," I said, but I could not keep his gaze.

"You will?" He seemed surprised. "My boy, you will make your country proud." I nodded, but in my heart I admitted that my country's pride might come at the expense of my mother's shame. I nodded and began to walk away, and Gnaeus returned to his masks and his contemplation.

I set off at once with a large coin purse no heavier than my heart. I wore my thickest cloak and pulled the hood up, tucking it in close to my ears. Fortunately, I blended in with most of the passersby in the stiff, cold air of coming winter. This was my only solace: that I wouldn't be recognized.

I made my way south, following the main via as best I could and occasionally needing to ask for directions from irritated foreigners, who knew the way far better than I.

I arrived at the Aventine to find a culture all its own. There was a smell of salt and dead fish ever present in the air, and the people seemed to have a very rough, foreign element about them—although they would most likely tell you they were the proudest and most ancient of Romans.

"Excuse me," I said, halting before a small butcher's shack, cutting my way past citizens angrily clamoring that it wasn't my turn. "I'm looking for a tavern run by a man named Caeparius. Any idea where I could find it?" I asked the butcher. The man rolled his eyes and threw a bloody towel over his shoulder.

"A few paces on your left, down thataway," he said with a nod.

"Thank you, sir." I began to step off.

"Hey, boy," he called after me, giving me a toothless grin. "Whoever she is that you're trying to hide from, she'll find out. Women always find out. They have spies everywhere." He chuckled, although I did not. He must have figured I was looking for a cheap whore at a tavern on a hill other than my own, looking to deceive my wife. He was wrong, but it forced me to reexamine my shame.

As I made my way to the tavern, I noticed how everything on the Aventine seemed lifeless. No shrubbery or greenery lined the roads or crawled up the walls as it did on the marble of the Palatine. Everything seemed to be old and brown, wood and brick.

To find my way to the tavern, all I had to do was follow the shouts of drunken men and the smells of opium and hemp wafting from the beaded door.

I ignored the graffitied depictions of fellatio on the wall and the propositions of the prostitutes as I passed by. Two rough-looking, toothless men stood at semi-attention by the door. They didn't bar my passage, but one of them snorted and spit a wad of thick mucus at my feet as I entered. I'm not sure what the man's intentions were, but if it was to repulse me, he succeeded.

Inside, the tavern was dimly lit, flowing with the booming laughter of sailors, thieves, and downtrodden and outcast ex-senators. I made my way to the bar, noticing that the floor was covered in some sticky substance—whether it was wine or bodily fluids I didn't know. The smell of the men I passed was saltier than the Mediterranean.

"Drink?" the bartender said busily as I approached. There was a great deal of meat hanging by ropes behind the bar, covered in flies. Bowls of prunes, nuts, old grapes, and rotten cheese were laid out on the bar.

"Sure. Whatever you have is fine." The bartender kicked his mangy guard dog out of the way to fix my cup and slammed the drink down in front of me, before moving on to other guests. I quickly found out I should have made a better request. The wine I received was the sourest, spiciest filth I'd ever drunk. The wine had clearly spoiled, and the man had dumped honey and spices into it to cover up that fact. He'd failed.

"You the lad I'm looking for, then?" a man asked, posting up beside me.

"If you're the man I'm looking for?" I said, refusing eye contact, looking instead at a mosaic on the back wall, featuring two men shaking hands. I imagined their interaction must have been just as unsavory as ours.

"The name's Gaius Servilius Glaucia." He extended his hand,

which I reluctantly accepted. I resisted the impulse to wipe my hand on my toga. "So you're Caepio's man, then?"

I nodded.

"You know, I'm probably related to them with a name like Servilius, somewhere down the line. But here I sit, leading the Aventine tribes in these huts and slums, and there they sit ... in the ivory of the Palatine, leading a nation." He never lost his grin. Glaucia obviously found himself funny.

"Let's cut the chatter." I pulled the coin purse from my belt and set it on the table. From the corner of my eye, I saw him rubbing his hands together in anticipation.

"What a sum! Your boys must be desperate. But I'll not take your money." I looked at him in confusion. He stared back at me with a coy grin and deep, empty black pools for eyes, like the dead fish that lined the Aventine market.

"Is that not why I am here?" I asked impatiently. Secretly, though, I hoped he would reply with something about honor and a desire to vote for the best candidate, without the need for bribery.

"I'm sure it is. But you're too late. This is Marian territory now, and I've been instructed to relay the message that your man is to stay away from the Aventine tribes from here on out. Got it?" He snorted vulgarly.

"Understood." I had nothing else to say to the man. I pulled out a coin for the drink and turned to leave, but the man grabbed my arm forcefully enough that I clenched my fists, ready for a fight.

"I can tell by your eyes that you don't like this work. No man of honor goes bribing, that I know."

My anger flared. "And what of you? Accepting bribes and rigging elections? A man of honor does that? You're correct that I don't like it, but you're a fool if you think you're any better. The only difference between you and me is that you seem to be enjoying yourself." I wrenched myself from his grip.

"Oh no, I'm no man of honor." He snickered. "Not at all. But I can see that you think you are. Just be sure not to spend too much time with the gorgons or you'll risk becoming one of them your-self. A man who commits crimes with remorse is no better than the one who does so feeling nothing." I brought myself close to his face, trying to restrain my anger. The smell of wine on his breath was so pungent I nearly gagged. "And eventually you'll feel nothing too."

"You know nothing of me or what I'm fighting for. Keep your philosophy to yourself." I gave him a light push before stepping off. "And inform your man that the Caepiones will respond." I stepped through the tavern, pushing aside the drunken gamblers and prosti-tutes. It had been a long time since I'd felt anger like this. My favorite Zeno quotes of self-control and peace swarmed my thoughts, but I couldn't seem to talk myself out of my rage.

When I returned to the domus, I found Gnaeus standing in the atrium, apparently waiting for me.

"Is it done, then? Have we secured their votes?" he asked anxiously.

"No. Their votes were already purchased by the Marians." I walked past him, afraid I might say something beyond my station in my anger.

"Damn him!" he spat. "How is that possible? I just arranged the meeting last market day!"

"I cannot tell you. But he threatened me, saying our people are no longer welcome in their territory." Gnaeus looked dumbstruck. He followed me into the peristylum. I cupped water from the foun-tain and splashed it over my head, hoping to cool myself. Gnaeus's mouth was agape, as if waiting for happier news or some silver lining. "Something ought to be done, sir, or Marius will have bought the whole city by the Saturnalia." I faced him. He looked away and seemed to be contemplating a strategy.

"I think it is best if you leave Rome for a few days, Sertorius." He nodded to himself. I'll admit I was perplexed and a little angry that I wasn't to be involved in the planning.

"I can help, sir. This is my Rome now, too."

"Oh, I know. That is precisely the plan. Why don't you return to Nursia with news of good tidings, of a new era? Inform them of the measures we are taking here and that with the election of my son they can expect prosperity to return to Nursia."

"If that is where I am needed most, sir," I said, pursing my lips to hide my growing excitement.

"It certainly is. Tell them grain will follow close behind you." I had half a mind to embrace him. My sense of loyalty to the Caepiones was growing by the day. If he truly meant to help my home, there was nothing I wouldn't do for him. I extended my hand, which he heartily accepted.

"Thank you, sir," I said. "I'll pack my things immediately."

SCROLL VI

October 648 ab urbe condita; three months until election.

The following morning I was crawling out of my skin to get on the road, but first I needed to make a stop. Following the directions I'd received in a letter, I went directly to the Esquiline Hill and then down to the Subura, heeding crude street signs to a block of insulae. They were, perhaps, better constructed than some of the others I'd seen in Rome, but they were nothing compared to a domus like Gnaeus's. I stopped before a brick building several stories tall and supported by large Greek columns, half scarlet, half the color of cream. After checking a sign hanging from a terrace, I started across the threshold but was stopped by an obese man with a stained tunic.

"Ay, what's your business?" he said, hoisting a club onto his shoulder.

I ignored the man's threatening pose. "I'm here to visit a friend. His name is Lucius Hirtuleius. Any idea where I might find him?"

"Third floor, second room on your right. Should have his name on the door." The man sounded bored as he returned to his stool at the foot of the steps. "Any trouble and I'll know the reason why." I made no response as I passed him by.

I made my way to the third floor, pausing only to admire the childish artwork on the walls. There was a relatively fresh scene depicting Gaius Marius receiving a crown from a Numidian, with the title "false king" scribbled above it. To his left stood another Roman, towering over the fallen corpse of a regal-looking Numidian. This Roman had the name SVLLA scribbled above him.

On the door I presumed to be Lucius's, I found a long list of tenant names, all of them crossed out save the last: "Lucius Hirtuleius." I couldn't help but smile as I knocked on the door. I'd missed my old friend.

After a brief moment, the door cracked open and Lucius peered out.

"Quintus? What are you doing here?" he asked, perplexed, as he opened the door wider.

"Not so happy to see me then, eh"

"Of course I am!" He sprang to embrace me. "I'm just surprised, that's all! Come in, come in! What on Gaia's green earth has brought you here?"

"To see my old friend!" I said happily as I entered his simple home.

"Well, let me show you around, then," he said, and he began pointing to his bed, his window with the small hanging garden he'd constructed. Despite the small scale of the place, he was obviously very proud of it—and I was proud of him.

"Perfect for a young man," I said, clapping him on the shoulder.

"I'm sure it's nothing compared to your royal villa, eh?" He laughed. "Please, sit!"

"I haven't received a letter from you in a few weeks now. How was the conclusion of your training?" I took a seat at his table.

"Couldn't have gone any better, Quintus, I assure you. The whole thing was miserable, but now that it's done, I can lie and say it was the most fun I've ever had!"

"So you've sworn in and everything?" I asked, amazed at the difference I saw in my young friend. He'd arrived in Rome a boy, naïve and perhaps even foolish, but now he was a man—a soldier—bringing all his youthful bravery and toughness to fruition. I was, perhaps, a little jealous of his experience.

"Took the oath last week. I'm proud to say I'm officially a man of the Colors! Well, tell me of your time with Rome's finest. How is my elite friend doing these days?" he said, rising to pour us both a cup of honey-water from a clay amphora.

"I wish I had some noble stories to tell, but unfortunately politics is more boring than you'd expect. Things move at the speed of pond water."

"*Gerrae*! I'm sure that isn't true. What have they had you doing?" he asked. I admit I was too ashamed to mention the bribery, and there wasn't much else to tell.

"I've really just been a pair of eyes and ears, drinking in everything I can. I've received my first task, though, and I'm setting off today," I said, his smile forcing mine.

"Tell me then!" He leaned over the table and pushed my shoulder.

"I'm to return to Nursia and give a rousing speech of hope and prosperity to our kinsmen in the name of my patron, who is a consul-elect."

"Really now?" His smile gave way to a look of despondency. "Which candidate is your man?"

"Quintus Servilius Caepio, son of Gnaeus." Suddenly a very strange look crossed Lucius's face, a seriousness that was entirely unusual to him.

"I hadn't remembered they were your father's patrons," he said, swirling his honey-water around in his cup.

"Why? You know of them?" I asked, somewhat offended that he wasn't more excited for me.

"Yeah, I've heard of them ..." He looked away and bit his lips. He seemed unable to respond.

"All right then, brother ... was it something bad?" I prompted.

"Yes, Sertorius. They're just like all the nobility—concerned with their own interests and crippling the state." The conviction of his reply baffled me. I'd always respected my simple friend for his unwavering convictions, but this time I was appalled.

"Correct me if I am wrong, brother, but did you not come to Rome to be a soldier? Not a politician?" I sneered, awkwardness enveloping the room like a plague.

"I did, unlike yourself. But I had to say something, Sertorius."

He shook his head and looked down. It was the first time, to my recollection, that we had ever disagreed on anything. He always used to follow me with devotion and fidelity, no matter the interest or concern.

"So you've heard a few idle rumors in the barracks and you presume to know what's going on in the Senate House?"

"I've heard more than rumors."

"Like what? What have you heard?"

"Quintus, you cannot possibly believe that spoiled urban patricians like the Caepiones will ever help Nursia! You've backed the wrong patrons," he said, turning finally to me. I felt every defensive response rush to my head, but I did all that I could to calm myself, for our friendship if for nothing else.

"Then who do you think can?"

"Gaius Marius." His eyes met mine.

"Cac! Marius? *Marius*, Lucius? You've already been brainwashed by the legion, I see." I stood up and pushed my chair in, barely able to contain my disappointment, anger, and shock.

"I've been brainwashed by no man, Quintus. I know Marius personally and I've come to respect the man a great deal. He is the future of Rome." Many unkind comments sprang to mind; I wanted to accuse him of conspiring with a renegade and of judging me on faulty knowledge. But I decided it was best to let it go. No words could sway my dear friend once he came to a conclusion, and so there was nothing I could do. He would have to find out who the villain really was for himself. I was sure that his strong morals would eventually cause a rift to grow between them.

"I am sorry, friend, but I must be going," I said, grabbing my cloak and throwing it over my shoulders. "I came to ask if you would like to accompany me to Nursia, for old time's sake." I made my last attempt.

"I'll not go on the orders of your patrons, Quintus. I'm sorry. Besides, I'm needed here."

"All right.… . I'll be off then," I said, making my way to the door.

Lucius said he required a handshake and an embrace before I was to leave, and he bade me farewell with, "Until next time," but honestly I wasn't so sure anymore. Just then, there wasn't a whole lot about which I was certain.

I don't remember much from my journey home. I paid little attention to the scenery, as my mind was consumed with troubled thoughts. I do, however, remember that every step became colder and colder. My time in Rome had left me unprepared for winter at higher elevations. As I made camp each night, chilled to the bone and trying to warm my hands over the fire, I remembered my journey to Rome only a short time ago, laughing alongside Hirtuleius as we discussed things both past and to come. Now, I sat all alone, listening to the angry voices in my mind.

As I neared Nursia, I was greeted by the smell of pine trees; in my youth, it had been such a comfort to me, but now the scent was so very unfamiliar compared to the musk of Roman air. I hadn't been gone long at all, but I felt like a stranger there. For the first time, I felt as though I had no home, no place to call my own.

I approached the old wooden gate I used to run by as a child and received only a curt nod from the sentry posted there. I crossed the threshold into Nursia. The air was so still and cold that a white, ominous presence seemed to surround the village. Men, women, and children lined the streets, huddled under blankets, but the only real signs of life were the quick, shifting movements of coal-black birds as they pecked incessantly at something on the cobblestone path. I moved through the streets with great reluctance, as if some force were restraining me, warning me of danger, and urging me to turn back. I could barely stand to look at the faces all around me, but nor could I pry my eyes away. I couldn't recognize a single person. To this day, I have no idea if I'd somehow never come across those people before, or if their misfortunes had rendered them unrecognizable to my eyes. They watched me with expressionless faces, as stony and cold as the death masks on Gnaeus's walls. I am unashamed to admit that tears fell freely from my eyes as I passed by, feeling like I had walked into at a large burial or a slave camp.

Do not take me for a hypocrite, Reader. I know I've told you I am a Stoic and therefore see suffering as neither good nor bad, intrinsically, but rather I believe it can even be useful. The Sabines had been suffering for an endless sea of generations and that didn't bother me—for my ancestors and their brethren had sacrificed their peace and security for something larger than themselves. They suffered numerous toils and endless depravities in the fight for the freedom of our people and later, when they paved the way to extend Rome's borders to nations across the Mediterranean. No, what grieved me so deeply was that this suffering was so pointless, so needless, so utterly avoidable. I'll admit mine is a poetic soul, hopelessly optimistic at times, but I could find no evidence of greater meaning for this pain, no silver lining. What good could come of children starving and freezing in the streets, without even their parents to comfort them? Something had to be done, and that made my mission all the more grave and serious.

I made my way to the center of the town; we called it the marketplace, but now, after experiencing the wide throngs of Roman shops, guilds, and storehouses, I realized it was little more than a few fruit and vegetable stands. I went halfway up the stairs that led to the town square, made an about-face, and paused.

"Citizens of Nursia!" I shouted. My voice carried endlessly in the lingering silence of the village. Nothing seemed to stir. "Citizens of Nursia!" I shouted again. A few moments passed before heads began to peak out of windows and a few confused people walked over from the side streets. I waited, despite my discomfort, as more people heard the growing murmur and began to make their way toward me to see what the commotion was about. Even some of the poor, lifeless creatures from the street rose and approached curiously.

"M-many of you know me. For those of you who do not, my name is Quintus Sertorius, son of Proculus. I've r-recently left my

home here for Rome, where I've been working to bring aid to Nursia."
I was shaking badly and my stutter had reared its ugly head. I tried
to resist it at first, feeling mortified, but eventually gave way to it.
"I am grieved, friends, d-deeply grieved. When I left Nursia, things
were bad. Otherwise I might have stayed. What I see today is a truly
unbearable sight. I have loved and valued this village as my home for
the past two decades, and I believe I always shall. That is why I have
attached myself to the patronage of Gnaeus and Quintus Caepio, the
very men who secured our aid in the past, when my father was still
alive.

"I know many of you may scoff at the idea of those in Rome
caring enough to help you, as they sit in their pleasant homes, eating
and drinking. But unfortunately, things in Rome aren't any better.
Everywhere you go you will find the starving, the sick, the thirsty ..."
I lapsed into silence as I remembered the hopeless faces of Rabirius
and his friends. "And I've found that even those who are more fortunate have not forgotten about those that aren't. I know it's easy to
blame them for our trials, their lethargy in aiding us, but I find that
most men, rich or poor, would rather prosper through the h-hap-
piness of others than through their misery. Our patrician allies in
Rome are extending their hands to you. They send a message of hope,
begging you to hold on a little longer, to continue this fight until help
arrives. And that is the very reason I am here—to promise that help
will arrive soon. Grain and supplies will be coming from our bene-
factor Quintus Caepio. He hopes that you will help to ensure he is
elected to office so that he can continue to lend aid not only to us but
to all Roman people, domestic and abroad." I took a few steps down
so I could look directly into the throng of Nursians that was continuing to grow.

My stutter vanished as elation overcame me. "We have lived
through a hard time, brothers and sisters—even by the accounts
of our ancestors. We have endured loss, sickness, poverty, and
the deaths of our loved ones. But I am here to proclaim a new era!
One of peace, one of prosperity! One of the Roman people coming

together—rich and poor, blessed and cursed, provincials and city dwellers—for the common good of each other and of this great nation we are honored by the gods to occupy. I urge you, friends, to fight! *Fight!* Press on until you can do so no longer. There are calmer seas ahead, greener pastures. Do not give in to despair, to grief. Push on, for a new day is rising!"

They roared with applause. I wept. They wept. Many approached and embraced me, whispering, "Thank you, thank you" again and again in my ear. I felt that I had done nothing to deserve their thanks—nothing had yet been done to change their circumstances—yet I was deeply honored to have restored just this small bit of hope to my home. For the first time since I had left Rome, I considered my own trials infinitely unimportant compared to this. I made no empty promises that day; I meant every word.

I spent quite some time there in the town square, speaking with as many Nursians as I could, embracing those I remembered (I have to imagine it was most of them) and vehemently shaking the hands of those I did not—pleased to meet more of my people. Eventually, through the throng I spied a familiar face: my mother. She waited patiently behind the others, bearing a gentle smile and glistening eyes. When she noticed me looking at her, her face lit up and her tears began to flow freely. I apologized to the man I'd been conversing with and bolted toward her.

"Mother!" I cried, as I ran into her arms.

"My boy, my sweet boy!" she sobbed into my shoulder, while I pressed her as hard as I could to me. I remember vaguely that the crowd around us clapped and cheered our embrace. I had never been so grateful to see her. I inwardly shamed my younger self for taking my family for granted. I turned to find my sister-in-law Volesa standing at my mother's side, clutching my baby nephew, all bundled up, to her chest. I hugged her gently and leaned over to kiss Gavius, who looked up at me with wildly curious eyes, as if he'd just woken from some life-altering dream. I searched for words, yet couldn't find them.

"Don't forget *us*, you bastard!" a voice shouted behind me, and I turned to discover my friends Spurius and Aulus. I held open my arms and locked them both firmly around the neck.

"Aulus, Spurius, my old friends!" I laughed, as we wrestled, "How could I forget you?"

"I was about to ask what brought you home, but I guess we know the answer!" Aulus said with a genuine smile, looking me up and down, perhaps trying to notice a difference. I turned to my family and told them I'd be home shortly, and they nodded and headed for our house.

"How have you been, Quintus? How is Rome?" Spurius asked, positively brimming with excitement.

"I've fared well, brothers. I cannot complain at all. But I am deeply gladdened to return home, despite the conditions of the village."

Aulus nodded. "It has been rough, truly."

"The worst I've seen it," added Spurius. "Which I assume is obvious."

"Oh, how is Hirtuleius? Fighting and scrapping with the best of them, I presume?" Aulus asked, giving me a wily grin.

"You'd best believe it. He has also attached himself to some important men, except he wears a soldier's cloak and I wear a toga." In that moment, I thought of my old friend with nothing but goodwill.

"Really? Well, excellent!" Aulus said, and he and Spurius exchanged a look of mutual shock and pride.

"Has he been struggling with the condition of old Manius? I figure that must be hard on him," Spurius said, catching me off guard.

"What? What's wrong with Manius?" Lucius' grandfather was old, but I was still surprised to hear that something might be wrong with him. My heart began to race.

"You haven't heard, then?" Aulus looked to Spurius, deferring to him the job of giving bad news.

"Manius is very sick. He'll likely die any day now. I cannot believe you haven't heard. It makes me wonder if even Lucius has."

"If he has, he has not mentioned it. Excuse me ..." I said fumbling over my words. "This burdens me."

"That as much as everything else has added to the solemn spirit in Nursia. He may be a mean old man, but he's been a pillar of this village for nearly a century. I think Nursia has relied on his strength more than we've known," Spurius replied sadly, his brother nodding.

"I apologize, friends, but I must return to my family. Can we have a drink before I leave?"

"We'd like nothing more." We embraced again, though more subdued than before. I set off toward home at a quick pace, knowing that I had to see Manius for myself. He'd always been so strong, so tough. In my youth, his mythic persona seemed somehow to eclipse death, but unfortunately I was learning quickly that no man can escape death, no matter his strength.

I hurried home but felt I couldn't move fast enough. I spoke with my mother and sister-in-law for but a moment before I apologized and said I had to go see Manius. They lowered their eyes and said I had best go soon, which amplified my fears.

I held back tears as I pushed out into the bitter cold of Nursia and followed the familiar, well-worn path to Manius's house. It was along this path that I used to run as a child, when going to play with Lucius. We would pretend to be soldiers and generals, waving fallen tree limbs like great swords.

Before I could reach the door, Lucius's younger brother, Aius, burst across the threshold and ran to me, as if he had sensed my arrival. He fell into my arms and was already crying. He tried to speak but the only managed a gurgling sound from deep in his throat. My young friend had always acted well beyond his age. An old soul, we called him. But here he seemed as broken and lost as any child would be. Both his parents dead, his brother moved on, his only provider now beginning his journey across the River Styx to the afterlife.

I held him to my chest as he wailed the high-pitched, helpless cry of a babe. It broke my heart.

"He is dying. What will I do?" What a valid question it was.

"Take me to him," I replied.

He turned and led the way back into the house as cold and barren as Nursia's streets. Manius had always kept a spartan home, with only the barest necessities and nothing at all for pleasure. He kept chairs with no backs so as to necessitate proper posture, the mosaic tile on the floor told of no aquatic adventures or tales of the gods. It was how this house had always been, yet still there was something different about the place. Perhaps it was only that there was hardly any light. The candelabra that usually brightened the dark home were barren, and the dark clouds outside didn't permit any sun to shine in through the windows, either. There was a particular smell, a musk, which seemed to be the very essence of sickness. I could tell his condition was bad, perhaps worse than I was prepared for.

Young Aius led me to Manius's bedroom, where I strained my eyes in the darkness to make out the figure crumpled on a straw mattress on the floor. He'd been withering for some years since he lost most of the mobility in his legs, but now he seemed at risk of dissolving altogether. His legs and arms were pursed together tightly, as if he were trying to compress himself into the smallest form possible.

"Grandfather, you remember Quintus Sertorius, don't you?" Aius said, trying to sound cheerful. The old man's eyes were still alert, and he looked up at me, shaking slightly, for a long moment before he nodded his head and rested it back against an old straw pillow.

"Manius, how are you, sir?" I knelt by his side and reached for his hand. I think this kind of affection would have been promptly refused earlier in his life, but now he made no attempt to pull away.

"He was coughing constantly yesterday, violently. He hardly ceased from dusk till dawn, but since late last night he has been silent, hardly making a sound. Even his breathing is shallow," Aius said from the doorway. I had very little experience with the sick and the dying, but I knew this wasn't a good sign.

"When did all of this begin? Or better yet, how did it begin?" I turned to Aius.

"I don't know. He woke up one morning and was feeling particularly feeble and told me to work outside by myself until he could get up. He refused any help. When I returned at the end of the day, he was still here in his cot, shivering and sweating, his head radiating heat like a fire." I turned back to Manius and looked in his face. Although his eyes were still alert, he seemed to have no idea where he was or what was happening. "He didn't react to anything," Aius said. The corners of his lips and the areas under his eyes were black as coal. It reminded me of the faces that lined the streets outside, and I wondered if it was a result of the fever.

"Aius, would you bring us some well-watered wine?" He nodded and shuffled away, and almost instantly Manius began to convulse. His bony legs and arms began to twitch in an almost epileptic rage. I pulled him up by his shoulders and into my lap. Even in his withered state I had a hard time keeping him under control. Spit and bile bubbled from his lips and ran down his chin. When Aius arrived at the door, I heard the amphora and cups clatter to the ground.

"Come and hold his hand, Aius," I said as calmly as I could, ignoring the wine spilling across the floor. He ran and knelt beside us, sweeping Manius's hands up between his own. Manius slowly returned to his docile state, his shallow breaths returning in irregular patterns.

I cannot say how long we stayed there. Hours, I guess, maybe even half the day. I do know that what little light had filled the room seemed to die away, and later on some of it reappeared. Manius shifted between angry, restless twitching and utter stillness. Several times we both craned our necks to see if he had stopped breathing, but time and again his chest continued to rise and fall like an easy tide on an early morning. Aius wept quietly but did his best to maintain his composure, knowing how much his grandfather had always valued strength and self-control.

As time passed, I could see a slight yellow tint begin to cross Manius's face, starting around the eyes. Suddenly he began to convulse again, but I felt that this time was different. His tongue pushed through his lips and his eyes looked up at the ceiling, so intently I thought they might disappear behind his eyelids.

"If there is anything you would like to say, Aius, I think now is the time." I still do not remember exactly what he said. Through bitter tears he told his grandfather how much he appreciated all that he had done for him—his care and his tutelage. He told his grandfather of his undying love, which I assume was the first and only time they had shared such words, and swore an oath to carry on his legacy. I remember trying to calm myself as I pressed my eyes shut, trying to hold back the warm waterfall of tears that flowed regardless.

"I thank you as well, sir," I remember saying as Aius finished. Shortly after, a deep, low breath arose from Manius's chest as if it was being driven from his body, and then he went limp. Aius finally let his emotions go, and he fell back against the stone, sobbing. I slowly returned Manius to his cot and pulled the sheet up over his face.

I tried not to think too much and had to keep pushing away the thoughts that seeped into my mind. Was I like Manius? Would I be respected and admired? I felt unclean. How could I be wading in the political filth of Rome when I had been reared among such noble men? The thoughts continued to flow, and I tried to push them away. I tried to dwell on Gnaeus's words about being a great man or doing great things. *Perhaps*, I thought, *I am not to be afforded the luxury of having both.* But even then, I knew it wasn't true.

It is funny how death, like the ending of a play or an epic poem, redefines everything that precedes it. In life, Manius had been a cold, unbending man, who we all feared as much as we respected. Now, in death, we remembered him as a statue of the old Roman ways. His death represented the passing of the old breed of Romans, the strong, unyielding, quiet kind.

Aius and I both returned to my home and told my mother of his passing, but she didn't seem surprised. At once, we began preparations for a funeral, and the very next day we burned him on a pyre before the same faces that had cheered me the afternoon prior. We mixed his ashes with wine and interred them in his ancestral burial ground, on a grassy knoll atop a hill that overlooked Nursia. It comforted me to think that Manius would oversee my old home, protecting and guiding our people the way he'd always done, just as silent in life as he was now in death.

How easy it must be for you, Reader, to disassociate yourself from these woes, as it often is for me so many years later. But so very long ago, those sights left me forever altered. To lose Manius, to see the burden of my people, left a scar on my heart that has never fully healed. It created in me an attachment to the very land beneath my feet, a need to do what I could to leave Italy better than when I was welcomed into it. Despite such intense feelings, it is difficult to put myself in those shoes again. Perhaps it is because my mind has refused it, or just because memories—even the bitterest, most formative ones—fade away with the passage of time. But after rereading some of my personal correspondence, I am reminded of the pain that was so prevalent at that time.

After the funeral we were left to answer Aius's question of what he would do. He was too young too live alone, too young to leave for Rome. There was no alternative. My mother and I decided it was our duty as his clansmen to take him in. He would be well cared for, I knew, by my mother and Volesa, even though we were enduring hardships of our own. But, then, what are friends for if we are unwilling to suffer alongside one another?

We returned to my family home immediately after Manius's ashes were interred. Aius followed reluctantly, looking back at Manius's house. Within no time at all of our arrival, Aius was fast asleep on a couch in the triclinium.

I felt much the same as he did, and found a couch of my own, dropping down onto it like a sack of old wine. I was too exhausted to do much of anything, but too wired to sleep. I spent a few moments staring at the old walls of my home, as if shades of my youth circled around me, reminding me of both happy times and sad, the things that shape us into who we become. Finally, my mother came in and sat down beside me, smiling at the sight of me home again. It was the first moment of rest we'd had since my arrival, and there was a natural understanding, a peace between us, that I can't explain.

"So tell me about Rome, my son," she said quietly, so as not to rouse Aius across the room.

"There isn't much to tell, honestly. It is all that I had hoped, in a way. I've been given a great opportunity, but perhaps it's not exactly what I'd expected."

"And what of our patrons? Are they good to you?"

"They are. I'm growing increasingly loyal to them for the good they have done me ..."

"Yet you are not sure you trust them," she said.

"I find that good or bad can both be taken in stride and handled accordingly, but ambiguity is a hard thing to conquer. What am I supposed to do when I don't know what is right?" I looked to her for an answer and realized for the first time that my eyes were incredibly weary.

"But you do know what's right, my son. Look within yourself. You've been raised to value what is right, and you are a good man. I don't say that simply because you are my son, but because you are the hope for so many people. Search within yourself. Your instincts will always lead you on the right path."

"I only wish it was as easy and as noble as that sounds. Thank you, Mother." She stood and knelt to kiss my head, and I guess I fell asleep shortly thereafter, because I don't remember anything else from the evening, nor did I come to until late the next morning.

When I arose, I strode through the corridors of my home the same as I did the Caepiones', in search of something I couldn't find. I finally approached the shrine to the household gods in what used to be my bedroom. I lit the candles and knelt before it, closing my eyes and resting, feeling as if my father were there with me.

"I pray that I will be led down the right path, that I shall see right and wrong and choose the former. I ask that you'll guide me to help my people, to better my country. If it pleases you, I vow my life—if only you will use it for good." At length I stood.

I spent some time that day catching up with my mother and with Volesa and the baby. We cheered and gasped as Gavius stood upright and began to walk between us, a feat that surprised me, since he'd hardly been able to crawl when I left for Rome. I walked around the house and smiled at the dents in the walls and the scratched paint where Titus and I had caused some mischief or other in our youth, the paw print in the cement on the floor where my ancestor's dog had stepped during the house's construction. All these things reminded me why I loved my home, but they also reminded me of why I had to leave.

I packed what little I had left and told each of them farewell in their turn, trying to keep the moment as calm and peaceful as possible given the emotional turmoil we had endured. "Goodbye, Mother," was the final thing I said from that doorway, giving my home just one last look before I turned away, eyes facing west, to Rome.

SCROLL VII

November 648 ab urbe condita; two months until election.

I arrived at Caepio's domus around dusk three days after I left Nursia. The home was relatively empty when I entered; a few slaves leaned against the walls, talking idly, and only straightening as I neared.

"Sertorius!" I heard Caecilia's voice from the tablinum. She rushed out to embrace me. "How was your journey? How was your home?" she asked, brimming with delight.

"It was good to see my family and friends again," I said, as she patted my shoulder.

"Well, we are happy to have you back home. Yours is a most welcome presence here." Her cordiality caught me off guard.

"I'm very honored to hear you say that, madam. I have great respect for this house, and I hope that I have done my humble part."

"Humble no longer." She leaned in close, a sly grin on her face. "I overheard Gnaeus and Quintus speaking a few days ago. They both agreed that despite your origins, you are a man who commands respect. They plan to utilize you more often in the future and seek to continue assisting you in whatever way you need."

"I-I'm taken aback, madam. I very much appreciate your trust in me."

"Very good," she said. "Forgive me, I must be getting ready. Gnaeus and Quintus are dining on the roof, if you would like to join them." She pointed to the staircase. I was eager to do so, hoping for some further praise.

I set my bags down and marched up the stairs to the roof.

"Sertorius! You've arrived. We were beginning to worry about you," Quintus said upon sight of me.

Gnaeus waved me over, saying, "Come and have a seat." Both he and Quintus were tucked under heavy woolen blankets, and their faces were pink from the wind. "How was your first speech?" he asked, pouring me a cup of wine.

"It went well, I think. The village cheered and all expressed how much they look forward to the aid you've promised. I would say Nursia is now among the staunchest of your supporters." I took a sip of the wine, pleased to discover it was far better than the swill I'd tried to drink on the Aventine.

"Very good. How exciting that must have been for you!" Quintus said. I was overjoyed to find both my patrons in such good moods. I stared over the vast ocean of temples, insulae, and state buildings to the horizon, where the pale blue sky convalesced into a silk apricot that covered the coast.

Suddenly Gnaeus spoke up. "Sertorius, we've been invited to the home of Aurelius Cotta for a wedding ceremony this evening, and you are more than welcome to come along."

"Really? Who is getting married—anyone I've met?" I asked, sounding more ignorant than I liked.

"The daughter of Cotta, Aurelia, is to be married to a man I don't believe you've met," Quintus replied. "His name is Gaius Julius Caesar. It's not the best match in my opinion, but I would never say that. The Julii are an ancient and respected family, but there's been little to tell of them for over a century now. Regardless, I'm happy for Aurelia."

"I don't believe I've had the pleasure of making her acquaintance yet, nor that of Gaius Julius, but I'd be happy to join and offer my congratulations." I was honored by the invitation.

"Master Sertorius?" came the peculiar voice of Crito from the entrance to the roof.

"Yes?"

"I'm sorry to interrupt, sir, but some mail arrived for you while you were away. I've laid it in your room. Just wanted to let you know." I nodded my thanks and returned my attention to Gnaeus and Quintus.

"Go on, boy, we know you want to read it." Gnaeus grinned.

"Thank you, sir." I sprang to my feet and made my way back downstairs.

"Sertorius, you might want to begin preparing yourself presently. We'll be leaving within an hour or so," Quintus shouted from above.

"Certainly, sir," I called back and continued downstairs. I hurried to my bedroom to find a single letter beside my pillow. Instead of wax on the seal, it was dried mud. Despite the rough insignia, I made it out to be the image of my family from my father's ring, now worn by my brother, Titus. It seemed a life-age since I'd heard from Titus, and I was overjoyed to run my fingers over the soft parchment before breaking the seal and poring over the familiar, rough penmanship.

Greetings, brother,

I have heard that you are now under the tutelage of the Caepiones. I am very proud indeed that you have taken the first step in what I believe will be a long career for you. The politician's toga will suit you adequately. I am sure they have been very kind to you and that you are adjusting fine. Still, I implore you to remember your values. I will not tell you how to live your life, but I want you to remember that loyalty to dogs is no better than disloyalty to good men.

Things here in Gaul are about what you would imagine. This winter has been boring and frigid, nothing but marching and building and sleeping in mud. I look forward to the beginning of war season again, when we can take the fight to the Cimbri. If it wasn't for Volesa, Gavius, mother, and yourself, I would very much like to stay here. A soldier's life suits me, just as it did our ancestors. Perhaps you will join me here, if you ever decide that life among Rome's finest is beneath your station. I look forward to our reunion, brother.

Titus, Prefect of XI Cohort, IV Legion

I sat back and pondered my brother's words for a long time, not for the first time wishing that he would be more direct and forthcoming. It irritated me that he was trying to discourage me from what I was doing with the Caepiones, but it did make me think. I had to silence my mind before I started to dwell on the subject for too long. Regardless, I was happy to hear from him.

Imagining the two of us fighting on the open frontier for the glory of the Republic gave me a thrill that politics didn't seem to ignite in me. After a moment, I set down the letter and changed into a new toga. Despite Titus's misgivings—and Lucius Hirtuleius's for that matter—I was doing something I knew was for the good of Rome, and therefore I had to prepare myself for whatever lay ahead.

I'll admit, for all my professed excitement, I was dreading another dinner party with the nobles. After the truth of all the emotions I'd experienced while home in Nursia, I wasn't particularly looking forward to a night of the nobles' duplicity, no matter how genial they were.

"I thank you again for this invitation, patron," I said to Quintus, as he helped his wife into a litter before crawling in himself.

"Dear me, you're part of the family now, after all," he said with a wink. Though I was flattered, I couldn't help but notice that they were all carried in litters while I walked behind.

Two slaves led the way, one with a cane to whip away undesirables, the other with a lantern, though it was still light outside. We moved slowly and deliberately, like a funeral procession, toward the home of Caesar II, where that night's feast was to be held for the man's son and new daughter-in-law. It came to my attention that the formal ceremony had been conducted the night prior, an event from which I, no doubt, would have been excluded. This was the social celebration. Gnaeus explained it as, "Verbal consent fulfills the legal expectations, the sharing of the hearth fire and water fulfills the religious expectations, and this celebration will fulfill the social expectations, and the first night … the practical expectations." He winked again.

We arrived in the Subura, where I was surprised to find the noble residence of Caesar. I would have figured a patrician like our host would have a home on the Palatine, where all his colleagues resided, but one could at least say that this home was triple the price of the shabby townhouses that surrounded it.

We ignored the heckling of citizens on the road and halted before the domus. My patrons took their time getting down from their litters, and we waited there to be addressed. One of Gnaeus's slaves beat the door ring to signal our arrival, and the steward slave answered.

"Greetings, masters! Welcome," the slave cried, bowing low and holding the doors open for us. Quintus waved the litter-bearers away, and they found their place along the adjacent wall among the litters of the other guests.

The home was packed. Compared to Gnaeus's domus, this home was small enough to make one feel quite enclosed—especially with the thick gathering of nobles. We moved slowly, formally, through the house, as if we were admiring artwork in a museum. Caecilia took the time to critique everything she saw. I started feeling antsy walking behind those old nobles and quickly squeezed my way through to the less-crowded tablinum. Much like Gnaeus's desk, Caesar's was covered in legal documents and recently read texts. The only item of note was an old sword and scabbard on the far wall, sitting atop a small Greek column of ancient stone. I analyzed it with deep interest. It was certainly timeworn. It was the color of rust and looked as though it might dissolve in my hands.

"My ancestor—whose name I bear—brought that home from Sicily during the Punic Wars," came a voice behind me. Startled, I stepped away. "No, it's all right. That blade has stood the test of time—I don't think there is anything you could do to harm it." The man stepped closer and admired the sword as well.

"I don't believe we've met. I'm Quintus Sertorius, client of the Caepiones," I said, extending my hand.

"Have we not? I always pretend so at these dinner parties. Much easier that way, nay?" He accepted my hand lazily and took a long pull of wine. "I am Sextus Caesar, brother of the recently enslaved man ... married man, I mean," he drawled, noticing the confusion on my face. I forced a laugh. "Client of Quintus? He must have you deep in the electoral filth then, huh?" He smiled, revealing wine-stained teeth.

"Not really. They keep me out of it for the most part—I assume because I am so new to all this."

He laughed. "Or to keep you from wading in the filth before you've been properly broken in, more like!" He slapped my shoulder rather aggressively. I tried again to laugh. I was glad to have a private word with a transparent man, rather than be consumed by the noisy chatter of a room full of walking masks, but the way Sextus Caesar looked at me was unnerving. Behind his persiflage there was a coldness to him that is difficult to describe.

To my relief, Gnaeus and Caecilia entered the room, arm in arm.

"Your Grace." Sextus bowed low, not minding that he spilled some of his wine.

"Ah, Sextus. How are you?"

"The gods bless me."

"Not jealous of your brother, then?" Gnaeus tried to jest.

"Oh dear me! Of course not. I'd rather be shackled in a prison cell than shackled to one woman. Besides, a disappointment like me? My father would sooner marry off one of the guard dogs to a patrician ally." Sextus was evidently very amused with himself, but we all had a hard time responding to this. "Don't let me keep you. Find your way into the triclinium whenever you can. Hurry and get the honey-wine before it's all gone." He bowed again and stumbled out, leaving Caecilia and Gnaeus to exchange an indiscernible look.

We left the tablinum and followed the procession through the peristylum to the entrance of the triclinium. I found myself bewildered by the procedures of high society, as Gnaeus and Caecilia lined up beside each other and Quintus and Junia followed behind with Marcus at their sides.

As we entered the dining area, the butler slave shouted, "Gnaeus Caepio and wife Caecilia! Quintus Caepio, wife Junia, and son Marcus Caepio!" The guests gave a dandy clap and cheers of awe rose from the room. The slave stared at me with a raised eyebrow as I trailed after my patrons without an introduction.

Two beautiful slave girls led my patrons to couches in the center of the room, both in places of honor to the left of the open couch reserved for the bride and groom. I made my way to the wall and leaned there, observing the nobles in their natural setting.

I'll admit that whoever was in charge of the decorations had done a splendid job. Garlands of scented white rose petals draped the walls, accented by silk shrouds hanging from the ceiling. The music of lyres, flutes, and tambourines accompanied the anxious buzz of gossip.

"Honey-wine from the foothills of Mount Vesuvius, the finest Falernian grape in Rome." A slave knelt before me, extending a silver chalice filled to the brim.

"Thank you," I said. Two slave girls removed my sandals and placed my feet in a bowl of water filled with perfume and rose petals. They dried my feet with steaming linen towels.

"Thank you, master," one of the girls said in a thick accent. She was beautiful, presumably a German of some kind. I was awestruck; Caesar's slaves were adorned only in the richest silk and were better kept than any I had ever seen.

Time went on as the patricians exchanged greetings and discussed current affairs, all the while picking delicately from the appetizers on the small, round tables placed before their couches. Finally, a hush fell over the room as the bride and groom arrived at the threshold. "Gaius Julius Caesar III and his new wife, Aurelia!" The guests all erupted in happy applause, and both the bride and groom bowed low before turning to give each other a quick kiss. They stepped down into the room and embraced their new fathers; Aurelia took the hand of the man I learned was Caesar II, a man half the height of most of the others and twice as hairy, while Julius embraced old Aurelius Cotta joyfully. I found myself smiling.

"Thank you all for coming here tonight to celebrate this momentous time in our lives. This is a happy day, friends! The union of our families will promote prosperity, not only for ourselves, but for all of Rome!" Julius said and taking his wife by the hand, he led her to the head of the room. I got the impression that everyone knew what was to follow, but I had no clue, given my complete lack of experience with patrician weddings—and for that matter, weddings in general. A scarlet tarp was brought forth and unraveled at the feet of the newlyweds, and then a sheep as white as Nursian snow was led forward.

A dagger was placed in the bride's hand and Julius stood behind her, taking her delicate hands in his own.

"I sacrifice this lamb to the households gods, so that their favor will rest on our union forever more," Aurelia said, her voice innocent and as sweet as the honey-wine. Hers was a striking figure: tall, slender, every tassel of her hair perfectly set. It amused me to think that such a creature could have been formed from a feeble man like Cotta, but his wife Rutilia proved how it was possible.

Julius guided Aurelia's dagger to the lamb's throat. The bride locked eyes with her new husband and didn't look away as together they sliced the lamb's throat. It bleated a single cry and the beast collapsed. Applause thundered through the room as the bride and groom walked off to clean themselves, while the slaves fell to cleaning the scene they'd left behind.

The first course arrived—stuffed lobster and moray eels drenched in hot sauce—but I refused what was offered me, deciding instead to introduce myself to those I could. I've always been rather quiet around strangers, not naturally personable in such circumstances, but I knew the opportunity to mingle with the upper crust of society was too great to pass up.

I introduced myself to Cotta's son Gaius, who was discussing Aristotle's *Nicomachean Ethics* with his uncle, Publius Rutilius Rufus.

"It's good to meet you, friend," Gaius Cotta said as he shook my hand. He was awkward and lanky, more like his father than his mother, although perhaps half his father's weight. His hair was shaggy and unkempt, and I remember that he seemed to have a perpetual cold. His uncle Rufus, on the other hand, was a soldier if ever I'd seen one. Rufus stood at attention all the while, even as he greeted me. He met my gaze with cool, calculating eyes. "Are you a soldier?" he asked.

"Who? Me? No," I stammered. "I've thought about it but haven't made my way to the registrar yet."

"Well, you've got the build for it. You look like a soldier," Rufus said, returning to his conversation with his nephew. My thoughts returned to Titus's letter. Suddenly, Rufus's words seemed like prophecy. After all, no one had ever told me I looked like a politician. I didn't fit in here in Rome, but I imagined a camp in Gaul at my brother's side would suit me just fine.

I made my way around the room, joining conversations wherever I could and finding each as awkward as the last. I could not always control my stutter.

After making rounds for a while, I noticed two stunning women speaking with each other in the corner of the room. I thought about approaching then, but even considering doing so was enough to make my palms sweat. Fortunately, they noticed my attention and came over to me.

"Greetings, I don't believe we've met," one said, extending her hand. "I am Julia, sister of the groom." I accepted her hand and bowed my head.

"And I am Illia, the youngest of the Caesar brood." They were both gorgeous. Julia, the elder, had pronounced cheekbones and the noblest eyes I'd ever seen, and her skin and lips looked soft. They both had golden, radiant hair, straight and well kept at the top and as wavy as the Tyrrhenian Sea at the bottom. Illia looked much like her sister, but there was more youthful vitality in her eyes, less wisdom and perhaps more girlish mischief.

"I am Quintus Sertorius, client of the Caepiones."

"Welcome to our home," Julia said with a smile.

"Are you from the city?" asked Illia.

"I am from Nursia. I am here to learn from my patrons all that I can, but I have considered joining the legion," I said, testing the idea that seemed so fresh that night.

"Gods, you should meet my husband. You would get along with him just fine," Julia laughed.

"Is he here?"

"Bona Dea! No," Illia giggled and touched my shoulder. "Do you not know who he is? Gaius Marius?" I am certain my eyes revealed my shock.

"*You* are married to Gaius Marius?"

"I am. It will be two years this April."

"Don't worry," Illia jested. "You're not the only one who is surprised."

"Most of the men here don't think very highly of my husband," she said.

"He seems to be a brave man, ma'am." I averted my gaze. How strange this was. Aurelius Cotta had sat with the other nobles, berating Marius and his lot, and all the while marrying his daughter to the brother-in-law of the Man with Two Names.

"It's because my father is the cleverest bastard of them all." Sextus Caesar appeared behind me and put his arm around my shoulders, startling me badly. "He married his eldest daughter to the most famous man in Rome and his son to the richest aristocrat's daughter. Gods, even little Illia here is betrothed to Marius's co-conspirator Sulla, who is in Africa with him presently." Sextus swayed from the effects of his wine. "And I—I'm just the debauched eldest child who hasn't yet been of any use to the old man." He chuckled and belched.

Julia shook her head. "Nonsense, Sextus! You always talk like this. If Father thought for a moment you had the slightest interest in marriage he'd have you the finest bride in Rome."

"Maybe you're right." He turned to me. "But I like my whores."

He winked as his sisters rolled their eyes.

"Enjoy your evening, Quintus Sertorius," Illia said, batting her eyelashes as she led her sister away by the arm.

At the end of the night we bade our hosts farewell and returned to our litters.

"Patron, I have something I'd like to discuss with you," I began before I even knew what I would say.

"One of those conversations? All right, what is it?" Quintus asked as the rest of the family climbed into their litters.

"I'd like to stand for military tribune."

"Dear me," he laughed and looked at me in bewilderment. "Why would you want to go and do something foolish like that?"

"I feel it's a natural first step in beginning my career, and I believe it's my duty."

"But we need you here."

"I believe that I've done all I can to help you in your electoral campaign. I can wait a few weeks until the voting begins, if you would like?" I heard myself almost pleading.

"No, no. You should stay here. We need you, and Rome is a far more fitting place for your talents than the muddy forests of Gaul or the endless deserts of Africa. Let the men with no ambition do the dying." Quintus climbed into his litter and snapped his fingers for the journey home to begin, and I followed from a distance, swallowing both my pride and my frustration.

SCROLL VIII

December 648 ab urbe condita; two weeks until election.

The weeks leading up to the election are a haze to me now. I do not have much correspondence from that time, and so have little to refer to. I couldn't bring myself to write home without news that relief would soon be headed that way, and I couldn't bring myself to write Titus either. I told myself it was because I was upset at the contents of his letter, but in truth it was that I wished to tell him I would join him in Gaul as a tribune following the elections, and of course, that was not the case.

Regardless, little of real note took place. Quintus started spending less time around the domus and more time in the Forum. Whereas before he'd preferred to spend his hours reading poetry with his dear friend Reginus, he now did such things as speaking from the rostra. As I've mentioned before, I found Quintus to be a strange candidate for oratory—though it didn't matter much. His speeches and their contents were essentially irrelevant, since his bid was all but bought ahead of time.

Gnaeus continued to handle all of their clients at the morning levy, promising them great things to come with the fresh season. He was optimistic, even joyful—going so far as to commission a large bust of Janus for his tablinum. Caecilia, meanwhile, dined often with Rome's most noble ladies, and Junia kept feeding the birds.

I'll admit that during this long while I debated going to see my friend Hirtuleius. The situation was difficult: duty required me to tell him of his grandfather's passing, but due to our last confrontation, I was uncomfortable at the thought of approaching him. Even without the bad news I brought, I did not know how he would receive me. Finally, my better nature won out, and I set off for the Subura to see my old friend.

"Sertorius! It's good to see you!" Hirtuleius greeted me as if nothing had happened between us.

"You as well, my friend. How have you been?"

"Fortuna smiles on me, as she does you, I hope?" I shrugged in response, and he continued, "Well, how was your visit home?"

"Honey and spice. It was good to see our fatherland, as you'd suppose, but it wasn't easy. I'm afraid things have gotten worse." At this, Lucius dropped his gaze. "And ... I have something else to tell you."

"Speak freely, amicus."

"It's best you take a seat," I said. His expression became grave as we both sat at the table where we had so recently argued. I leaned over and placed my hand on his knee. My heart broke for him even before I spoke. "Your grandfather, Manius, has left us to join your ancestors."

Lucius's eyes strained shut. After some time, he inhaled deeply and looked up, as if the very spirit of Manius, with all of its stoic virtue, had flowed into Lucius's veins.

"I suppose I shouldn't be surprised. I shall have to make a sacrifice to Dis Pater." A silence followed, but he didn't seem to notice. "I'll have to visit his grave when I return home. Was he interred on the ancestral grounds?"

"He was. All of Nursia sent him off with every honor that can be bestowed on a man. You would have been very proud."

He cleared his throat. "Thank you for coming to tell me."

"It was my duty, although I confess it's no pleasure to relay such news. I grieve with you, amicus."

"And what has become of my brother?"

"He is staying in my home, under the care of Volesa and my

mother." Lucius seemed relieved, and he locked eyes with me.

"You and your family are good people, then. I've always known that, but I am truly in your debt."

"There is no debt, Lucius. This is what friends must do for one another during times of struggle."

When we returned to happier topics, I told him of the Insteius twins, and we shared several laughs about old times and childhood memories.

"Listen, I've got to get going," he said, catching me off guard.

"Oh, I understand. I've stayed longer than I meant to anyhow."

"No, no, I just have prior engagements. But you should come with me."

"Where to?"

"To the Field of Mars. I'm meeting with General Marius." He must have noticed the look of calculation on my face, because, "Gerrae! He can't infect you with his presence, can he? It won't hurt to meet the man."

"Yes, but ..."

He raised his eyebrows and gave me a wily grin. "But what?"

"It could be dangerous for a client of the Caepiones to be seen with him."

"Wait ... spies? Where are the spies?" I couldn't help but chuckle as he looked dramatically around the room, even going to his small window and peering out. "I don't see any spies. Besides, Marius has his own reasons to be discreet. Come on, then. Let's go."

I could hardly refuse. Besides, I much preferred Lucius's company to anyone else's, so we set off at once to meet the most famous man in Rome.

On our way, Lucius explained why Marius was still at the Field of Mars. Marius—certain of an impending victory over the Numidians in Africa—expected a Triumph for his service. He would doubtless be awarded one, Lucius said, but if Marius entered the sacred boundaries of Rome, he would lose his imperium and thus his right to a Triumph. Instead, he was merely "visiting" his troops in Italy to see how they were developing—though of course, we all knew he was also lobbying for the election of his son-in-law—while his quaestor, Lucius Cornelius Sulla, mopped up all the enemy remnants in Africa. According to my friend, Marius secretly desired to hold out until he could be awarded the command of the north, so he could receive a double triumph should he conquer that territory as well. However, Marius refused to ask for this honor, worrying he would be perceived as overly ambitious, and instead relied on his friends in Rome and his almost mythical reputation to earn him the title. It all seemed a little vain to me, but after everything I'd heard about the man, I decided I needed to meet him before drawing any conclusions.

The Field of Mars always smelled of fresh leather—especially when a large force was training there. A sound like distant thunder always followed the marching drills of the trainees, and as we approached, we heard the chattering and laughter of idle guards.

When we arrived at what was clearly Marius's tent, Lucius snapped smartly to attention and saluted the sentries posted there.

"Lucius Hirtuleius, reporting to see Imperator Marius."

"And who's your friend?" one of the sentries demanded in a Corsican accent, glaring at me intently.

"Quintus Sertorius, a companion of mine. I vouch for him." At length they nodded and stepped aside.

Marius's tent was more like a small home—larger even than Lucius's insula—though it was very spartan. Everything in the room was of some utility to military matters, and unlike Gnaeus's tablinum, Marius's table was neat and proper with all the military reports organized in an orderly fashion like an obedient column of soldiers. Lucius led the way to a backroom and we entered. To my shock, Marius was lying upon a table with an old Greek slave performing some kind of surgery on his right leg. His soldier's tunic was pulled up to reveal his thigh, drenched in blood. He had a damp rag on his forehead and a small wooden peg lodged tightly between his teeth. Between incisions, the slave dabbed at the blood with a dirty towel so that he could make sense of his work. It looked much like the butcher shop in the Forum Boarium, except this slave seemed far more frightened than any butcher I'd ever seen. In fact, he looked far more concerned than Marius did. The general lay completely still, grunting lowly every so often, but never squirming. This was my first impression of Marius's toughness, and it was a lasting one.

"Desist this at once, you old woman," Marius said impatiently as he spit out the peg. He tossed the rag at the doctor and told him to patch him up. "Clearly the cure isn't worth the pain."

"Sir." Lucius snapped to attention.

"Oh, Hirtuleius, I'm glad you've arrived," Marius said, sitting up. The slave began to thread, stitching through the various incisions. "And you must be Quintus Sertorius. It's a pleasure." Marius extended his hand, which I hastened to accept. The man appeared like a great eagle, with his head pressed backwards and arms like wings tucked to his sides.

"You know of me, sir?" I stammered.

"Do I know you? Dis, I feel like I know you better than my own wife from how often Hirtuleius praises you." Marius laughed as Lucius blushed. "What has brought you here today?"

"Quintus brought me unfortunate news. It seems my grandfather has died. I persuaded him to come along to meet you."

"Ah ..." Marius paused. "Unfortunate business—death, I mean. You're welcome to make whatever sacrifices you feel inclined to, on my coin."

"Thank you, sir."

"By Bellona, would you hurry up!" Marius's famously gruff voice boomed at the slave, who mumbled his apologies. "Sorry you arrived to this. I've had these tumors growing in my legs for some time now. I figured I'd cut them out, but it's no matter." Finally he stood and pushed the doctor aside, ignoring a few still-open wounds. "Pour us some wine," he said to another slave standing silently behind us. "So you're from Nursia as well, I presume?" Marius asked me. He quaffed his wine as though he was deeply parched.

"Yes, Consul. I have plenty of stories on my friend Lucius here, if you're ever in any need of them." Lucius punched my shoulder.

"I'm sure I could make use of them. I once had a friendship that reminds me of you two.... He died on our first campaign," he said, rather carelessly. The man had witnessed so much death, this was hardly a surprise. "It was in Spain. Have you ever been to Spain?" he asked us both, though neither of us had. "Hardy country. I'd prefer it to any other corner of the Republic, but those bastards can fight, I'll tell you." He waved at the slave, indicating for him to give us our wine. "My friend and I were born in the north, Arpinum. Have you ever heard of it?"

"I haven't, sir," I replied.

Marius grunted. "I didn't figure you had. Small place, probably not too dissimilar to your hill-country. Harsh winters, scorching summers, so few beds that my brothers and I had to swap out each night." He smiled at the memory. "Despite how small and insignificant my hometown was, my family was so lowly that I couldn't even have served in a local magistracy. So I began the only path to a career that I saw possible: to fight, maim, and kill—like your friend Hirtuleius here. I fought with my companion under the late General Scipio Aemilianus, gods protect him, and by the time I returned, I was well on my way to where I am now. And do you know how I did this?" Marius couldn't contain his grin. Hiking up his sleeves and tunic, he directed us to the various scars that covered his flesh—even a deep old gash stretched across his forehead and through his left eyebrow. "It definitely wasn't how many men I killed, or by kissing the arse of some pompous old patrician, but by these scars, by sweat, and the glory that comes with it." He was obviously proud of his past. "I share this with you, Quintus Sertorius, because Hirtuleius has told me of your home and the state Nursia is in. I am not so far removed from my roots that I cannot empathize with you."

"I appreciate that, sir. I have great respect for anyone who can rise to prominence through merit," I said. Marius grunted again.

"Well, since I have shared, I'd like to ask you something now. What have you heard of me?" He locked his steel-blue eyes, cold and strong, on me, and I felt as if I was on trial, although his demeanor was nothing but amicable. My words caught in my throat for so long that finally Marius repeated his question.

"Consul, I've heard nothing but good things from my friend Lucius. But I've heard from others that you are attempting a revolution in the vein of the Gracchi." Marius clenched his fists, and for a split-second I saw the anger he would become famous for.

"Immortal gods! People say that, do they?"

"Nobles, mostly."

"That's ridiculous. I am no Tiberius or Gaius Gracchus, of that I can assure you. The Gracchi stand for the rights of the mob. Do you know what the mob is?"

"The people?" I shrugged.

"No. The mob is a hand-selected crowd of people—only those who support the cause of the mob leader. I don't stand for the rights of the mob, but for the good of all Rome. There is a difference."

"I see. But, sir, any kind of revolution has to have a figurehead. Even if you do not wish to support the cause of the people, they look to rally behind you." A smile cracked across his face, a look of badly concealed pride behind those blue eyes.

"Sertorius, in my fifty years, I have seen a great deal—of that I swear on Jupiter's Stone. I have seen that there need to be changes to the fundamental fabric of this society, and I intend to make those changes, no matter what foolish labels the dusty old noblemen attribute to me. Nor do I care what enemies I make or what friends I keep." His voice was conviction itself; there was no wavering in him.

"And what are these changes, Consul?"

"Well, for one, to cut down on the wretched bribery in this city. I want to see officials elected on merit, like I was, and not due to the size of their coin purse …" His voice trailed off as he noticed something about my expression. "What is it?"

"Permission to speak frankly, Consul?"

"Yes, speak freely," he said impatiently.

"I was sent to the Aventine Hill to deliver a sum of money to the tribal leaders there for the assurance of their vote—an act I am not very proud of. But when I arrived, they claimed you had already purchased their loyalty."

Marius burst into raspy laughter and stopped as abruptly as he had begun.

"Is that what they told you? No, it's not true. I am a declared enemy of that treachery. You have only to look at the state records of my time as tribune or praetor to see proof of that. The only thing I did was have my people visit the head of the Stellatina and Oufentina tribes. They were told that if my son-in-law is elected—and I am allowed the leverage to continue my military reforms—that members of their families would be able to serve in my legions. Currently, only those with ten thousand *asses* of property can serve their country— which is a whole pot of nonsense. I have passed measures that this outrageous number be lowered to four thousand asses, so that any man with a little backbone can serve. If I have no representation in the upper echelon, the nobles will doubtlessly work to undo what I've done. I told the Aventine this, and that under my regime they will have a place to make a better Rome and to make a better living for themselves than wrangling fish from the Tiber."

"Is this not a bribery of sorts?" I asked, rather sheepishly.

"You may call it what you wish, but I merely stated facts," he snarled. Hirtuleius shifted nervously at my side. "Sertorius, you have not seen the state of our military. Despite what reports would have you believe, it's weaker than it has been since the second war with Carthage. This is because the land-owning citizens that once fought to make this country great have now abandoned their people's cause to seek their own interests. Fewer and fewer come to the registrars to join the legion, and those that do are entitled and pompous, with no discipline, no patriotism about them. In Spain I remember the wealthiest soldiers served as the cavalry. They were so arrogant, so insubordinate, that General Scipio Aemilianus could find no use for them. He had to rally up his own band of soldiers to serve as his guard, for he couldn't even *trust* the spoiled cavalrymen. This is the state of Rome, Sertorius, and it will only get worse. But as the fervor for service dwindles in the hearts of the rich, the streets are continuously being filled with the poor who would relish the opportunity to wield a sword."

"That is very interesting, Consul," I said, unable to meet his gaze—though, I had to admit it made sense. Of what I had learned from my time with the Caepiones and their allies, I could hardly imagine those entitled men taking orders and obeying with military bearing.

"Besides, I can't really be held responsible for including the *hoi polloi* in the legions, even if it is where my personal sympathies lie. The real cause is the massive losses our men have suffered due to the blunders of incompetent noble leadership," he said, and I had no rebuttal. "Pour him some more wine," Marius ordered his slave. "Hirtuleius, there is a reason I selected you, and Sertorius, there is a reason I've taken a vested interest in you as well. You boys are a lot like me: outsiders who grew up inconspicuous and seemingly unable to better there own station in life. In time, I think you will see Rome for what she is beneath the shadow of the nobles. I hope that in time you will join my cause, Sertorius. I can see that you have a warrior's blood coursing through your veins, and I don't say that lightly. There will always be a place for you on my staff. Perhaps as a military tribune, or even quaestor in time, given your family." This offering shocked me deeply. Everything in me wanted to jump at the opportunity. It was as if Marius had somehow received intelligence that I had been seeking a military tribuneship—although I knew my patrons had thought so little of it that they hadn't mentioned it again.

"I am deeply honored, Consul…. I'm not sure what to say."

"Then say nothing. Just know that the offer stands. I want to show you something. Mago, bring me one of the barrels," he said to a slave in one of the rooms across from us. A Numidian man with a gentle face but massive shoulders—possibly the biggest human

I've seen to this day—carried into the room a large wooden barrel, setting it down between us.

"Anything else, sir?"

"No, Mago, thank you," Marius said. It surprised me to see a consul thanking a slave; although this man stood with a dignity that I took to mean he hadn't been a slave for very long. Marius cracked the lid of the barrel and scooped up grain that trickled through his fingers like water. "This is for Nursia, Sertorius. It's grain from Africa. I've got miles of it, and I intend to send it to several ailing cities throughout Italy. I intend to give this gift whether you join me or not, but I wanted you to see that you would be joining a man of action rather than a man of fine words." I had to bite my tongue. To see the very grain that could feed my people and stimulate the Nursian economy gave me such hope. But I couldn't do it.

"I am sorry, Consul. I deeply wish to accept your offer. And you may be right about all that you have said. Perhaps my patrons have sought out only their own interests. I do not know whether they are good or bad, but I do know they have been good to me. And I cannot betray what they've done for me."

"Very good. Loyalty, fidelity, honesty.... I like you, Quintus Sertorius. I trust that you'll think over my offer. It still stands, should you ever decide to make a change."

"Again, I am deeply honored."

"Save all that." Behind us, the flaps of the tent opened and several men poured in. I stepped out of the way so they could salute Marius. At first I couldn't place them, but after a moment their names began to appear in my mind.

Gaius Julius Caesar, the newlywed; his brother Sextus; Publius Rutilius Rufus, who had asked me about philosophy; Gnaeus Mallius Maximus, the man running for consul. I began to tremble. Even before I spoke I could feel the stutter forming on my lips. These men had seen me at the wedding. They knew me, and they knew my patrons.

Marius introduced me to them and I accepted their hands as if we had not yet met. Rufus and Sextus Caesar seemed to have forgotten me, but Gaius Julius looked suspicious.

"It's a pleasure to make your acquaintance," he said and forced me to meet his eyes.

"You're more than welcome to join us, Sertorius. We have plenty more wine. I'm sure it's soldiers' swill compared to the Falernian you've been drinking, but it's ample and you can have as much as you'd like."

"I appreciate your offer, Consul. B-b-but I best be leaving." I shook as I made me way to the exit.

"Go with fortune," Marius said, and the others echoed the sentiment. I saw Julius watching me until the tent flap folded closed behind me.

I didn't stop shaking until I arrived back at the Palatine. If my patrons discovered that I was so much as in the presence of the Man with Two Names, they might have me killed.

I was relieved to find the domus empty. I listened for Quintus and his friend Reginus reciting poetry in the peristylum, Caecilia's distinguished laugh from the triclinium, or Gnaeus berating a slave for the temperature of his wine in his tablinum. But all was silent.

I gathered a wool cloak from my room and made my way to the roof. I sat and looked up at the stars, thinking how Lucius had done the same thing on our journey here to Rome. My breathing was erratic, and I couldn't keep my legs still.

I stared across the vastness and grandeur of Rome, the shadow of night cast over it. I focused on the hearth fires burning in the windows of small houses below us on the hill. Just as I began to calm myself, I heard footsteps behind me.

"Gods!" I shouted, startled, and turned to find Junia.

"Looks like we're all alone," she said taking a few slow, graceful steps toward me. "Quintus and his parents have gone to visit Scaurus for the evening."

"I find it strange to say we're alone in a place like Rome." I turned back to the sea of buildings before me. "This house has about as many slaves as Nursia does villagers." I tried to jest.

After a moment she took another step toward me. "I always feel alone in Rome." We both fell silent and the sounds of a sleeping city blared in my ears.

"I must go." I said, rising from my chair. But before I could go far, she grabbed my hand. Her touch mesmerized me.

"I feel less alone when I am with you." I felt dizzy. Despite the cold, my body suddenly felt warm. After a moment of hesitation, I turned and placed my hand on her hips. I watched her gaze shift across my face and eventually settle on my lips.

"Junia." I stepped away. "We can't do this. I can't do this." I distanced myself further. "Your father-in-law and husband have been good to me, they have taken me in and … and …"

"I have been stuck in a loveless marriage since—" Her lips began to quiver.

"I know, Junia. I know. Quintus isn't perfect, but I know he cares for you. He is a good man." The moment the words left my mouth, her lips stopped trembling. Her eyes dried.

"No, Sertorius," she said, "he is not."

SCROLL VIV

Lucius Hirtuleius—December 648 ab urbe condita; three days until election.

After Sertorius left, Marius's business with me was nothing unusual. He updated me on the various speaking engagements planned for Maximus and his allies, and we discussed protection for the various events. We had encountered no foul play thus far, but it was clear to me that Marius was cautious, perhaps even waiting for something to happen. He prepared for Maximus's political campaign much as he had his victories over Jugurtha in Numidia, from all the stories he told me.

Two days later, however, I heard a great clamor at my door. I slid a dagger into the back of my belt and approached.

"Who goes there? What's your business?" I pressed my weight against the door.

"It's Mago, young master. I'm sorry for the disturbance." I hastily let Marius's body slave in. His dark skin glistened with sweat, and I supposed he had run all the way from the Field of Mars.

"What is it, Mago? Has something happened?"

"No … quite the opposite. Well, yes, I guess …" He stopped and caught his breath, placing his hands akimbo on his hips. "I'm not sure what has happened, but Marius said it was incredibly important that all of you assemble at his tent right away. He's sent couriers to all of his allies, and they should be arriving soon."

"Gods. That doesn't sound good. I'll grab my cloak."

"Perhaps it isn't, but Marius was overjoyed when he told me to go."

I grabbed my cloak and bolted from my home, Mago trying his best to keep up despite his exhaustion. I arrived along with Marius's allies. They had not taken the time to assemble litters, or even an entourage; Norbanus showed up without his toga. As we entered, the only sounds were of hushed voices and the crackling of torches in the wind. I saluted but did so silently and said nothing else. In the dim light of Marius's tent, I finally made out the general standing in the corner, whispering to Maximus.

Marius caught sight of us. "Thank the gods you've come. I'm sorry for the disturbance at this hour, but you'll be very pleased with the news."

"You better have ample wine." Norbanus grinned, and Marius snapped his fingers at a nearby slave.

"Make sure they're all sated, but not too much. This is a conversation for sober minds."

"Well, what is it then? Don't keep us waiting all evening," Rufus said.

"Gather 'round then, gentleman," Marius said and we all crept up to his desk. "I have been contacted by a man named Lucius Reginus, who claims to be on very intimate terms with the consul-elect Quintus Caepio. Given Julius's marriage to the daughter of Aurelius Cotta, that makes us extended family with the Cottae and the Caepiones to boot. Reginus said that in the interests of the state, he wishes for a parley between our two parties." He suddenly stopped and looked around, before leaning in and continuing in a quieter tone, "It appears that the Caepiones have fallen out with the Metelli, to some extent, and wish to come to a truce with us, to ensure that Quintus Caepio is elected with Maximus as his co-consul, rather than allowing Metellus Pius to have the second chair."

Rufus shook his head. "That seems hard to believe…. Numidicus and Gnaeus Caepio are like brothers."

"To all *appearances*, yes. But from what Reginus said, the Cottae and Caepiones have discussed things with the Father of the Senate, Marcus Scaurus, who has never liked Numidicus, and they've decided it's not in the best interests of their alliance to allow his son to be elected. They stated his age as the reason, but it isn't difficult to see that they're simply tired of the Metelli. They're a plebeian clan that has risen to consider themselves equal to the patricians."

"But Scaurus is married to Pius's first cousin, is he not? This would be quite a betrayal," said Rufus.

"A scandal, more like." Sextus Caesar smirked.

"Yes, Rufus, you are right. And that is why I was sworn to secrecy. They said that this must be handled with the utmost confidentiality. I'm only cleared to discuss it with you gentlemen here. No one outside this tent is to know."

"And what makes you think that this Lucius Reginus is worth trusting?" Julius spoke for the first time.

"I've checked my sources. It seems he is hardly ever away from Quintus Caepio's side. Some whisper they are actually lovers, but that is no matter. He came bearing a sealed letter with the Caepiones' insignia on the wax. It gave us instructions to meet in Ostia tomorrow after dark." Marius took the parchment from a fold of his toga and passed it around.

"This sounds incredibly dangerous, Marius. You of all people should know how an enemy sets a trap. What if they try to attack you en route?" said Rufus, ever the soldier and pragmatist.

"I agree. In the letter, I'm directed to take a boat from the Aventine port. Supposedly it will be provided by our ally Gaius Glaucia and we will be rowed down the Tiber to Ostia, without the sailors having any information of our voyage. But I find that too dangerous. So I say that we take the Via Aurelia—" He ran his fingers along a nearby map. "—here, down to Ostia through the northern gate. As for once we enter the city … we have arranged protection from an ally of mine, Saturninus, who is the grain monitor there and has a detachment of guards under his command. Any objections?" Marius scanned our faces.

"If you trust that this is the best idea, then we will follow you," Rufus said finally.

"This shows me that the nobles' position is desperately weak. I do not think they would suffer one pleb to serve in office in the place of another unless they felt confident that only one patrician could be elected. This is what we've been waiting for!" Heads nodded silently. "It's settled then. Hirtuleius, round up ten of our best men and meet us here no earlier than the second watch. Understood?"

"Yes, sir."

"Good. You must guard Maximus with your life. The future of Rome hinges upon it."

"Understood, General." With that, we were dismissed. Some of the men, notably Maximus, stuck around to speak with Marius further. It was difficult to gauge how Maximus felt about the whole ordeal, but he surely trusted Marius to his core. I returned home to a restless night, and the next day prepared myself for whatever the gods had ordained.

There was something strange about the air that night as we reconvened in Marius's tent. There was a stillness—a mist seemed to linger there and glisten in the light of the full moon. Maximus had persuaded Marius to stay behind, saying his presence was an unnecessary risk, so I set off with only the consul-elect and ten men under my command. We moved silently through the maze of tents to the Via Aurelia in the northwest of Rome. Everywhere men were sleeping, the only sounds the occasional snoring and the crunch of our sandals on the Italian dirt.

"Men, form a protective column," I whispered, and the boys split, five to the left and five to the right, on either side of the road. Maximus took the middle and I guarded his flank.

My heart raced.

We found the road to be completely deserted. In those days, the roads were far too dangerous at night for the average traveler, but I wasn't particularly concerned about brigands. They would not attack a well-trained column of Roman soldiers, whatever the hour. Still, as we passed between rows of endless ancestral tombs, it felt as if we were being watched from all sides. Perhaps the dead themselves had returned to earth to witness our journey, knowing that the balance of power in their ancient families now hinged on the success or failure of our mission.

We moved at a slow, cautious pace for half an hour until I called the column to a halt.

"Sir, this is where we are to cut off the main road for Ostia. Any orders?" I asked Maximus quietly.

"No. Lead on." Maximus seemed cautious as well, swiveling his head often, his eyes extremely alert, but there was also a serenity, a calm bravery about him that gave me peace.

I signaled for the column to make a turn off the road and continue along the well-worn dirt path toward Ostia. At the sides of the road were large overgrown fields of grass and thick weeds. I specifically remember hearing insects buzzing, and once, the rustling of some animal gave us all a fright. Finally we reached the point where we were to turn again off our path through a patch of briar directly to the Ostian gate. I signaled the turn with hand gestures alone, and we kept silent as we moved along. I went in front of Maximus, pushing aside most of the weeds and vines before he came to them.

Suddenly, we heard shuffling from all around us. I didn't give the command to halt, but the entire line stopped and began to crane their necks at the noise.

A stillness enveloped us. Then suddenly a tumult sounded and I heard the stomping of feet.

"Sir, there's someone in the fields," I hissed. "What would you like us to do? Perhaps they've set a trap for us."

Maximus's jaw flexed for a moment as he contemplated the

matter. "No, it's probably just a beggar we've frightened. Besides, no one knows our path of travel, do they? We have to press on." I knew he was calculating the reward and deemed it worth the risk.

"Come on, men, keep moving," I said.

Then a flaming torch shot past us. And another.

War cries arose from the briar around us, and I heard the sound of swords unsheathing from all sides. Helmets glistened in the moonlight. These were no bandits.

"Defensive positions!" I shouted—no need for silence any longer.

I wrangled Maximus into the center of the column. The men formed a circle around us.

In a flash, men sprang forth from the vegetation as though they had been catapulted. The clatter of their swords against our shields was deafening. I'd been prepared for this moment, but nevertheless, my focus couldn't stop switching from one spot to the next, and soon I realized we were surrounded.

"Sir, get down!" I shouted at Maximus as more torches flashed past us, but I found that he too had brandished his sword and was standing his ground. He was calmer than us all.

The men on the left began to falter. I rushed to help.

I could hear the soft noises of sword penetrating flesh, and the screams that followed, but in the night it was hard to tell who was slaying whom.

I ran to the position right behind one of my companions from training camp and lunged over his shoulder to stab one of our assailants through the collarbone. The man wailed as blood poured from the wound like water from an overturned vase.

I swiveled to the left to catch a fat man rushing my flank. He stabbed at my side, but I dodged just in time so that he only sliced the inner part of my arm. I bull-rushed him with my shield, pushing him backwards, but he was a great deal larger than I, and I lost my footing on the loose earth. I stumbled to the ground and dropped my shield, lucky to have held on to my sword. The man was immediately on me, slicing wildly with his dagger. I followed his movements as I scrambled to my feet and stepped back slowly. He lunged, but I evaded the strike and plunged my gladius into his gut. The man fell forward to the tip of my blade and collapsed into me, blood spilling from his lips over my shoulders. I lost balance and stumbled back over the side of the road into a ditch.

I landed hard, the dead man crashing down atop me and sending the hilt of my gladius directly into my ribs. The breath in my lungs shot out in a fury. Everything went black. I tried to blink myself awake. I was in a haze, a dream. The fury continued about me, but I couldn't free myself from the dead man. My ribs throbbing, my left arm nearly paralyzed.

When I came to—probably just a few moments later—I heard only a few footsteps on the dirt above me.

I had failed Maximus. I had failed Rome.

My grief roused me and gave me enough energy to finally push the corpse away.

"You best stop all this nonsense about being consul, Mallius Maximus, or otherwise this tumult might continue into your home. It would be a real shame if something happened to that ill-born daughter of Marius." I slowly began the climb from the ditch to the road, and spied two men standing above the ailing consul-elect. "We will keep you alive tonight as a gift to Marius, but there will be no such niceties in the future. The Caepiones and the Metelli send their regards to your chief." I sprang to my feet, bloody sword in hand and rushed them from behind. I jammed my blade through one's back.

The other leaped into action. I pushed the ailing man from my sword into his companion, who threw the man aside and lunged forward. I swung my blade up in time to deflect his, and on the recoil he stabbed at my gut. With my shield hand I grabbed the blade of his sword and tried to hold it from me.

The blade dug deep into my flesh. Veins split.

I held onto the assailant's blade with all the strength I still had, and plunged my own sword beneath his arm and through the back of his torso. He shook violently. His eyes rolled back. Then he collapsed.

I stumbled for a moment, until the adrenaline finally waned and the pain returned to my hand, arm, and ribs.

"Sir, are you all right?" I nearly collapsed, but my terror held me upright. There was no reply. I could make out Maximus's glistening brown eyes in the moonlight, and I could see rhythms of breathing as well as a slight tremor of his flesh. He was alive, but he wasn't in good shape. I ran to his side and hoisted him onto my shoulders, as we had been taught to carry casualties in battle. Ignoring the pain in my ribs, I moved like the Marathon runner for the Field of Mars.

When I arrived at the tent, I found Marius sitting at his desk, unable to sleep on such a night. At my entrance, Maximus still slung over my shoulder, I saw Marius's face morph from excitement to terror.

"Gods!" It was the only thing he managed to say as he rushed toward us. I moved past him to the back room, where I lay Maximus down on Marius's cot. "Run and get a doctor!" Marius finally shouted to one of his slaves. "What has happened?" he demanded of me. I could tell from his voice that, despite his distress, he was hoping I could tell him we'd been attacked by a simple party of ruffians, that he had not been betrayed.

"Attacked by agents of the Caepiones and the Metelli. They said they send their regards." In the blink of an eye, Marius's famous rage appeared before me, as if he were possessed by the spirit of Mars himself. He backhanded an amphora of wine. He picked up his side table and threw it across the tent. He scattered his parchment all across the room and slammed his fists onto his desk.

"I swear by the sons of Dis that I will hang their heads on pikes in the Forum!" His voice could have been heard across the entire Field of Mars. "Someone has betrayed me. One of my own men has betrayed me! And when I find out who …"

He tried to collect himself but his fury was not to be abated. While Marius shouted curses, I grabbed someone's cloak from the ground and tucked it between the cut on my arm and my damaged ribs, doing all I could to stay conscious through the pain, ignoring the wheeze in my breath. I sat at Marius's desk and scrambled to find pen and paper.

> To Sertorius:
>
> *Amicus, I have bad news. Your patrons have ordered an attack on Marius's ally Maximus and have successfully killed ten of my comrade. They've terribly injured the consul-elect and have left me wounded. Don't worry about me—I'll be fine. Now you have to look to yourself, to ensure that violence like this does not come to you in time.*
>
> Lucius Hirtuleius

I rolled up the letter, placed it in a carrier, and handed it to Mago. "At first light you are to ensure that this reaches the hands of Quintus Sertorius directly. Do you understand?"

"Yes, master."

"On your life—no one else must see it, for his safety and ours."

"Yes, master." Suddenly, my duties complete, my weariness and pain entrapped me and I collapsed onto the floor of Marius's tent.

SCROLL X

December 28, 648 ab urbe condita; one day until election.

When I returned home from Marius's tent that evening, I received a most welcome letter. It was from my mother, telling me she had arrived in Rome for the elections, along with Volesa and my nephew, Gavius. They were staying at an inn on the Caelian Hill, and she bade me to come visit them when I could.

I was thrilled. It was a chance for me to show my mother the work I had been doing, the man I had become. But regardless of how much I desired to spend time with my family, there was a great deal I needed to do in the domus. I was serving as an aide to Quintus and Gnaeus, running whatever errands they required of me and accompanying them to the Forum, where they spread word of their impending victory in the election. The Metelli and Aurelius Cotta spent a great deal of time with us, and smiles and good cheer abounded as they began to celebrate; it was as though Quintus and Pius had already won the election. I found such an abrupt shift in emotion odd. They'd displayed nothing but anxiety and discomfort since the beginning of the campaign, and a great fear of failure had loomed. But now, suddenly, they felt certain of their victory.

It wasn't until the next day that I learned why.

That morning I accompanied Gnaeus to the morning levy. Quintus, meanwhile, was attending a meeting of the senate, wherein they discussed procedures for the elections that would begin in three days, if the signs were auspicious.

After Gnaeus had received all his clients, he asked me to accompany him to the peristylum.

"Sertorius, I am very glad that you have been a part of this campaign. It has been a pleasure working alongside you and seeing you grow into a man. I think you'll have a bright future in Rome." He sat down cheerfully on a bench beside the greenery.

"I'm deeply honored to have served Rome in whatever capacity I could, sir," I replied.

"All this fuss will be over soon enough, and when things have settled down, we shall see to it that Nursia is rewarded for their loyalty.... And we shall see that you are rewarded as well."

"Master Sertorius," came Crito's voice from the atrium. "A letter has arrived for you. The messenger is waiting at the door."

I hastened to follow him.

"I swear, you could have written a volume on Rome with all the letter-writing you do!" Gnaeus shouted good-naturedly after me.

At first, I did not recognize the man at the door. He was clad in a simple tunic and bore a hood that shrouded his face. What little of him I could see was so grim that it made my stomach drop.

Finally I placed him. It was Marius's body slave—the massive Numidian.

He brandished a scroll and placed it firmly in my hand.

"Read this quickly, young master," he said. I was so perplexed that I could not reply until he had already turned on his heels and departed.

I took no time in breaking the seal and poring over the letter. I cannot describe the effect it had on me. My heart sank deep into my stomach, and I lost all the strength in my hands, so that the parchment slipped through my fingers and drifted to the floor. My feet carried me back to the peristylum.

"Tell me it isn't true," I managed to say at length, stumbling, bracing myself against a column. I shut my eyes and clenched my fists, doing all that I could to restrain my anger.

"Hmm?" Gnaeus said carelessly as he analyzed the flowers.

"Tell me!" I shouted. He whirled around, his expression one of extreme displeasure at being addressed this way by only a provincial client.

"Before I can tell you anything, I need to know of what you speak. And while you are at it, mind your tone, *boy.*"

"Is it true that you ordered an attack on the consul-elect Gnaeus Mallius Maximus?"

"I have done no such thing!" He sounded appalled.

"Then why have armed men beaten to within an inch of his life the largest threat to your political maneuverings? My closest friend was nearly killed in the attack!"

"Sertorius." Gnaeus wagged his finger at me, barely holding in his irritation. "I do not know of what you speak."

"*Is it true?*" I screamed, forgetting entirely my place. I could hold back my anger no longer. Gnaeus's breathing came heavy and quick, his eyebrows furrowed and his glare menacing.

"Sertorius, by Jupiter's Stone and on the masks of all my ancestors, I have no idea what you are talking about!"

I was perplexed. Could Marius have really made up such a tale to win my allegiance? Could Lucius? Regardless, I couldn't imagine that Gnaeus would make such a vow if he was lying.

"He is telling the truth, Sertorius." Suddenly, Caecilia appeared behind me. "I know because it was *I* who ordered the attack."

"You harpy!" I shrieked. "Is your son really so weak that his mother must use violence to ensure his election?"

"Mind your tongue, you impudent wretch!" Gnaeus spat and lurched toward me with clinched fists. Still, I thought I could see a look of disappointment in his eyes. At that moment, Quintus arrived in the doorway, catching only the tail end of our conversation.

"Sertorius, what business is it of yours what I do to be elected?" Quintus asked calmly. "You know nothing of politics and even less of Rome."

"No, but I am receiving a quick education. Excuse me, patrons, but I believe my services will no longer be of any use to you."

"Sertorius," Quintus said firmly. "Do you know how the patron–client relationship came to be?" I glowered but didn't reply. There was nothing left to be said, but he continued on: "When Rome was founded and foreigners began to flock to the city, they allied themselves with the established families to ensure that their rights were protected. If you betray your patrons now, after all that we have done for you …will your *friend* feed your city? Will your *friend* further your career? You will have no guarantee of your safety here."

"Are you threatening me?"

"No, I am warning you."

I paused for a moment, trying to collect myself. Gnaeus threw up his arms and strode from the garden.

"I have a new patron who will protect me. Of that I assure you. My time here is done." I began to leave, too, of a mind to collect my things and escape immediately.

"Sertorius," Quintus said again as I reached the doorway. "I've heard that your family is visiting Rome for the elections. It would be a tragedy if something were to happen to them, especially the little boy," he said lightly. Apparently their growing appreciation of me hadn't resulted in trust; they must have been reading my correspondence. I paused for a moment and then moved back to face him.

"You may threaten me all you like, but you will not threaten my family. You've made a grave mistake, Quintus Caepio. I will end you."

In a swift, fluid motion, Quintus pulled a dagger from the folds of his toga and offered it to me. "Do it then! Do it, if you are so foolish!"

"I am not a murderer." This time I responded coolly. "Unlike some in the house." I shot Caecilia a poisonous look, which she returned. "And I don't mean *you*." I buried my finger in his chest. "A weak suckling babe like you will self-destruct in time. I have only to outlast you. No, I mean this house. Your family. Your connections. As long as I have breath in my lungs, I will make you regret your decision."

"Be careful or you shall find that your lungs empty sooner than you might expect," Quintus snarled. I met his glance, finally feeling under control. I believe I had *him* under *my* control, too. He was weak, his threatening persiflage proved that.

"Get out!" Cecilia yelled. "*Get out!*" She pointed to the door. I did an about-face and strode calmly from the garden, grabbing what little I needed. On my way to the door, I saw Junia and Marcus standing together in the atrium. I went to them and grabbed her hand.

"I may never see you again. But I will sacrifice to Jupiter that you are both safe in this foul place." I kissed them on their cheeks and turned quickly, before the Caepiones could change their minds about letting me go. And I left that house forever.

I have at times been slandered for my decision to leave my patrons, but I feel no remorse. I was not enticed by Marius's offerings, as some have said, but left of my own accord, not out of blind anger or lust for power. Who better for a two-named man to ally himself with than the Man with Two Names?

As I stepped out into the streets, an unfamiliar feeling of certainty greeted me. All the ambiguity surrounding my life for the past several months was gone. I felt decisive again.

It wasn't until a few moments later that I became terribly, terribly afraid for my family's safety.

It's difficult to remember how I really experienced things without the lens of hindsight. I never doubted my decision to break with the Caepiones; they had left me no other choice. But I'm sure you can imagine the immense fear I experienced as I hastened to the Field of Mars. Any safety net I'd previously known had now vanished. My most powerful friends were now my most powerful enemies. What if Marius redacted his former offer? What if Marius's power was not nearly strong enough to guarantee any kind of future in Rome?

As I arrived at Marius's tent, I found a man standing before the general and the consul-elect Maximus standing behind him. Maximus had a crutch under one arm and a bandage concealing half of his previously well-oiled hair.

It took me a moment, but eventually I recognized the man from the wedding, Rutilius Rufus.

"If I had any more evidence, I would kill you where you stand." Marius's voice was commanding, livid.

"It could have been anyone, Marius. What about the Caesar brothers? Gaius Julius just married into that family!" the man pleaded.

"They're my family. They would never betray me. But you—you have doubted my every move since we left Africa. It's clear that you are discontented with my leadership."

"Marius, I—"

"Do not speak another word. You are going back to Africa, where you'll remain until I decide what to do with you."

Rufus shook his head, mouth agape, trying to find something else to say.

"Get him out of here," said Maximus. One of Marius's slaves pulled Rufus away by his arm. But: "You know, it really could be Gaius Julius," Maximus said reluctantly.

"I know. I know." Marius bit his fingernail and looked down intently, still not noticing me. "We'll have to keep an eye on him, but at least the others will know treachery will not be tolerated." Then the general looked up. "Quintus Sertorius. Why are you here?"

"Consul, I have come to pledge my loyalty."

A small grin creased his lips. "Mago, bring me parchment," he said, then scribbled something hastily.

"Permission to ask what you are writing, sir?" I said anxiously.

"I'm writing a letter to the registrar, officially naming Quintus Sertorius a military tribune." My words caught in my throat. "Tribunes are traditionally elected by the popular assembly, but things don't really work like that anymore. Besides, I *am* the popular assembly." Marius grinned. "Welcome to the Colors, Sertorius." He stood to shake my hand, and Maximus hobbled over to do the same.

"I am honored, Consul."

"You might not thank me once you've donned the colors. Military tribunes don't see much action anymore, and they don't have much responsibility. But at least it will further your career, and you'll look nice in that shiny armor." Marius winked at Maximus. "I'm assuming that you have broken your alliance with the Caepiones?"

"Yes, sir. It ended the moment I received Lucius Hirtuleius's letter informing me of what happened."

"Good. Then I assume you won't mind if I now ask you to tell me what they are planning?"

"Unfortunately, sir, it seems that their trust in me had been waning for some time, and they didn't inform me of all their maneuverings. Regardless, I do think they won't hold back from further violence if Maximus continues to run. They threatened as much as I was leaving."

Marius bit his lip and nodded his head. "Yes. We've been discussing whether or not it is a good idea. They have used this distraction to gain an advantage with the urban tribes, and our chances don't look good. If we withdraw Maximus's bid now, we can save face by citing his injuries, but if we proceed and are defeated it will be a great dishonor for us all."

"Wait, sir, why don't you have the Caepiones arrested? They are clearly guilty—they even told me as much!" My fear grew. If Quintus Caepio and Metellus Pius were now elected, both of the most powerful men in Rome would be sworn enemies of my family and myself. That was a danger I was not prepared to face.

"Unfortunately, there were no assailants left alive to testify and we can't obtain a legal confession without torture. We would have no hope of conviction, and it would be seen by the Senate and the people alike as a pathetic attempt to distract everyone from our failure to get Maximus elected.

"Regardless, sir, we cannot withdraw now. The Sertorii are now aligned with your cause, and the way we vote will persuade other Nursians, and how the Nursians vote will persuade other Sabines. That is a great loss for Caepio among the rural tribes and a great victory for Maximus. Let's roll the dice and see this out." Marius couldn't conceal his grin. He looked over his shoulder at Maximus, who nodded. I said, "But to persuade them, I will need solid evidence that my people will be fed, sir."

Marius lingered a moment and then snapped his fingers. "Mago, make arrangements for the grain to be delivered to Nursia and the surrounding villages immediately. Send two centuries of our best men to ensure it gets there safely." Now it was my turn to fight back a smile. Whatever doubts still lingered about my decision vanished. "If we proceed, though, we'll need a method of protecting Maximus from further attacks, and doubtless, we cannot be seen having soldiers running around the city. That would not bode well at all with the people—not to mention its illegality. Maximus has no lictors of his own, and I cannot allow mine to leave my side without a vote from the Senate, which would assuredly be blocked by our enemies."

"I know just the men," I said.

"Oh?" Marius cocked an eyebrow.

"Old soldiers. Tough and well weathered. They would be honored to ensure the legality of the proceedings."

"And these friends of yours would do this out of the goodness of their hearts?"

"I have no doubt that they would, but let's discuss terms and I'll offer them to the men as soon as you permit me."

I hastened to the Forum. I am sure the people on the roads assumed I was running away from some great threat, and perhaps I was. I arrived shortly at the Temple of Mars, which Rabirius had dubbed his "home." Just as I'd expected, he was there.

"Greetings, Quintus Sertorius!" He perked up as soon as he saw me. "Where is your young friend, Marcus?"

"Unfortunately, I don't believe Marcus will be accompanying me any longer." I could see the disappointment on the old soldier's face. "But perhaps he will come to see you on his own."

"Well, no matter. Have a seat! Tell me how you've been," he said, wiping dirt off the steps.

"It's been a hectic time, friend. And I'm afraid worse things lie ahead."

"Oh?"

"Yes. In fact, I have a favor to ask of you, and an offer to make."

"Anything for you."

"We need your help, and the aid of your friends. There is a threat looming over one of the consul-elects, and I want you to help protect him. I want you to cut your hair, shave your mourning beard, and pick up your shield once more."

He was greatly surprised. "I ... I ... well, I wasn't expecting to hear that today!"

"I know. I understand the risk involved, and so I cannot force you to accept. But my offer is that if you do accept, you and those that join you will be enlisted into the newly formed *evocati* under General Gaius Marius. You yourself will be a prefect of centurion rank and wield the vine staff, if you accept." His jaw dropped, and he couldn't immediately reply.

"Mighty Mars, reenlist ... I would like nothing more, but I'm not sure I'm fit for it. I might be able to fend off some urchins on the streets, but I don't know that I ..."

"You won't have to fight. You would be there to train the men, keep the younger fellows in line, and to serve as a reserve cohort in case things get rough."

His eyes glistened. "I'll do it, then. And I know my men will follow me."

"How many men can you muster by tomorrow?"

"Maybe twenty, depending."

"That's more than enough. Meet us at the Field of Mars tomorrow, and we will march together to the assembly. I will ask that three of your men be available to go to the Scarlet Inn on the Caelian Hill. My family is there, and they too are being threatened."

"No harm will come to them."

"You are a good friend, Rabirius," I said and shook his hand.

"It will be a pleasure to serve alongside you, young master."

I made at once for the Caelian Hill, with greater anxiety still. I tried to keep from my mind all the terrible images that appeared: of arriving at my mother's room to find her, Volesa, and Gavius drowning in a pool of their own blood. But to my relief, there was no commotion at the inn, and I found my way up the stairs to the little room in which she had informed me they were staying—not unlike Lucius's insula.

As soon as I entered, Gavius waddled to me and clutched at my leg. Volesa and Mother, however, both stared at me in shock.

"Quintus, what's wrong?" Mothers can always discern when something is the matter with their child.

"Titus was right, Mother. The Caepiones are monsters!"

"What has happened?" Volesa had fear in her eyes.

"They have resorted to treachery to ensure that Quintus Caepio and his ally Metellus Pius win the election. They attacked the candidate Mallius Maximus on the road a few nights ago. Lucius was with him and was beaten terribly. Their entire company was slaughtered save for Lucius and the consul-elect."

"Bona dea!" they both gasped.

"Mother, have the heads of the Sabine tribes arrived in Rome?"

"Yes, yes."

"Do you know where they are staying?"

"I do."

"Thank the gods. You must write to them immediately and tell them to no longer vote for the patricians, but for Mallius Maximus."

"I will do as you ask, but we have only a few hours of daylight left and the voting is to begin at dawn. I'm not sure if we can reach them all."

"We must." I leaned forward and took both her hands. "Everything depends upon it."

"What about the grain the Caepiones promised Nursia? We need it desperately, Quintus," said Volesa.

"Marius is sending grain to Nursia as we speak." Their faces brightened, just a little. "I'm not sure the Caepiones ever intended to help us, and if they did, it certainly wasn't a priority, so long as they had our votes."

"I see." Mother looked down.

"Mother, we must reach the other families in time. If both patricians win, we will have no protection—and there will be repercussions because I broke with them. If Maximus cannot win and continues to lend support to Marius's proposals and our family, we are likely to see bloodshed. I will likely be killed. And they will stop at nothing to restrict support to Nursia." Again they gasped.

"Quintus, why do they want to harm you so badly? You've been good to them until now."

"Because there is nothing patricians take more seriously then their own *dignitas*, and they feel I've insulted them greatly … and, then, I also said I would destroy them."

Volesa clapped her hands to her mouth and groaned. Mother only stared back blankly.

"Mother, after you send out the letters, you must not leave this room. And no one is to be admitted in. No one at this inn can be trusted. Bar the doors and remain here. Three men will be coming to guard the doors, but even they must not be allowed inside.

"Are we in danger?" Volesa cried, clutching Gavius.

"I am not sure." I made no mention of Quintus's threat. "But I would not put any violence past the Caepiones at this point." I bent over and kissed Gavius's head. He was smiling, oblivious to the commotion. I envied him. "I'm sorry but I must leave."

"Why can't you stay here with us?" Mother asked, reaching for my arm.

"I wish very much that I could. But I must return to the Field of Mars. Our new patron, Gaius Marius, has asked that Lucius and I join him there and stay with him so that we can begin planning for tomorrow—and whatever eventualities lie ahead." I embraced my mother and kissed her forehead. My hands trembled and I couldn't shake the thought that I might never return to her—or that she might not be there when I did. "Goodbye. I'll return as soon as I am able."

SCROLL XI

December 29, 648 ab urbe condita; day of the election.

That was one of the only entirely sleepless nights of my life. We stayed up the whole evening, drinking wine to the point where we were more dehydrated than intoxicated, and trying to make decisions that had never felt more important.

We waited anxiously for Marius's allies to arrive, but after some time had passed, his friend Norbanus was the only one there.

"Where are the Caesar brothers?" Marius asked Mago, a hint of irritation in his voice.

"I just received word from Gaius Julius—he sent a letter. He says he won't be coming. His remains with us, but he can't be seen to oppose his new wife's family so soon," Maximus answered instead.

"What of Sextus?"

"No word."

"No matter. We need to get moving."

The long hours spent planning did nothing to assuage our concerns. And then, before we knew it, apricot clouds lined the horizon and the sun was upon us.

Rabirius and his men packed together just outside the tent, and we could hear them whispering anxiously.

"Are we ready to move?" Maximus asked. Marius hesitated. There was nothing left to do, nothing left unsaid, but he was reluctant to let us leave, knowing he couldn't go with us into the city.

"If it wasn't for the damn Senate enacting a measure to ensure the voting was done in the Forum, it could be done right here on the Field of Mars, where my soldiers could keep an eye on the proceedings." Marius had said this several times already. "Yes, it's time for you to go. Mago, go with them. If there is anything I need to know, return to me at once. Understood?"

"Yes, dominus."

"May Fortuna guide you," Marius said at length. He was the only one of us who appeared unmarred by the lack of sleep—a trait that accompanied him as long as I knew him.

I could tell by the look of them that Rabirius's men were joyful to feel like soldiers again. It was remarkable how quickly they had cleaned up. That they were veterans was obvious by their stance and by the way they moved in unison. Most bore old injuries. Rabirius himself had a restricted leg that I hadn't noticed until now.

"Thank you all for your service to Rome today, men," Maximus said to them. "You are doing an honorable thing. Now let's move." Maximus limped more than any of the others, dragging his right leg behind him and clutching his left arm to his chest. If anyone had any doubt as to the validity of the attack on Maximus, they need look no further than the injuries he had sustained.

The wind that had seemed so still for weeks was suddenly tempestuous. The sky was an ominous gray despite the rising sun, and powerful gusts sent the flags lining Rome's high walls snapping above us. There was, too, a light drizzle of freezing rain, and occasionally I thought I heard thunder, though the others didn't seem to notice. I figured there might be a storm, given the conditions of the sky. That would have been interesting, for who knows how the augurs would have interpreted this? Depending on whom you ask, lightning is either a terrible omen of a bad year ahead, or a portent for great things to come.

The moment we passed through the gates, a vast throng appeared before us. I had never before seen Rome so crammed full—packed to bursting with both city dwellers and Italian citizens. I recalled the elections I had attended with my father when I was a child, and I couldn't imagine there to be even half as many people then. The entire Roman nation had turned out to decide the fate of the Republic. Very few present knew all that this election meant, or of the violent proceedings that had led up to it, but something about the solemn way the people moved toward the Forum—the epicenter of Rome—told me they sensed there was something important at stake. The air was thick with the gravity of the decisions about to be made.

The crowds split like an earthquake around our party, allowing us to move through with ease. I remember the people's concerned glances as they watched the injured consul-elect move through the crowd, a determination in his eyes so rare to see at that time. The multitudes followed behind us, as if they had joined our party, and the torchbearer Maximus led the way.

But before we could reach the Forum, a handful of seedy-looking men sauntered into our path. Most were cloaked and hooded, their hands hidden behind their backs. Our entire procession came to a halt.

We stared at them and waited for their move.

Rabirius took up a position beside Maximus and pulled his gladius from his scabbard—just enough that the steel glimmered in the early morning light.

The men before us nodded at each other. Tension rose and strained at us until, finally, they stepped off the path and made way for us to proceed. There was a murmur of approval from those following behind us.

I looked over at the consul-elect. His hands were shaking, but it was impossible not to notice the grin etched onto his lips.

As we arrived at the Forum, I began to spot the different candidates climbing the steps to the Capitol. I saw Quintus, trailed by the clients I had come to known through the Caepiones' morning levy. I saw Metellus Pius, his father close behind, and a number of quaestors and legates who I remembered had served under Numidicus in

Africa. Maximus, however, had no clients of his own, and ascended the steps only with Lucius, Mago, and myself, leaving Rabirius and our guards at the bottom of the one hundred steps.

Above us, I spotted Dalmaticus, looking ridiculous in the long robes of a Pontifex Maximus, standing alongside the college of pontiffs, the augurs, and the high priests. Dalmaticus wore none of his usual bravado and brashness.

We were shown to our places, as were Quintus, Pius, and the straw candidates. We turned to the vast crowd and waited for the proceedings to begin. I couldn't recall ever being as nervous as I was in that moment, fearing I might faint and tumble down the steps, which would doubtlessly have been seen as a curse from Apollo on our party.

The *Flamen Dialis* stepped away from the rest of the priests and threw up his arms and his head back to the heavens. He began a ritualistic prayer to Jupiter Optimus Maximus, asking for his blessing that he would guide the proceedings of the morning. A bull with gilded horns and a laurel crown was led out before him, along with the *rex sacrorum*, who would perform the sacrifice. The beast began to thrash against his handlers. We didn't turn to look, but the bull's stamping filled our ears. I saw Maximus grimace and look down. The crowd gasped and fell silent, and the vast ocean of motionless faces watched anxiously. There was no worse way to start an election than this, for the beast was supposed to offer itself without restraint. In general practice, the bull would have been heavily sedated beforehand, but apparently it hadn't worked as desired. The priests tried to calm him as the bull was led to the scarlet mat. The rex sacrorum said something about blood, how it made the crops grow and the rains fall—an ancient prayer. For the first time I felt I was a part of history.

I turned just in time to see the priest's dagger cut deeply through the bull's throat. Blood spewed like a flood, and the bull crashed to the marble with a thud that reverberated through the entire city. They gutted the sacrifice and began searching through its entrails, haruspicy being taken of the liver. Time came to a complete stand-still. The silence became an ominous mist over the Forum, and everything outside of where we sat began to feel unreal to me. I caught sight of blood trickling down from the sacrifice above us, flowing with the rain past my feet.

What could be taking them so long? The candidates and their parties alike grew restless, and we all couldn't help but steal a glance up at the priests to see what was wrong. Many of them crouched around the bull and analyzed its entrails. Something was certainly wrong. The haruspicy had frightened them. They pulled out more and more of the beast's organs and ran their blood-soaked hands through them. No one had to say it; I knew everyone feared that the elections would have to be postponed. Maximus's face especially told of his concern.

Dalmaticus threw up his hands in exasperation and made for the priests, suddenly more in keeping with his usual character. His tone was hushed so that no onlooker could hear him, but the veins in his neck bulged so that no one had to guess as to what he was saying.

"The gods are with us!" the Flamen Dialis finally shouted, and the crowd, for the first time, erupted. "The proceedings may begin. The Collina Tribe has been chosen by lot to vote first."

The selected tribal elders of the Collina Tribe sallied forth into the wooden voting pens.

"It's in the hands of the gods now," Maximus said under his breath, as much to himself as anyone else.

One by one the tribal representatives moved forward to the voting pens, anxious for their turns. Each and every time, I searched the faces of the men who entered, wondering how they might vote. I've never been much of a man for prayer, but in that moment, I could think of nothing else to do. I went through a long list of gods—from the ancient Sabine ones to the urban Roman ones. To each in turn I prayed for their hand to be on the proceedings. I remember that my prayers slowly devolved into pleading, begging even.

The four urban tribes and the thirty-one rustic tribes went one after another. The process took so long that the rains went and came again. Went and came once more. The sun appeared, then disappeared behind the clouds. When the final tribe voted—Lemonia, I believe—Marcus Aemilius Scaurus and the presiding consul, Ravilla, collected the ballots and took their places atop the capitol. The gathering stayed silent as the men drew each bid, Ravilla's booming voice announcing each to the Roman populace. Each bid had a first and second choice, many of those who voted for Caepio had Pius along with him, or vice versa, as was to be expected. The bids that bore Maximus's name as the primary had as the second choice some no-name—a straw man running not to win but to push forth some political agenda or to gain support from a certain sect of Romans, such as the publicani.

Thirty-five tribes in all. If the election could be secured within the first eighteen votes, the day was concluded. My heart sank as I realized this was a distinct possibility; the urban tribes voted unanimously for their patrician patrons, and their votes held weight. But as Ravilla sounded off the next several votes, it appeared that Maximus would be hanging around.

I recently found a letter I'd drawn up hastily after the proceedings that day, recounting that after the fourteenth reading, these were the standings:

Quintus Servilius Caepio	11 votes
Caecilius Metellus Pius	7 votes
Gnaeus Mallius Maximus	5 votes
Lucius Claudius	2 votes
Spurius Larcius	2 votes
Aulus Gabinius	1 vote

Seven more votes for Caepio and he would be locked in as the senior consul; just eleven more for Pius and he would join as the subordinate. With twenty-two tribes left to vote and none of their allegiances known, I felt myself growing weak. I remember trying to refrain from dry heaving, trying to wipe away the cold sweat pouring from my hairline. The only good sign we received was that, as the election went on, more and more of Caepio's votes had another as the secondary preference. It seemed that some of the aristocrats didn't like the idea of a man as young as Pius being the most powerful magistrate in Rome, and although they had feigned complicity, they refused to be bullied into allowing him this power. The fifteenth tribe—and oh I remember it clearly!—was Quirina, my own. I felt like collapsing as Ravilla pulled forth the Quirina vote and analyzed it for some time.

"Quirina votes: Gnaeus Mallius Maximus as primary, and Lucius Claudius as secondary!" A gasp shot up around the Forum, followed by shocked whispers. It had been believed that if any vote was truly secured, it would be ours. For as long as my father had lived, and perhaps much longer, the Caepiones had considered themselves patrons of the Sabine tribes. But no longer. For the rest of the ballot readings, I felt a weight lifted from my shoulders—for even if Maximus was not elected, I knew I had done my part. Now all I could do was hope my mother had been able to reach the other two Sabine tribes in time.

The proceedings continued, and its movement was much like the slithering of a serpent, moving at once this way and then violently the other. It would be some time before we felt certain which way the proceedings were going. By the twenty-eighth vote, Caepio had won. Dread overcame me, but that was to be expected. The votes now appeared as such:

Quintus Servilius Caepio	18 votes
Caecilius Metellus Pius	14 votes
Gnaeus Mallius Maximus	13 votes
Lucius Claudius	6 votes
Spurius Larcius	4 votes
Aulus Gabinius	1 vote

The twenty-ninth vote belonged to the Clustumina Tribe, one of the two Sabine tribes incorporated into Rome alongside mine centuries earlier. They voted for Maximus and Aulus Gabinius. I nearly wept. I whispered aloud my gratitude to my mother.

Again the crowd seemed stunned. I stole a quick glance at Quintus Caepio, who seemed more irritated than anything else, but beside him Pius had turned the same shade of red as a soldier's cloak. He looked as angry as the bull that had just been sacrificed.

Three further votes passed, and the ballots read:

Quintus Servilius Caepio	18 votes
Caecilius Metellus Pius	16 votes
Gnaeus Mallius Maximus	15 votes
Lucius Claudius	7 votes
Spurius Larcius	4 votes
Aulus Gabinius	2 votes

I'm sure that if given the opportunity, some of the tribes would have changed their votes to ensure Pius was elected alongside his colleague, rather that doing as they had promised and voting for a nobody like Aulus Gabinius. But it was too late. The fate of Rome would be decided with the last three votes—those of the Scaptia, Sergia, and Voltinia tribes. Maximus was a ghost beside me, all the color drained from his face. The odds weren't good. All the urban tribes had gone, yes, but the Sergia and Voltinia were among the oldest rustic tribes, and their loyalty generally resided with the nobility—those that had awarded them citizenship lifetimes before. Scaptia was called with the thirty-third vote. They were the first Sabine tribe incorporated by the Romans, so I was unsure where their loyalties would lie, even if mother had reached their elders in time.

"Scaptia votes primary Quintus Servilius Caepio ..." I'm ashamed to admit I let out an audible moan, a whimper even. My stoicism fled from me in the face of certain defeat. They didn't even know what they had done. "... And Gnaeus Mallius Maximus as secondary." The crowd erupted. I'm not sure if they really cared for Maximus, or had even considered him an option coming into the election, but this proceeding was like watching a bout between gladiators, with several twists and turns.

I grabbed Maximus's arm lightly. "That's all the Sabine tribes, sir." I looked over at Metellus, glaring at Caepio with bulging eyes, as though he were a centurion and Caepio an unruly soldier.

Caepio tried to calm him, but Ravilla continued: "Sergia votes Caecilius Metellus Pius as primary and Gnaeus Mallius Maximus as secondary." Old soldiers, I assumed. Those that had served under Pius's father in Africa, but alongside Maximus. I squeezed my eyes tight and clenched my fists. My breathing came erratic and shaky, and I felt that the throng before me was as nervous as I. At that moment, I caught sight of the Voltinia tribal elder turning to leave through the crowd. I tried not to take any meaning from this, as the final vote—Voltinia's—was pulled from the silver amphora. Ravilla stared at it for a long time. Perhaps he was perplexed by its contents; perhaps he was trying to draw out the tension of the moment.

"Voltinia votes Gnaeus Mallius Maximus as primary and—" the crowd erupted. Ravilla could barely be heard over the victory cries of those who had barely known of Mallius Maximus the day before. It was a victory for the people regardless, and as Gnaeus had once told me, "The mob loves seeing their betters suffer." It turned out that Voltinia's second vote was for Aulus Gabinius, and the election was done. Maximus had won. Marius had won.

"By the auspices of Jupiter Optimus Maximus, I present to you your new consuls!" Ravilla's voice was drowned out by the crowd. I followed Maximus as he immediately went over to greet the other candidates in a display of unity of the state. Pius shot Maximus a look so venomous I thought he might lunge forward and attack, but instead he turned away and pushed through his entourage, ignoring Maximus's extended hand. Quintus Caepio just stood still, arms folded. Perhaps he was feigning disappointment so as to not upset his allies, or perhaps he was disappointed to have begun his term of office with a moral defeat.

"I congratulate you, colleague," Maximus said, with the friend-liness of an old farmer, failing to mention the man's complicity in the attacks that had nearly killed him. At length, Caepio accepted his hand.

"Let's not go about forgetting our places," Quintus said. "Your tricks and schemes may have gotten you here, but they will not sustain you. Go and tell your master I said that." He nodded to the Field of Mars.

"And I am very pleased that your tricks and schemes did not work as well for your co-conspirator." I said nodding at the defeated Metellus Pius, who was trying his best to escape the crowd. Caepio finally looked at me.

"After all that we've done for you ... your pig-spawn tribes betrayed us. We shall not forget what you've done, Quintus Sertorius. Don't *you* forget that."

"Sertorius, why don't you and Mago go to tell Marius what has happened? Lucius and our guards can stay here with me. I'd like to address my people," Maximus said, turning his back on his new colleague.

We arrived to find Marius working diligently at his desk.

"So what has happened?" he asked without looking up.

"We've won. Caepio and Maximus were elected as consuls," I said, unable to contain my delight. Marius exhaled deeply and leaned back in his chair, relief the only emotion discernible on his stone-like face.

"Good. Then I guess it's time to prepare." He returned to the work before him and beckoned us forward. "I'm sure you men are parched. Have some wine." It surprised me that Marius was not more excited, but this was before I really got to know him; he was a man who took both failure and success in stride and looked to what was next. He once said, years later, "A victory means nothing, lad, without following it up with a second and third." And it was true. There have been thousands of consuls over the years, many of them all but erased from memory and time—men who posterity will never know. Perhaps that's why Marius's ambition was not halted, as his own term of consulship had ended with the election of Maximus. Despite his calm calculation, something about him made me believe he was more joyful than he let on.

Shortly thereafter, Maximus returned, and Marius cried, "My boy, I am so proud of you." He wrapped his thick forearms around his son-in-law's neck and clasped the back of his head. "I am honored to call you my son."

"Thank you, Marius," Maximus said, blushing like a child under such praise. "If not for your aid, I'm certain I would never have won."

"Cac, I say. Rome needs you as much as you need her, and the gods would have gotten you here no matter the circumstances."

"Regardless, I am deeply grateful."

Marius returned to his desk, saying, "If my guess is correct, you'll be going to Gaul soon enough."

"What, why? What makes you think that?" Maximus sounded perplexed, but also perhaps intrigued.

"The gods have ordained it. There is no use sending a consul to fight in Africa, where I will return to my men and lead what's left of the conquest. But the legions in the north are in bad shape, and although the Cimbri have been silent for some time, I don't think they will be for much longer. The province will be divided by lot, but I feel it in my gut that you'll win. With any luck, Caepio will rig it that way to get you out of his hair so he can strut about like the first queen of Rome." We all laughed. The relief of victory—like the feeling of escaping death in battle, which I would later come to know—had put us all in high spirits.

"If I am to be sent there, Marius, I'll remember your instructions and apply them to the best of my ability."

"Yes, do that. And you must remember one other thing, which I have not yet taught you ..." He stood and held up his finger. I found it humorous that these two, not ten years apart in age, really did look in that moment like father and son. "All great men have great passion. Through today's election, you've proven that you are a great man. But if it is not tamed, the passion that comes with excellence can destroy both greatness and the man who wields it." He smiled and looked up, choosing his words carefully. "Sertorius, I want you to hear this too. I've won many battles in my life, but the first and hardest was the victory over myself."

"You are as wise as you are brave, Marius. On Jupiter's Stone, I swear to keep your advice at the forefront of my mind at all times. I ask that all of you ensure I stay on that course."

"And ... one other thing," Marius said. "In defeat, be calm and work to discover how you may yet wrest victory from its jaws. In victory, be calm and work to discover how you might yet keep what you have fought for." Marius had never appeared so philosophical. He was clearly working very hard at it, and when he finally burst into laughter, we all did too. "I'm proud of you, men," he said at length and slapped us all on the back—even Mago. "Let's drink some damn wine and celebrate what Fortuna has given us."

PART TWO:

The Road to Arausio 648-649 ab urbe condita

"They want the centurions not so much to be venturesome and daredevils, as to be natural leaders, of a steady and reliable spirit. They do not so much want men who will initiate attacks and open the battle, but men who will hold their ground when beaten and hard-pressed, and will be ready to die at their posts."—Polybius

SCROLL XII

Outwardly, tempers cooled after the elections, although I imagine the tumult continued for some time in the home of the Caepiones.

Gaius Marius left within a week or so for Africa, taking Rabirius and his men with him. He said it would give them an opportunity to become reacquainted with life in the Colors without the risk of imminent danger. Marius was confident that the war in Africa would soon be over.

Maximus and Quintus Caepio were both inaugurated under Jupiter Capitolinus, and within a week they drew lots. Maximus was given the command of the war against the Cimbri and Teutones, while Quintus was to stay in Rome. Maximus told us his joy at the thought of becoming an imperator, like his father-in-law. However, the most rewarding part of that moment in the Senate House, he said, was seeing the look on Quintus's face.

"To rob him of all the glory and fame he is so desperate for is all the revenge I need," Maximus said, beaming.

My next step was to be assigned to the legion, and I remember fondly the period of my life that followed. My first experience with the military—I think of it with the same joy a man feels when remembering how he first met his wife. One of my favorite quotes by Socrates has always been, "It is not death which is difficult to escape, gentlemen; no, it is far more difficult to escape wickedness, which pursues us more swiftly." Perhaps I had this quote in mind at the time, for having escaped the wickedness of politics, I was undeterred by the threat of death that came with a military life.

The fear, the joy, the difficulty in learning how to behave; I struggled, of course, but such struggles thrilled me. The first few weeks of my military career, however, were anything but enjoyable. I took the military tribune's oath and donned my armor for the first time, and so was let loose into the ranks. I didn't know the first thing about being a soldier, and tribunes don't receive any of the training the foot soldiers do. I attempted to learn whatever I could from watching the other tribunes, the centurions, and even the rank and file, but to my disappointment no one was willing to take me in and train me in the most rudimentary details of military life. So I learned slowly. Lucius stayed on under Maximus, as a *contubernales*, and I would have asked him for instructions, except that he was too busy with logistics and planning and we were so often kept apart.

The majority of my brothers in arms treated me with contempt. The military tribunes, with whom I spent most of my time, would barely hold a conversation with me. The soldiers and centurions too were disdainful, although it was formal disdain, due to the fact that I was their military superior. Eventually, when I had exhausted all my ideas for making acquaintances, I called over a centurion—a man named Gnaeus Tremellius Scrofa—and asked his opinion. Covered in scars, Tremellius exuded an aura of experience and discipline: a proper soldier. I wanted to know what I could do to earn the trust of my comrades.

"Permission to speak freely, sir?" he replied. This kind of formality made me uncomfortable; Tremellius was nearly twice my age and had experienced more of life than I had ever wanted to.

"Please do."

"There is nothing you *can* do. The other military tribunes dislike you because you are all in competition for promotions and special orders. The soldiers don't like you because military tribunes are so distant and lofty atop their fine horses; they can give the command for men to die and yet are in no danger themselves. And we centurions hate tribunes because they are almost exclusively incompetent, lazy fools, who give dangerous and vainglorious orders, get my men lost on patrols, and eat far too much of the scant food this army is afforded. But most of all, sir, we really hate tribunes because they have been given a position they did not earn—unless you count being the cum-stain of some rich old senator as entitlement enough to lead good men to their deaths." He looked emotionlessly at me. "Does that answer your question, sir?"

At length I nodded, to which he saluted and spun away from me.

I carried on in this capacity for a few days, feeling even more alone than I had in Gnaeus Caepio's house. Finally, I decided to approach Maximus.

"Sir," I saluted as I had seen others do. "I am sorry to bother you, but do you have a moment?"

"For you, I can make time. What can I do for you?" He set down his scroll and looked up, appearing every part the natural successor to Marius.

"I would like to resign my commission, sir." He stared back blankly, seeming to search for the humor in my statement.

"What?"

"Yes, sir."

"You've only been in the army for a week. Has military life been so difficult? You've taken an oath, Sertorius. It is illegal to go back on that."

"I have no intentions of leaving the army, sir, but I would like to relinquish my command and join the ranks." He nearly spit out his sip of wine.

"You'll have to forgive me if you are joking, Sertorius, but I am puzzled. Why would you want that?"

"I am not joking, sir. I have discovered that I am in no place to lead these men. I want to earn their respect before I lead them."

"Sertorius, you *did* earn it. You earned it by birth, by right of helping me get elected."

"We both know that's not enough, sir," I said, and he finally slouched back in his chair.

"I'm surprised to say the least, but if nothing else I admire your spirit. I'm not sure how Marius would feel about this, but I'll consent if it's what you really desire." He paused and seemed to consider the issue. "This might be good, in a way. Perhaps you could report to me how the men feel once the campaign starts and things get rough. I don't expect you to betray any confidences, but you can help me do what I must to keep the men happy."

"I can do that, sir."

"Is there anything I can do for you in return? I feel I must give you something, since you'll be sacrificing a great deal of money as well as authority."

"Just give me a chance to prove myself in battle, and if I do so adequately perhaps I can take an officership then."

"There will be plenty of opportunities to prove yourself in battle, I assure you. And perhaps I can work to put you in the right places to earn the respect of the men."

"That's all I ask, sir."

"Well, there is currently a group of recruits training. They've been at it for a few weeks but will be finishing their training shortly before we step off. Does that work for you?"

"Perfectly, sir."

"Consider it done, then."

I'd wondered how Rome had managed to conquer more than any nation that came before her, without being a military society such as the Spartans or the Thebans, but I soon realized that this was because Rome had a military society all its own within the larger culture. I was introduced to this life not when I first donned the colors, but when I was introduced to the Mules beside whom I would fight. All foot soldiers were called Mules for two reasons: because they carried gear like Rome's favorite pack animal, and because a mule is born of a male donkey and a female horse, symbolic of the mixed and low bloodlines of the common soldier. At first, the term was intended as an insult, but eventually Mules assumed the title with pride. I cannot properly explain what it was like to be a Mule, nor the sense of honor it evoked, but after some time with one's comrades, the shared suffering, the soldier became fully bonded with the moniker and his peers. The more drudgery, the colder the seasons became, the more it rained, the closer Mules became.

Unfortunately for me, the Mules I met at the beginning of February were anything but my comrades. As Maximus mentioned, they had been training together for a few weeks already, and in soldiers' sandals, a few weeks feels like a thousand years. They had all discovered each other's idiosyncrasies and distributed nicknames accordingly.

During my time in the military I have found that each unit has the same cast of characters: there is the overweight and lazy joker; the athletic strongman; the prankster; the worrier; the rebel who thinks he knows how to break all the rules; the soldier with sarcastic quips at the ready; and the patriot, who is doubtless mocked more thoroughly then all the rest combined. Unfortunately, when I was brought into my unit—Second Century, Third Cohort, Legio IV— the men had already assumed their roles, and they didn't seem to believe there was room enough for me. I was dubbed simply "the new guy" and was treated as such for some time.

We immediately set off on a rigorous training regimen, which always carried with it a sense of urgency. As soon as one task or objective was completed, we were on to the next. We would complete close-order marching drills and then immediately receive orders that we were to begin focusing on weapons proficiency. The next task was always more vital than the last, and the following task would be of greater importance still. We were often told that the new objective would be grueling and few of us would be able to endure it, but most of the time we bound together and overcame the challenge. Although they didn't favor me, the Mules in Second Century still went out of their way to assist me, unlike the military tribunes.

Eventually I did enter their good graces. One evening after we were released to our tents, Lucius Hirtuleius came by to visit and we talked for a while. Afterward, around the fire, some of my comrades questioned me; apparently they had met Lucius before.

"How do you know him?"

"He's a good friend of mine. We grew up together," I said, plopping down on a log.

"Wait … wait … are you the one he used to talk about? Some important senatorial fellow? That can't be you," one of them asked, perplexed.

"Well, I'm not a senator, but yes, I assume that was me."

"Then why in the hell are you here? Why are you a damned Mule?" another demanded.

I was reluctant to divulge this information, but then, I didn't see how it could hurt. "I joined the military for a few reasons, and I was given a commission as a military tribune. I was only in the role for a few weeks before I decided I wanted to earn the right to lead. I don't really know the first thing about being a soldier, but I will learn."

They exchanged glances. Some of them shook their heads in disbelief, while others bellowed their laughter. I assume some must have thought I was telling a flagrant, boastful lie, but word soon spread throughout Second Century, and I was never again treated as an outsider. The name "New Guy" was ditched in favor of "Stallion," because I gave up my horse to march with the Mules.

I won't bore you with too many stories about my training. It's considered unfashionable to talk of training after one has finished and left for campaign, so I won't break tradition here, but I can't stress enough how important this experience was for me. As I said before, I cherish my memories of this time.

Perhaps it's worth mentioning that my recollections of my time in the military will be slightly different than what I have written of my political life. I suppose the reason for this is because military experiences are deeply personal, perhaps so more than any other realm. When telling these stories, I feel the urge to attach some moral to them, but of course, for the sake of veracity I cannot. When wearing the soldier's kit, nothing outside of the military seems to exist; nothing else is real. It is simply imagination and memories. A military story doesn't really end, because they rely far more on the experience of what happened, than on what truly happened. I find myself replaying these memories again and again in my mind—not only the heavy combat but the most rudimentary, boring moments as well. Occasionally I speak of my first days in the Colors, but I cannot ever seem to get the details right. I tell and retell so that the listeners may feel what I felt, but of course this is impossible. I share this now because some of the things I will tell you may not coincide perfectly with historical record. It is impossible to distinguish what actually happened from what only seemed to happen—so for any inaccuracies or embellishments, I apologize. My desire is that you will feel what I felt, that you will know the feeling of blistered feet after a thirty-mile quick march bearing sixty pounds of full kit. I want you to know the deep sense of belonging one feels when wielding a shield beside his brothers; how the most idiotic of jokes could keep you laughing for weeks; how one loses all sense of time except as it pertains to the next meal, next letter, next cup of wine, next night of sleep.

I learned all that I needed to during my training. I became proficient with the gladius and the scutum; I was soon able to march in rhythm with the rest of my century; and I learned how to pack the proper gear for a movement. I memorized formations and specific orders, going over them in my head each night. Perhaps the most important things I learned on the Field of Mars were the nicknames the Mules had for damn near everything. The Cimbri and Teutones, who we prepared to fight, were known as "Reds" for the color of their hair and the complexion of their skin. The name was meant to dehumanize the enemy; we hated them as much as we feared them, and we often boasted of our desire to kill a Red. Our soldier's wine was known fondly as "piss," to honor its quality; we didn't have a term for good civilian wine, since we never had any. Close to everything associated with military life had a name that resembled its nature to us, but would have meant nothing at all to an outsider.

I'm ashamed to admit that the thing we did most in training was complain. I tried to avoid it—especially because I knew I might one day lead these men—but complaining was integral to the culture of being a Mule. Every one of us did it from time to time.

Complaining was the best way to bond with your companions. We ridiculed the officers, the food, the sleeping arrangements. Acknowledging the lowly nature of our situation highlighted the fact that we were going through it together, and we bonded through adversity more so than through similarities or personal sentiments.

We spent the remainder of February training, and when March arrived, we knew it was time to leave for the north. We were all excited. We talked of nothing else. And though no one admitted it, everyone was scared. Not so much of death, but of being so far away from home, in a strange country, when so many of us had never left Italy. But all in all, we were ready to leave, ready to put ourselves to the test and see if we had indeed become real soldiers. I think I was perhaps the most anxious to leave, since it meant that I would be seeing my brother, Titus, again.

The officers conducted the annual ritual of announcing war on the Cimbri to begin the war season by throwing the ceremonial spear across the boundaries of Rome into the Field of Mars. The ranks were given license to applaud, chant, and in all ways display our bloodlust.

On the third of March, the first auspicious day of the month, Maximus led the Third Cohort from the Field of Mars toward Gaul, to reinforce my brother and his Fourth Legion. Somehow, I believe I knew even then that I would not return the same man. I don't mean to be trite, but I knew the course of my life would be forever altered after leaving Italian soil. And by the gods, I was right.

SCROLL XIII

One of the first things I noticed as we mobilized was that even though it was war season in Rome, the weather conditions were hardly conducive to military actions in the north. The higher elevations in northern Italy and Cisalpine Gaul created the driest cold imaginable. Even in March, when Rome was enjoying a new sun, bright flowers, and warm air, the north was nothing but frost and dead vegetation. The further we went, the fewer colors there were to look upon. Eventually, the color of dirt and the rare tree replaced the olive orchards, and the chirping little birds gave way to the buzzards that feasted on the carcasses of animals that hadn't been able survive until summer. The scarlet tunics we all wore were anything but original or creative, but they bore the only color we saw for some time, and that scarlet reminded us of home.

Maximus was gracious enough to let us converse as we marched, so long as we didn't forget our military bearing. Most of our conversations consisted of jokes and mockery, usually coupled with boasting and claims of greatness. If you ever supposed the brotherhood of soldiers is forged in battle, you are mistaken. These moments—these petty conversations—make life in the Colors what it is.

Although Maximus gave us this small liberty, we quickly discovered that when it came to discipline, he took after his father-in-law.

From Rome, we went along the western coast, toward Genua. If you are familiar with Italian geography at all, you know that this path was through friendly territory. Still, Maximus ordered that we set up camp the same as we would in enemy territory. "I will not be the fool that allows an entire cohort to be destroyed due to a lack of precaution," he would say whenever we grumbled, and he would say the same thing later when he had four legions under his command.

It wasn't until we were a few miles from Genua that Maximus ordered the Third Cohort into formation and addressed us all.

"I'm proud of how we've been marching, soldiers. We've made good time and are ahead of schedule. I am sure some of you are already developing new blisters, and if not yet, I promise that you will." He paused for us to laugh about the validity of his statement. "But hard days are ahead and I need the best out of every one of you. If you think it is cold now, wait till we reach Narbo—then you'll really experience cold. If you believe we've been marching too much, then I regret to inform you that we will be marching a great deal more— and a great deal faster. I'm ordering a forced march from here until we reach Massilia, where we will meet up with Legio VIII and IX. That means thirty miles a day, no breaks, no stopping." Some of the men groaned. "I know. I am not looking forward to it anymore than you are, but it is imperative that we reach Narbo before the snows melt, so that our strength will be at four legions should the Reds decide to give us a go. Prepare yourselves accordingly, for trying days are ahead of us. Now, remain in formation, and you'll be assigned to your *contubernium*." We snapped to attention and saluted, and he returned the gesture and stepped away. A tribune took his place and began calling out names.

This was the first time we had been assigned to our smallest combat teams: the contubernium. If you have never served in the Colors, I doubt that you'd be familiar with this term. Though many believe that the century is the smallest maneuver element, this is a misconception. The century, which in theory consists of one hundred Mules (I generally remember it being no larger than eighty at this time), is not how the military is really *experienced*. You experience everyday life through your contubernium, which is a unit made up of eight to ten men, with whom you do damned near everything.

We anxiously waited for our names to be called, hoping that

we would be assigned to a good group of men. I considered myself blessed when my name was listed with several of the men I had grown close to during training, and I was grateful to have avoided some of the troublemakers.

My contubernium was made up of seven new recruits, myself included, and one veteran, who had served in several campaigns, most recently in Africa under Marius. The new recruits were Proculus Velius, who we called "Bear" not just for his ridiculous height, frame, and body hair, but because of a story that he'd singlehandedly killed a bear when out hunting as a child. At nineteen, he was the youngest of our band, and his naïve and innocent personality reflected that. He was clumsy, but never careless, as he always sought to make the others proud. He was actually my tent-mate for a portion of the campaign, so I came to know and cherish him a great deal.

There was also Caeso Alfidius, who we all called "Grumble," which he did with a certain drawl. He did everything lazily, and to him everything was subject to mockery. He had a dark and ironic sense of humor, but he made us laugh nevertheless.

Another was Hostus Naevius. It's hard to describe a man like him on paper and expect to be believed. The man was nearly perfect at everything he did. We called him "Pilate" because of his unrivaled excellence with a pilum, but he could have been nicknamed for just about any aspect of military life. He was a brilliant swordsman, marched in perfect order, was the best swimmer in the whole damned cohort, and was the fastest runner and most accomplished wrestler in the military games. He was a wonder to us.

Next was Tullus Canius, who we called "Terence" after the comedic poet. Of all the nicknames, none was more fitting. Like Grumble, Terence was always looking for an opportunity to make others laugh—except his humor was decidedly more clever and witty. Also, the man's impressions were unbelievably accurate. He could pick up on a person's most minute idiosyncrasies and imitate them perfectly. These alone could keep us laughing for weeks.

Another Mule assigned to our contubernium was Marcus Axius,

who we called "Ax" for short. He wasn't as unique as some of the others were, I suppose, but he was a damned good soldier to have in your company. I'm not sure I ever really heard him talk much about Rome or the Colors at large, but he bled Legio IV, Third Cohort, Second Century. He believed in each man in our contubernium and would have staked all his earnings on us against any Red. He was the kind of man you'd want at your side when the enemy was in your sights.

The last of the new recruits was Paullus Fulvius, who was dubbed "Flamen" for his religious piety and moral devotion. Naturally, these tendencies made him something of an outsider in our group of bawdy young men—not to mention that at twenty-seven he was the eldest. This suited him just fine, however, as he was a relatively closed-off person. He spent the majority of his time writing letters home, but when I had an opportunity to converse with him one on one, he was a pleasure to be around.

The only one of us who had ever served before was Gaius Basilus, who we occasionally referred to as "Bass," but generally we refrained from doing so, out of respect. He was the leader of our contubernium, or our *decanus*. I've never met a man who looked so much like me. He could have easily been mistaken for my brother, perhaps even my twin. The only noticeable difference between the two of us was his gait, the military discipline that kept with him whether he was in front of a formation or by himself on guard duty. He had the saddest eyes of any man I've ever known, so much so that it almost worried me. I couldn't understand it—none of us could, until we too experienced combat for the first time and took our first lives.

Maximus was definitely right about one thing: the blisters. Overall, our training had prepared us for everything we encountered at the beginning of our campaign, but several days of thirty-mile marching with full kit was enough to wear down even the strongest of men. We tried to ignore it with laughter. Grumble kept making jokes about how our gear was inspected each night and was expected to be perfectly oiled and shined. "We gonna spit-shine the Reds to death?" he said, with thousands of variations. Somehow this never lost its humor.

Days during a forced march are unique in that they all blend together. Each day is met with fresh anxiety and discomfort, but the longer you march, the more you begin to see the same things reappear. The same barren plains, the same snow-covered hilltops, the same dead trees, the same mud-thatched villages with wild-eyed spectators. Sometimes we wondered aloud if it was all a cruel joke and they were really just marching us in circles—a continuation of our training, perhaps.

Every night we made the same fort, going through the same motions to do so. We would receive the same orders, given as if they were new, to scavenge wood and set up our tents in the designated places. Each time, one of the Mules—usually Grumble—was a little bit careless on this detail and returned with less wood than requested, and each time, Bear, who worked harder than a charioteer's horse, would give away some of his copious quantities of wood to cover up the neglect of the others.

It was ten days of hard marching until we arrived at Massalia. As we neared, we all craned our necks to get a decent view of the bustling city on the water. It was the first real bit of civilization that we had seen since Genua. We were disappointed, to say the least, that we were not permitted to visit the Greek city, knowing that this would be our last chance to experience anything familiar during the campaign, save maybe Narbo.

We continued north to the plains between Massalia and Aquae Sextiae, where two of our legions were stationed. Even from a distance we could smell the leather of thousands of legionaries.

Before the camp was a huge train of pack animals, slaves, and merchants. They clamored around our line, inspecting us, the merchants trying to solicit new customers. The familiar noises of camp greeted us: the thunder of stamping horses, the clamor of sword drills, laughing soldiers. The Mules there gathered around us more vehemently than the outsiders had, circling like Mediterranean sharks. We tried to maintain our bearing, but couldn't help stealing a few glances.

They were ragged. Unlike our armor, theirs was scuffed and begrimed. Many of them bore the stubble of a beard, and I even noticed a few wearing animal pelts over their shoulders. The degree to which they ignored regulations shocked us.

Maximus ordered us to halt. He swung gracefully from his steed and asked a few tribunes where he could find their commander. We stood at attention as the Mules of the Eighth and Ninth stalked closer still.

"Hey, what's your name?" one wild-eyed Mule asked Flamen.

He hesitated but replied, "Paullus Fulvius."

"I don't give a damn. You'll be dead before I can remember it." The Mule spit, and his comrades roared with laughter. My face flushed with embarrassment. Although I hadn't been directly addressed, I knew the Mule's words were meant for all of us. I looked away.

"But see how well they stand at attention? What good little boys and girls," another said with a toothless grin.

"They'll make good sport, won't they?"

"Oh, but have you seen how nicely their armor is shined? They look ready for a damned Triumph!"

"They'll make beautiful corpses, I bet. Lovers of Venus on the funeral pyre."

One of them slithered up to Bear. "Aye, everybody leave off this fat one. He's mine!" he shouted to the others. "You ever been with a man before?" The Mule licked his lips. Bear, to my left, shuffled anxiously. His face was wrenched with so much anxiety that I was afraid he might cry. "I won't tell anyone if you play real nice." Bear remained at attention, as we had been instructed, but he couldn't have squirmed any more. Finally, a few ranks up, we watched as the centurion Tremellius—the same I'd talked to when I too was a Tribune—broke rank in proper order and approached the heckling Mules.

"Soldier!" his voice erupted. He buried his fingers in the soldier's chest like a knife. "You take one step closer to this formation and I'll have you flogged. All of you, get back to your drills and leave my men alone." They tried to chuckle this off but it didn't gain any traction.

"You damned replacements are all the same," one of them shouted, as they skulked back the way they had come.

"Welcome to the Colors, boys," Grumble said.

"Think he'll really try something?" Bear finally managed to whisper.

"If he does, I'll bury my dagger in his gut. Don't worry." Ax broke formation to pat Bear's shoulder.

"Quiet, men. You're at attention," Tremellius spoke up from the front. Needless to say we all fell in and shut our mouths, feeling like babes both consoled and chastised.

Maximus finally returned to our column. "Here we are, men. It's been a long few days, hasn't it?" We nodded. "Well, it isn't over yet. We'll only be staying here overnight. Tomorrow we leave for Narbo. This time, we will not be conducting a forced march, but we will be planning for future maneuvers in enemy territory. So we'll cover far less ground per day, but we'll increase security measures." He ignored the audible groans from the ranks. It is sad to think now of our lack of discipline, but at that point, we hadn't endured the real nature of warfare. It was all still a game to us, in a way. "Disperse yourselves among the Eighth and Ninth, get to know your new comrades, and then you'll be shown to your quarters for the evening. We'll have an accountability formation before you're dismissed for the night, so ensure that your gear is in good order. Dismissed." More groans as we fell out of line.

"Welcome to the Colors, *boys*!" Grumble chuckled again.

"Shut the hell up," was the only reply.

SCROLL XIV

As one might expect, meeting our new "comrades" didn't go as smoothly as we would have liked. Very few of us even tried to meet the others, and those that did were ridiculed until they left. We quickly came to understand that this was typical of the way replacements were treated. And we couldn't blame them; after all, we'd only been brought in because their friends had been killed. Once they learned we were actually replacements for Legio IV rather than them, they loss interest in mocking us—in fact, they lost interest in us entirely. When addressed, they would exhale deeply and look away until the foolish Mule gave up and returned to our side of camp.

The next day we left for Narbo, as planned. And since we didn't have to march thirty miles a day, our new pace seemed almost relaxing. Still, our bodies were sorer than we'd ever known, and the repetitiveness of the road made us all cranky.

We just wanted to fight. Before joining the Colors, I'd never truly desired to spill another man's blood. Of course, every boy dreams of being a brave warrior and fighting for his country, but those kinds of ideas work better in your fantasies, fit better into poems and children's stories, than in any actual consideration of the brutal nature of sword against flesh. As I've said, I'd never relished the idea of combat. But after joining, that changed somewhat. I'm sure outsiders would ascribe this to the culture of the Colors, but I couldn't disagree more. I believe it was due to the inanely dull nature of most military matters. You join to be a soldier, a warrior, dreaming of valor and stories to tell your womenfolk. These kinds of aspirations make marching around quietly in frozen mud agonizing. The more we marched, the more we shined our gear, the more we wanted to fight something. The longer we were called on to scour the tree line in the distance, the more powerfully we wanted to see war-painted Reds, ready for battle.

Unfortunately for us—or so we thought—Narbonensis Gaul was friendly territory. Even the villagers no longer glared at us, but rather applauded as we passed by, the children playfully running alongside for as long as they could keep up. Pilate and Ax would point out the prettiest girls along the road and laugh about how much they'd have to pay for a few hours of indulgence.

The one redeeming trait about Narbonensis Gaul was the warmth that came from the coast. The climate was far more agreeable to us than Northern Italy and Cisalpine Gaul. The majority of the snows had melted and flowers had begun to bloom. We appreciated the colors and scenery, although we were all too manly to admit it.

The nearer we came to Narbo, the more anxious I became to see Titus. It had been nearly three years since we'd last seen each other, and I had no idea what to expect. Would he now be like the Mules of the Eighth and Ninth? Battle-hardened or battle-scarred? I could barely fathom how much I'd changed in three years, and I was not fighting the Reds in the north. He kept coming to mind during the march, but I could hardly recollect what he looked like. His face seemed jumbled, like a reflection in rippling water. But it wasn't his appearance that concerned me, but the state of his person. No matter what he would be like, I could hardly bear the length of the journey to see him.

Although it felt like an eternity, in reality I didn't have to wait long. It took us about a week, covering twenty miles a day, to near the city—the last friendly place we'd see for the remainder of the campaign.

When we arrived at the fortifications outside Narbo, we were once again greeted by the incumbent force. They gathered around to watch as we marched to a halt and stood at attention. We cringed, anticipating further mockery.

But the soldiers were silent. They looked on with sad, empty eyes, pink-rimmed and strained. It was the same look that had concerned me in Basilus. Some of these Mules lowered their eyes and shook their heads, kicking the dirt beneath their sandals. Eventually they turned and moved away, like a departing funeral party.

As Maximus addressed the current commander, I felt my gut drop. What if Titus was as lifeless as these men? What had they seen that had begotten such solemn spirits? This was not the humorous, lively culture of the Colors that I knew. I broke military bearing to crane my neck to look for Titus. No luck.

"Soldiers, we've arrived at our destination. Now the real campaign begins," Maximus said, smirking as he returned to the formation. "As a reward for your efforts thus far, there will be no accountability formation this evening, but do not give me cause to regret this leniency. Tomorrow morning we will hold a change-of-command ceremony, and then you will receive your orders. I have plans for the ensuing months, but I will be conferring with the current commander and other officers this evening before any decisions are made. What I will say is this: you will see battle soon." He left the center of formation and stepped closer to our cohort. "Your service thus far has been more than adequate, but I need the best out of you now. Soon, many of you will wet your swords for the first time. My orders for you this evening are to call on whatever god you choose and ask him for favor and strength in the coming days. You will need it."

He then addressed the Eighth and Ninth. "I apologize that your previous commander failed to prepare you for this campaign. You have been freezing your asses off in the north for a year or more now, doing little to nothing except wasting your own time. The military bearing you were taught has ebbed away. If you think this will continue under my command, however, you are mistaken. You will look like soldiers, conduct yourselves like soldiers, and fight like soldiers. Prepare yourselves accordingly. Dismissed," he said with a salute that was quickly returned.

The Mules around me broke formation rather sluggishly, not knowing what to do next. I, however, burst from the line in a sort of panic, fearing that if all the men from the Fourth and Fifth made it back to their camp before I could find Titus, I would never be able to spot him in the endless sea of armor.

The other Mules probably thought me ridiculous, searching frantically as I was, but I didn't care. Truthfully, I was still not even convinced that Titus would actually be here. Countless possibilities ran through my mind.

But then I spotted him. Except, what I saw was not what I'd been looking for. I had been searching for the bushy-haired farm boy, in a simple tunic and covered in dirt, but what caught my eye was the striking resemblance to my father. The same fair skin and hair, the same nobility etched into each line on his face, the same quiet, stern nature that my father was known for. The resemblance was uncanny.

"Titus!" I shouted and ran to him. Finally, he spotted me.

There was nothing discernible in his face. He stared back almost blankly. "Brother!" I cried, approaching him with hand outstretched, but he only scanned me and waited. Finally, he accepted my hand and pulled me close to him.

"What are you doing here?" he asked.

"Well, I ... I joined the Colors. You were the one that suggested it, remember?" This was hardly the reunion I'd expected.

"I see that ..." Silence crept between us.

"I guess I should stand at attention," I said after a moment, as I caught sight of his prefect's crest.

"Stop that. I won't have any brother of mine treating me like a superior ... except when I give you an order—then I expect you to comply." I winced at his tone. "Where is your centurion?"

"Right over there. Centurion Tremellius Scrofa." I pointed him out.

"I know him. He's been serving in Gaul since we lost the Battle of Noreia. He tried to leave the Colors, but I guess he couldn't. He's a good soldier, though—always listen to him." I nodded. "Centurion!" Titus waved him over. Tremellius smiled, something I'd never seen him do.

"What in the hell do we have here? A prefect now?" Tremellius laughed and shook Titus's hand, but he didn't forget to snap to attention and offer a salute. Even with the formality, there was a comfort between them I envied.

"Eh, that's what they tell me, anyways." Titus waved him off attention and patted his shoulder. "You received your discharge papers, though. Why the hell are you back here?"

"Missed the Colors, and I discovered that I hate civilians." They laughed.

"Do you care if I borrow this soldier for a while?" Titus gestured to me.

"Of course not. Has he done something wrong?" Tremellius's eyes hardened as he turned to me, becoming again the disciplinarian I had come to know.

"No, no.... He's my brother."

Tremellius shot us both a look of astonishment. "What? He doesn't look a damn thing like you!" He sized us both up.

"He takes after our mother, I after our father."

"I see. Sure you don't have another brother? Decanus Basilus looks just like the kid." He nodded to me. "Anyways, let me know if you want me to rough him up sometime or give him extra guard duty." He winked and punched my shoulder, turning to leave.

"Let's go to my tent," Titus suggested and turned on his heels.

His tent was at least three times bigger than the one I was used to, and fully furnished. Having ascended the ranks, it made sense. He poured us two cups of piss and handed one to me.

"How is home?" He propped himself up on his desk.

"Nursia is struggling, but General Gaius Marius has recently sent grain, so—"

"No, how is our *home*? How are Mother, Volesa, and my boy?"

"Mother is doing as well as could be expected with both of us gone. Volesa misses you deeply and doesn't fail to let us know." I tried to smile. "Gavius is thriving, growing every day. An oak tree. A young Hercules." Titus finally smiled and exhaled deeply.

"I miss them ..." He took a long pull of his wine and scratched his helmet-flattened hair. "Do I seem different?" He met my eyes for the first time.

"You do."

"I was worried I might. If I've seemed unhappy that you are here ..."

"Are you?"

"No, no. That's not it. I am pleased to see you, and I regret it if I haven't shown that properly." Titus had always been a closed communicator, just like Father. "I know I encouraged you to come here. I just hadn't considered that would mean we would both be here."

I was perplexed. When he noticed the look on my face he continued. "We are both in the *north*, Quintus. We are both fighting the Reds." But his meaning wasn't registering with me, and he knew it. "Little brother, Rome has never defeated these bastards. Ever. We haven't had a near defeat, inflicted huge losses.... We have been massacred every time our swords have met theirs." He rubbed his head. And for a moment, the candlelight illuminating his weary face, I thought I could see those same strained eyes. "I don't fear dying for Rome, brother.... No, I would be *honored* to die for Rome. But what if the Reds decide to leave Spain and come after us again this year? What if they test the Fourth, and we are annihilated like all the others? Mother will have lost two sons, Volesa will have lost a husband and the natural heir to her hand, and Gavius will have lost both his father and the man who would raise him." He poured more wine.

"I see." Such a possibility had never occurred to me. Death in combat enters the mind of every young trainee, but the thought of Titus dying was so ridiculous to me that I'd never even considered it. The thought of us both dying was unbelievable. "Do you have reason to believe the Reds will leave Spain? They've left us alone for a few years now. Maybe they've found some fertile fields and decided to settle down."

"Spain isn't big enough for the Cimbri and Teutones, Quintus. They'll be back, and I think that time is fast approaching." He paused, but the look on his face told me that he was debating whether or not to confide in me. "We received word a few days ago that Maximus is planning to order an attack on a Red ally tribe in Gaul. He sent word, asking for suggestions. He said he didn't care which tribe, but he wanted battle. I presume he became accustomed to enormous amounts of bloodshed serving under Marius, so he's preparing to continue the trend here."

"And you think this will provoke the Reds into returning?"

"The Reds already want to return. They want to destroy Rome, and they have no reason to believe they can't, given recent history. But some of their allies need convincing, and I think this will give them the means to do so."

"Do you think we can win?" I felt like a child, like I was playing dress up in my armor. He waited a long time to reply.

"I don't know. But by the gods, I am afraid of what will become of Rome if we do not. These will not be merciful overlords. When we conquer an enemy, Rome takes a few slaves, a few virgins, a little land, and some taxes. Eventually, the enemy can even enjoy the wealth of the Republic. But the Reds ..." He clenched his teeth. "You know I haven't fought the Cimbri directly since I arrived in the north—only their allies. But along our marches, we have seen the atrocities the Cimbri leave in their wake. They are more animals than men ... they make Gauls look like patricians by comparison." I downed my wine and asked for more. Titus said, "I don't want you to worry, little brother. You leave that to me and the other officers. The gods will protect us. I just hope that you and the rest of the replacements will be prepared. You're stepping in because a lot of good men have been slain."

"I don't have much to compare to, but I think the men I'm with are good soldiers. I am proud and honored to serve alongside them. I think they will serve admirably."

"We'll see how admirable they are when a spear tip is at their throats," he said quickly, almost with irritation. But he soon came to himself and looked at me with sorrowful eyes, although he didn't voice any apology.

We stayed together for a few more hours, trying to discuss more pleasant topics. We put back a great deal of wine as we laughed about old times, swapped stories about life under the Caepiones, and I told him of retiring my military tribuneship to become a Mule. Altogether, it was a pleasant evening, conversing this way. But the underlying fear never dissipated, so that when I finally saluted him and left for my tent, I realized how shaken I was. That night, I lay awake for hours, trying to ignore Bear's incessant snoring and trying to block out the endless thoughts that rushed through my head like an angry river.

Eventually I rose and took over for the Mules on guard, allowing them to go back to sleep. As I climbed the hastily constructed ladder to the sentry tower, I heard footsteps behind me. Bear gave me a sleepy smile and patted my back.

"Did I wake you?" I asked.

"No, no. I was awake. I try to pretend I'm asleep when I can't nod off. Sometimes I can trick myself." We turned and scoured the tree line. "What do you think our families are doing back in Rome?"

"Sleeping, I bet."

"Not on guard duty, anyways!" He chuckled. "I bet my mother is going to wake up in a few hours. She'll say her prayers to the household gods and shake my brothers awake so they can help prepare the butcher shop for market day."

"Your family owns a butcher shop?"

"It's my mother's new husband's. But ... she does most of the work. He'll probably stay in bed most of the day and chastise them for how little coin they bring in." I nodded. Silence followed. "Are you afraid of battle?"

I took a long time considering my answer. "I am, in a way. I just want to do well."

"Well, I'm not," he said, but he shifted uncomfortably. "Sometimes I am afraid to die though." He looked at me seriously. "I've never died before." After a moment, he chuckled at himself and I joined in. I shifted my view from the vast plain to the trees in the distance, thick ancient oaks. I no longer wished to see enemies hiding there.

SCROLL XV

The next morning the bugles startled me from a restless sleep. "Morning, Stallion!" Bear said, far too cheerfully for my liking. It was still dark out.

Shouts rang through the camp of. "Everybody up! Let's get moving, ladies!" We all reconvened outside of our tents and attempted to shave with our daggers in the darkness, using only the water in our wineskins.

"Now remember, lads, I expect your gear to be in perfect condition and your personal hygiene to be flawless." Terence was already beginning his impression of Maximus, itself nearly flawless. After preparing ourselves and gulping down some lukewarm soup, we formed up for the change-of-command ceremony. These kinds of formations were always tedious, but today, exhaustion made it absolutely unbearable.

We were put at attention and kept there for a great deal of time as the different century and cohort flags crossed the parade field in procession, the dull thumping of drums sounding off in the distance. I remember my eyes trying to force themselves closed as I stood there, nearly stumbling forward until Ax jabbed me playfully in the ribs.

The former commander of the Fourth and Fifth spoke, wishing his old soldiers well on their journey and giving them a final salute. Maximus then received the command and assumed his position at the head of our joint force—all four legions.

"I know it may be unprecedented," he began, "to give combat orders on my first day in command, but these are unprecedented times." My heartbeat increased and I listened intently, my conversation with Titus flooding back to me. "Warfare is upon us. There are enemies of Rome in our very midst. They have committed atrocities against the Roman people and have gone unpunished. This cannot be tolerated!" His voice carried, as loud and commanding as the drums had been. It rose with the morning wind and echoed across the camp. "There is a Gallic tribe called the Tigurini. These people helped the Cimbri completely annihilate a Roman force, killing my father-in-law Marius's consular colleague and two other consular-ranked Romans in the process! Thousands of Romans were forced to march under the yoke like slaves, whipped and spat on, and only permitted to die after they had been tortured, mangled, and dismembered." I had never seen Maximus so grim before. Everyone was silent; even the merchants and prostitutes lining our camp stood motionless. The pack animals, too, in the distance seemed to be listening to the fates that awaited us and the Gauls. "This cannot be tolerated! We cannot allow our brothers to die in vain! Are you with me?" The formation rang out; I joined them. We beat our gladii against our shields viciously. Even in my fear, Maximus's words were undeniable; the fire in his voice burned our very souls.

"Men, we are marching on Burdigala. They will receive that which they have given us! And we will make the world know that treachery to Rome will not go unpunished! This will serve as a warning to all others who defy us. So I ask again: are you with me?" We erupted—all four legions united under the cohort flags that lined the parade field. "Then Rome will never fall!"

He saluted and we returned it, offering up chants to Mars. It was time for war.

The first opportunity I found, I approached Maximus. I asked Centurion Tremellius for permission to address the commander, and he reluctantly agreed, saying only that I had better have my things ready with the rest of the Mules by the time of departure.

"We have no reason to believe that the Burdigalans were involved in the attack on the Romans there!" one of Maximus's legates hollered as I entered. Maximus exhaled impatiently and rubbed his eyes.

"Then how do you explain the fact that the gates were left open to Rome's enemies? The entire Roman garrison was either butchered or captured, and the citizens of the city were completely unharmed."

"The mercy of the Tigurini should not be mistaken for complicity," the legate said, causing Maximus to burst into a hopeless laughter.

"The Tigurini have no mercy. Them or any other Red. They butcher anything with a heartbeat unless they have something to gain from abstaining." Maximus seemed exasperated.

"To even be under suspicion of treason demands reprisal," another legate spoke up.

"By the gods, thank you." Maximus finally smiled.

I spotted my brother in the back of the tent, among a few other prefects. They stood behind their respective legates, their direct superiors.

"Permission to speak, Consul?" Titus stepped forward, his eyes fixed and stern.

"Speak freely," Maximus answered before Titus's legate could.

"I believe that this could be a dangerous move so early in the campaign. These men are not ready for a battle of this scale. The recruits are green, and the veterans are out of shape and undisciplined. I'm afraid of how either group of soldiers will react when put to the test."

I still remained at attention in the entrance, waiting to be invited forth.

"I agree with you, Prefect," Maximus said, his pointer finger on his lips. "I do. You are as smart as I've heard you are tough, but unfortunately I cannot call off these orders."

"Permission to ask your true intentions, Consul?" Titus went on. Some of the other prefects squirmed, but Titus was always bold in the face of authority. Maximus turned to Titus's legate and smiled.

"He's a smart one. You need to keep him around. My true intentions are this: to set the precedent early for what the remainder of this year will be like. There will be bloodshed, there will be sleepless nights and extra guard duties, long marches over perilous land. I want to weed out the weak from the beginning and establish the tone from the start: I am not like their previous commanders. I am not here to milk my province dry, sit on my riches, and allow Roman soldiers to sit around getting drunk. Soldiers fight, and that is what we'll do. To tell you the truth, I don't know how much strategic benefit there is in taking Burdigala, but I can tell you it will be a moral victory. These four legions obviously have no love for each other. A victory will bond them together. You say that the recruits are green? They won't be after they've taken their first life. The others are undisciplined? Fear makes all men disciplined."

"Very well, Consul." Titus stepped back into the shadows.

"But perhaps your enlightened brother could add something to our debate?" Maximus smiled and beckoned me forward. "How do the men fare?"

I tried to remain calm, though it was difficult with all the officers watching me and no doubt wondering why a Mule was directly approaching the consul.

"They are content, Consul, although they complain about the degree to which they are expected to maintain their gear." Maximus's contagious laugh rang out.

"Excellent. They hate it now, but after experiencing warfare, cleaning their gear will be a sweet safe haven, a calming interim amidst the uproar. And it will remind them of their discipline when they need it most. Anything else?"

"No, Consul. Altogether the men are doing well, morale is high, and we are ready for battle." I was mostly being honest.

"Good. Thank you. Now, what can I do for you?"

"Sir, when we attack Burdigala, how will we be breaching the walls?" I felt the room empty of breath as all eyes fixed on me.

"I have no intention of taking the time to construct siege

equipment, so we will be using ladders."

"I'd like to be the first to scale the walls."

Maximus leaned back and grinned. "So this is how you desire to prove yourself?" he said, almost to himself, nodding. "I admire your courage, young Sertorius, but what you ask is perilous. Every man who scales the walls of an enemy city first receives a military crown, but so many die in the process we rarely have the opportunity to give them out. Are you sure this is a risk you wish to take?"

"Yes, Consul. I've made up my mind." I couldn't see Titus from my position but I knew he was unhappy. I could feel his glare.

"And this is how you want to receive your commission as an officer?"

"Yes, Consul. If you and the rest of the Colors deem me worthy."

"There is none worthier. But by the gods I need another officer like I need an arrow to the chest. Between all their complaining and lecturing, I barely have enough time to eat and sleep!" He laughed, as did the officers. "I am only joking. But, unfortunately, military tribunes are never given their position in this way."

"That's fine, Consul. I have no desire to be a military tribune. I want to be a centurion," I struggled to say as my throat dried and my voice quavered.

"A centurion?" His eyes grew wide. "See how tough he is? I told you!" he said to one of the legates. "We can make that happen, Sertorius. I'll make sure that you are in position to scale the walls first, and if you make it out alive, I will make you a centurion before the men."

"Thank you, Consul." Such sweet relief overcame me, although I knew I would still have to reckon with Titus.

"Anything for you, friend." I saluted and spun on my heels. It was time to shine my gear and prepare to move out.

To say the least, the march to Burdigala gave me ample time to regret my decision. I didn't feel comfortable discussing this with any of my companions, and Titus never did come to argue with me about it. He must've understood that I'd made up my mind and wouldn't be swayed—though I am not altogether sure that is true—but I never mistook this for complicity.

After our conversation the night before, my decision to put myself at risk must have been a blow to him. Titus never talked much, and I had difficulty expressing myself to him, more so perhaps than with anyone else. But I think my decision to scale the walls first, despite the danger it would surely bring me, was my way of telling him how I felt.

I was always the second plan. Second eldest, I was the reinforcement, the backup plan in the event of the unknown. It was Titus who went to Rome first; I only took his place when he left. It was Titus who had the wife and child, the one who would lead our family and continue the Sertorii name.

I do not want you to misunderstand me; I did not resent him for this. It was simply how I viewed life. He *needed* to be sent back home, to those he protected and cared for.

I was only vital should Titus die first.

This was the way of my world, and I did not curse my lot. There was nothing that forbade me from doing all the things he had already done, or doing new things entirely, but I'd resigned myself to being my brother's subordinate. He was, and still is in my mind, a giant among men. In some ways, I was honored to be nothing more than his younger brother.

Of course, we couldn't speak of these things. We had an unspoken agreement not to divulge such sentiments, so rather I simply decided to scale the wall first. If one of us were to die in Burdigala, it would have to be me—the man who'd left nothing behind. Perhaps my mind has become jaded over the years; perhaps I don't remember why I made the decision I did. Perhaps I am simply trying to reconstruct the forgotten thoughts that lay behind such an extraordinarily dangerous decision. I did not want to die; honestly, I had never wanted to live more than I did as I resigned myself over to the Fates.

We crossed a vast geography of territory, leaving Narbo, entering Celtica, briefly crossing through Aquitania—the province bordering Spain—only to reenter Celtica and head toward our destination. I don't remember the journey at all. The jokes and the geography have faded from my mind, and all I am left with is the sick, hollow, pitiless feeling that echoed in my gut. I was always on the verge of vomiting. My knees were so weak and my head so light that I felt I would collapse beneath the combined weight of my gear and my fear, but somehow my feet continued to propel me forward.

I must have seemed pretty distant to the rest of the Mules at that time. I imagined they were whispering that I was too green for battle—that I had grown cold from fear before our first bloodshed. If they did think this, then they were right to a degree, but I suppose they didn't know the full extent of the situation until we arrived.

Fortunately, I wasn't the only one showing my nerves. I discovered this when we were released for food the evening before battle. Those short meals were often where the Mules bonded the most; even animals that eat together form a bond, and so it was for us.

We stood in line for what felt like hours, only to receive some hot soup with far less meat and fewer vegetables than expected. While we ate, it became clear that the other men shared my fears.

"Basilus," Bear said, looking up from his soup. "What is battle like? What is it *really* like?" Basilus swirled his soup around and stared at it for some time.

"The rocks are grayer afterward."

Bear looked at me in confusion. "What?" we all asked, and Basilus began to chuckle.

"The rocks. They get grayer, the trees greener. Look around you right now." He pointed across the vast expanse of Gallic farmland beyond our camp and to the forest full of trees that looked older than Rome itself. "You'll notice things after battle that you didn't see before. The entire world becomes alive. It's like everything is breathing."

"What else?" Pilate asked, shuffling closer and perching himself on his gear.

"You value certain things more. Like the things that you would have lost if you had died, or the things the world would have lost in you. You start dreaming about the great things you mean to accomplish when you get home, the things you want to tell others."

"But what about battle? During it, when you're right in the thick of things?" Bear asked anxiously.

Basilus looked back at his soup. "Well, words can't really describe that." We all looked at each other, wordless.

"I'll tell you this," Centurion Scrofa walked up behind us, helmet held tightly under his arm. "You do strange things after battle. Even after all these years, I tremble, laugh for no reason. It's a strange thing." He found a seat beside us. "I promise you this, lads: you won't ever come back from it. Not the same, anyways. I tried to go back, you know, but couldn't. Watching people go about their lives … so misinformed. Misinformed about the war, or virtue, about what really matters. They were misinformed about how much they would value their lives if they were inches away from losing it."

"Proximity to death brings along with it the proximity to life," I said looking up. It was a quote my father had taught me. It was probably from Zeno or some other old Stoic philosopher, but he said it was true of his own experience in war.

"Yes, it does," the centurion said, nodding. "So get ready to live, boys. For tomorrow, we will either live as kings here or in Elysium." He slapped us each on the back and we stood to salute.

No one said anything further, and one by one we fell asleep, the thoughts rumbling in our heads. I tried to imagine what the next day would be like, but couldn't form any solid pictures in my mind. I was not comforted by the fact that I would soon find out.

From a great distance I saw it: Burdigala. Our enemy. The city was not large, but the walls were enough to scare off most potential invaders.

They stood nearly fifty feet tall, to my recollection, and were wide enough to host three men abreast on the ramparts. I now realized why everyone had warned me against this decision. Seeing the walls that I would ascend, it all became real.

Somewhere within, there were men I would kill, or the man that would kill me.

A sobering thought.

The Mules let out a collective gasp—filled, like myself, with both a strange brand of excitement and a numbing fear. We all bounced on our feet and tried to keep hold of our senses. This was the first time I'd experienced those pre-battle conditions that still occur in me to this day: loss of feeling in the hands and feet, breath catching in the lungs and refusing to come out, the chill of profuse sweating over every inch of the body, the profound feeling of being completely withdrawn into oneself, alone and scared—even surrounded by all those men.

For this reason, I believe, Centurion Scrofa began to talk to us quietly. Between the thunderous stomping of Mules and the century of buglers, I could barely hear him.

"Whatever happens, men … don't you ever forget … and your brothers beside you …" He spoke not in the motivating war cry you might expect, but rather a calming tone that reminded me of my father when he comforted skittish colts. We came to a halt just in time for Bear and a few other men to empty their stomachs on the Gallic soil. "Watering the fields and we haven't won the battle yet?" Terence said, and for once everyone was too preoccupied to even chuckle.

Ax was muttering something to himself, staring forward.

Basilus, directly to my right, was open-eyed and unmoving save for the flexing of his jaw.

Grumble whistled a famous ballad of the Colors, about a dying general's last words to his men.

Warfare is nothing like it is imagined or told of in tales. Most of the time there is no beginning, middle, or end. No climax. For that reason, I have learned, most generals or legates never address their men before battle and instead let it begin as if it were the next step in the evolution of a march. But like his father-in-law, Maximus was no ordinary leader, and they both always addressed their men. Maximus, along with his horseman guard, wheeled around the formation and approached the center.

"There it is, soldiers." He unsheathed his gladius and used it to point at the city before us. "Burdigala: the city that killed thousands of your comrades, took three consuls away from Rome, and made the survivors march under the yoke to their deaths. We cannot let their crimes go unpunished—we cannot allow our brothers' deaths to be in vain." His scarlet cape fluttered behind him, cracking with every burst of wind. "When the battle begins, stay together, hold the line. Remember your training, and never fail to protect your brothers first. If we do this, victory will be ours this day!" In the distance we could hear the haunting echo of a battle horn, rallying our enemies to their arms and to the city walls.

"Where is Legionary Quintus Sertorius?" Maximus called, just as I had entered into a daze, staring at the city we were about to breach. "Legionary Sertorius?" he cried again, as I jolted from my thoughts and fell out of formation, my heart beating violently in my chest. As I arrived at attention directly beside the consul, Maximus swept from his steed and put his hand on my shoulder. "Legionary Sertorius has offered to draw first blood. He has volunteered to be the first to scale the enemy walls. Will you let him go alone?" Maximus asked and all four legions shouted their willingness to follow.

My fear, my weakness remained as powerful in my chest, but a certain pride overwhelmed me too. Maximus thrust his sword in the air and let out a lion's roar, taken up by the twenty thousand men before me. I was afraid, but I would certainly rather be the first Roman to scale a Burdigalan wall than any Burdigalan facing twenty thousand Romans.

"Remain at the front and you'll be led to the first ladder," Maximus said directly to me as the legates began issuing orders. He brought me in close for a moment. "The gods blessed me when they gave me a soldier like you. Keep your head and I have no doubt that this blessing will continue." He patted my back firmly and saluted, doing all he could to reassure me before turning away.

"Quintus!" I turned to see Titus approaching behind me, his scarlet plume nearly a foot above the guards on either side of him.

"Brother." I grabbed his arm.

"You'll be all right. Just remember that you are not going in alone. You're going in first. I'll be with you. Your men will be with you." He clasped my neck and looked me in the eyes.

"And father watches over us."

"And father watches over us," he repeated, pulling me in and patting my back as only an older brother can. "Be safe, little brother," he whispered in my ear before returning to his position. An *optio* then appeared at my side and instructed me where to go. I was hardly available, barely present, but I followed instructions. This was it. As the enemy began to appear on the walls before us, spears and axes in hand, I knew that the battle had begun. The war had begun.

SCROLL XVI

"*Tecombre!*"

The command was given. I broke from under the wall of shields, and a centurion helped me onto the ladder. I tested the grip of my sandals and grabbed as high as I could reach. I couldn't tell if it was the ladder or myself that was shaking.

Above me, the Burdigalans roared, already the tips of their spears danced and swayed above me, begging me to meet them.

"Move! Move! Move!" The shouts came from beneath me as the soldiers began to clamor up in close order, other ladders reaching the wall simultaneously. I whispered a quick prayer, to whom I don't know, but I asked for nothing more than for our lives to be preserved. I tried to keep my eyes fixed on the stone walls before me, becoming even more shaken whenever I looked down at the ground below or the enemy above. The plume of the soldier beneath me brushed my foot and I knew I had to move faster.

Left foot, right hand. Right foot, left hand.

As I reached the top, my callused fingers fumbled to find a hold on the ledge. A rock the size of a man's fist collided against my helmet, the noise deafening me, the pain nearly forcing my eyes shut.

I reached for my gladius, struggling to maintain my balance while defending myself with my shield. I fell awkwardly from the ledge to the wall and at once enemy warriors surrounded me. Spears jammed incessantly against my shield, pushing me back toward the ledge and the men coming up behind me. I held that shield as close to my body as a second set of armor, suddenly forgetting my training, attempting only to protect myself.

I set my feet and managed to get my gladius into position. I rammed my shield into the closest combatant. With a cry he pitched over the ledge, back into the city he defended. There was no time to contemplate or celebrate, for more and more filled his place.

A man the size of a gladiator pushed others from his path to meet me, a wooden club clenched in his grip.

He bashed it against my shield, and the pain reverberated through my hand, down my arm, my wrist bending awkwardly. Before I could move, he attacked again. And again. He made no attempt to get behind my defenses and strike my body—he meant simply to beat the life force from me.

Just as he swung a final time, I too swung my shield to meet it. The resulting pain was greater even than before, and I felt I would lose my grip on my shield, but in this second, my enemy was defenseless. If I didn't strike now, he and his companions might swallow me whole. Adrenaline, maybe even rage, pulsed through my limbs and gave me the power to thrust my gladius into his belly. It was met with resistance. I hadn't known that it required so much effort to pierce a man's flesh. I stepped into him, ducking beneath my shield as other assailants attacked from my left. I funneled all the bodyweight the gods had given to me into the hilt of my sword, driving it further and further into the man's gut. He grimaced, squirmed. His feet fidgeted beneath him and his knees threatened to give way. His core moved back, away from my sword, his chest pushing outward as a result. In a final attempt to save himself, or perhaps to bring a Roman with him into the afterlife, he beat my helmet with his club again and again. But his blows had no power to them, the strength in his arms already going slack, but the metal beat on my forehead and left a nasty gash on my cheek that I wouldn't feel until later.

I made the mistake of meeting his eyes.

Hate.

Hate filled them. I can only imagine what my own eyes revealed to him in that moment, as the light faded from his view. In one swift motion, his body collapsed in on itself. And then, he was immediately, ruthlessly, slung aside by another Burdigalan, the man's body trampled and swallowed up by hordes of his countrymen longing to avenge his death.

Along and behind me, Romans flooded the wall. Centurion whistles blew and orders were shouted, scarcely audible above the tumult. I stood my ground, meeting whatever foe approached me. I held my shield before me like a fortress, but the spears and clubs of the enemy were too many. They came from all sides. Nor were they trained attacks, but rather wild, savage jabs, attempting to perforate anything in their path. Some met my armor and were too dull to break it. But the blades sliced through the bare flesh of my arms in a volley. I don't remember the feeling, but I remember the cry that leaped from my throat as I thrashed violently to defend myself. As I lost my stance, it happened. A spear found its mark on my leg, just above the knee. The steel pushed forcefully through my flesh until it met bone, pulling back only to give it another go. I could not see the man at the end of the spear, but I swung my shield to smack the spear away.

The Burdigalans closed in around me. I was close enough to taste their frantic breath, to feel the spit of their curses on the exposed flesh of my face.

I suppose I would have died right there. I would have been swallowed up by the enemy before me and my memory swallowed up by the sands of time. But I flew backwards at the right instant, as if a gust of wind or the force of the gods had pushed me forcefully into the ranks of my men. In reality, it was a Mule who grabbed my cuirass and tugged me back into the line that was hastily forming.

Unable to catch my breath or thank the gods, I did as ordered and linked my shield with those of the men around me, stepping forward only when they did. The countless enemy soldiers bashed up against our line with all the fury, the relentlessness, of an angry sea on a rock bed, but we each found strength in the next man's shield.

Stones continued to pelt us like hail from the sentry towers above, finding their mark only occasionally but never failing to make their presence known.

"Push them back—push!" The shouts continued, as we lowered our shoulders and generated the power from our legs to send the enemy back to the ledge of the wall.

Realizing theirs was a losing battle, our enemy's resistance crumbled. They clambered to their own ladders and retreated into the city for a final stand. Those that remained to face us received several gladius puncture wounds and tumbled over the edge to their fatherland anyhow.

"Move into the city! March until resistance is met, crush it, and move forward!" The orders sprang from officers on all sides. We scrambled to the designated areas and climbed back down into the fray. The pain pulsed in my arm, throbbed with every heartbeat, with every shallow breath. But I was carried forward by the movement of the men—no stopping.

I found my descent down the ladder into Burdigala no more pleasant than my ascent onto its walls, my trembling hands and weak knees threatening to drop me every few steps.

When I reached the Burdigalan soil, the enemy had broken even further. Their resistance shattered, they scrambled in every direction.

"Loose ranks! Hunt the bastards down!" The soldiers around me reveled in the excitement of our orders, offering a few chants before quickly pursuing our defeated foe. I looked in all directions, not a familiar face among that endless swarm of Roman soldiers.

I glanced at my leg wound. My eyes rolled back at the sight of it.

I moved forward with the rest of the men, but with different intentions. I would be content if I didn't end the life of another Burdigalan, but I needed to find help. Fast. And there was none in sight.

We poured through the narrow city streets like a flood let loose. All around me the piercing sound of steel and human cries echoed along the corridors; banners, and century flags sped past me in blurs. Smoke rose from the torches launched through hut windows.

A haze overcame me. I'm not sure exactly what happened, but I found myself separated from our men. My entire body ached, the breath in my lungs stung like poisonous fumes. My head throbbed. Keeping my eyes open called for a war with myself, and steaming blood still oozed from the open wound on my leg, dressing my foot like a boot.

A shout sounded from behind me.

It was no fierce war cry, but the desperate wail of cornered prey.

I turned just in time to meet my assailant.

Before I had fully diagnosed the threat, his club smashed against my shield, forcing it from my feeble grip. My body spiraled backwards. I swung back to face the Burdigalan, my sword balanced before me. In my daze, I saw several of the same man standing there.

I stepped toward him only to be met with a fierce blow to the ribs, sending me into the mud hut behind me. My gladius flew from my hand; my helmet cracked against the wall. My vision flashed for a moment, and then he was on top of me. He pinned my right arm with his knee and clutched my throat with a mud-caked hand. He brought his club up again, blotting out the sun.

A roar ripped from me as I cast the man aside before he could crush me. I scrambled to mount him and slammed his head into the ground.

I fumbled for the dagger on my thigh and in one swift movement brought it up to him. Again and again, I pierced him between his ribs. The breath was driven from him and the strength of his grip on my throat loosened.

His arms went limp, as did mine.

Again I looked into a dying man's eyes. There was something peculiar about this moment. This man was about my age, and neither of us looked away. I said nothing, nor him, although it seemed as though he wanted to. I never heard the boy say a word, but it was as if he was desperate to tell me something, everything. His eyes were venomous but wet, his lips suddenly covered with scarlet, nearly black, lifeblood that poured from him in waves. His throat gargled;

his fingers quaked to plug the holes in his ribs.

I grabbed his head and slammed it again into the ground. Not out of violence, not out of hate. It was desperation; it was pain. He made me do this, I told myself. He could have run; he could have hidden. Why did he attack me?

He lay still and I fell off of him. I slid myself away from him and began to sob. Let me be clear, I did not cry. There were no tears. Something deep within me wept, my nature itself. I bit my tongue, blinked fervently the sweat from my eyes. Only a soldier knows this experience, and he knows it intimately.

In time I propped myself up on the wall and made my way to the sword and shield that lay scattered along the road, blood pooling in the cracks of the stone path all around.

Before me was a door blockaded by wooden boards. I stumbled my way to it and used the hilt of my gladius to hammer the wood away; it had been only hastily barricaded. Within, I believed, might be some form of aid. A blanket, a shirt, a rope to cut off the blood flow. Anything was better than waiting until the skirmish had concluded and I could receive care from the *medicus*. My only hope was that there would be no more angry Burdigalans within.

I entered, straining my eyes in the darkness, the brightness from the sun still burning in my eyes. I could make out shapes, but nothing definite. I bumped through the hut, into table and chairs, looking frantically for any piece of cloth. Suddenly, I heard feet shuffling behind me, and I could hear quick, shallow breaths. I turned and steadied myself, preparing for another attacker, but none met me. I focused my stare but only imaginary figures came to me. Fortunately, a breeze pushed the door open, sending a gentle beam of light along the floor into the corner where the sound had originated.

A girl. A woman, rather, was crouched there, a dagger poised in one hand and the other propping her up against the wall. We locked eyes for a moment, perhaps longer than I remember, for in my haze I was unsure if she was real or not. If someone was watching unaware, they might have thought we were having a contest to see who could tremble more. Despite her obvious fear, the girl never failed to meet my eyes.

I looked away. I let my shield slip again from my grasp, falling to a knee and resting my sword against the dirt floor. With my blood-soaked fingers I unbuckled my helmet and slid it from my head.

"Please, I need help," I said, holding my hands up in surrender. I nodded to my wound. She did not lower the dagger. I assumed she couldn't understand my Latin, so I searched frantically through my head for the Gallic terms that now escaped me. "Wounded," I said in Gallic, or so I believed. I moved my hand to the wound and revealed to her the blood oozing from me.

Suddenly a burst of light nearly blinded me—and the girl too, from the look of her. The door had swung open with a fury, two Mules striding in, swords in hand. They stopped when they saw the girl and leered.

"Tasty piece there," one of them said.

"It's hard to find cunny like her on campaign. Do you mind if we share?" the other said, a quiet laughter coming from his chest.

I grimaced. "No. Go away."

"What? Why? Every ass in Burdigala now belongs to the Colors, right?"

"Leave," I said. "Now."

"Greedy one, aren't you?" They laughed but shrugged their shoulders, leaving to pursue more prey.

I turned back to the girl. "Please, I won't hurt you." I managed to recollect some of my Gallic vocabulary. I could see the dagger shaking in her delicate hand, but her eyes remained alert, wary. I prostrated myself on the ground, like a slave before a queen. She could kill me if she liked, and she knew it. Slowly, she shimmied up the wall to her feet, her slender figure that of a goddess in my haze.

"On your back." Her voice was soft but forceful. I rolled over, struggling against the weight of my armor and lying my head against the back plate of my armor. I watched intently as she untied the leather belt around her waist. She knelt at my side and fixed it around my leg, just beneath my hip. "This will hurt," her words hoarse and barely audible.

I rolled my head away and gritted my teeth. "What's your name?" I asked as she twisted the belt tighter and tighter, biting it in her teeth to hold it in place. She did not answer me, but worked diligently on my arm. "I am sorry," I managed to say between grunts. Exactly what for, I did not know. She stood and went to retrieve my gladius. She knelt to grab it and balanced it in her hands for some time. She seemed to test its weight, pondering intently. I watched her every move. I was transfixed, fascinated. She could have killed me then and there, but I was unafraid. I was as at peace in that moment as perhaps I have ever been.

At length, she moved across the hut toward a small candelabrum in the corner, one I had not noticed before. She balanced the sword over the flame for some time, rotating it back and forth. She returned and placed the burning steel across my wound. I did all that I could to maintain my Roman composure, but the excruciating heat caused every bone in my body to cry out for mercy. She placed a delicate hand over my mouth and held it shut.

Perhaps she had simply heard enough bloodcurdling cries for one day.

She tore the sleeve off her tunic and wrapped up the wound itself. I was left with the feeling that my leg had withered, all the blood sucked out with leeches. But I was safe.

"Thank you," I whispered. "I know that you did not have to help me." She gave me a look I could not discern and moved away, back to the wall where she again crouched. Her clothes were humble, even compared to those of her kinsmen. Even before she'd removed her belt and her sleeve, she'd been wearing little more than rags, the soles of her sandals ripped and frayed.

"My name is Arrea," she said in Latin. Her voice the softest, sweetest sound I had ever heard. Something about battle, I supposed.

I hadn't imagined I would hear a woman's voice again. It graced my ears like a swift stream in the desert.

"You know Latin?"

"A little. You know Gallic?"

"A little." I sat up. "I am sorry for the lot of your people." These words were uncomfortable coming from my lips. It was a strange reality in warfare, one you find more often then you'd think.

"These are not my people. I am a slave," she said. I was surprised, for her eyes were full of dignity, the skin of her face still radiating youth, but this explained her attire.

The bugles sounded in the distance. The battle was won. Time for formation. I struggled to my feet, barely able to muster the strength. I picked up my gladius, still warm from the flames, and slid it into my scabbard. I donned my helmet and grabbed my shield. Yet I was hesitant to leave. Something had been left unsaid. Arrea watched quietly, devoid of emotion.

"Thank you, Arrea," I said, and exited the hut. On the stone pathway, I tried to ignore the corpse of the man I'd killed. I followed the bugles' call toward the gates, but turned when I heard shuffling behind me. Arrea.

"What are you doing?" I asked.

"Coming with you."

"What?" I was perplexed.

"It is Gallic custom. You killed my master, so you are my master now," she said. Even speaking the words of a slave, her eyes shone with the dignity of a free woman.

"Arrea, that no longer applies. You are free now. You can do as you like." I turned again and moved off. I heard her shuffling behind me, and she grabbed my arm. She fell to her knees before me.

"Please! Don't leave me. I have nowhere to go. My home is destroyed—I have no family. Please." She held my hand to her face.

"Stand. Please, stand." I helped her to her feet. "You can come with me. But I don't need a slave."

"All right." Her Latin was distinctly Gallic, especially in her tears. She stood and helped bear my weight. We moved forward to the gathering legions, leaving the corpses and the blood and the devastation in our wake.

SCROLL XVII

I struggled to the line, my knees weak and hands trembling. The formation before me was a blur. Though Arrea had stopped the blood loss, I'd already lost a great deal.

I stumbled around until I spotted the Fourth Legion standard and made my way to the Second Century. The men smiled when they saw me and sighed with relief. We couldn't help but glance over our shoulders, silently counting the faces of our companions. Ax broke the line to pat me on the shoulder, and Pilate gave me a curt nod. Both had tears in their eyes.

Maximus took his place at the head of the army, watching us in silence for some time. "Men, I am proud of you." He repeated this a few times. "This was our first engagement of the war season, and you have all conducted yourself as only Roman soldiers can. When you first donned the colors, you became a member of the world's greatest fighting force, but after what you have done today, you have joined the halls of heroes that extend back through time to the founding of Rome itself. Your ancestors smile upon you today. Not only that, but your brothers who died at the hands of these Burdigalans can now rest. You have served admirably and courageously. This war is not over yet, but if you continue to conduct yourself the way you did today, it soon will be... ." He paused. "If you continue to conduct yourselves the way you did today, those Red bastards don't stand a chance!" The legions cheered, and Maximus smiled deeply, genuinely, looking at his legates with a mixture of pride and admiration.

"Where is Legionary Quintus Sertorius?" he asked as the

applause died down. My mind was swimming too much to register the words. Flamen had to nudge me. "Legionary Quintus Sertorius, post!" I fell out of formation and began to make my way to Maximus. Ax followed shortly behind to steady me.

"Sertorius, are you all right?" Maximus asked under his breath when I arrived.

"Yes, sir. Just a scratch. I'll be fine by tomorrow." He nodded and returned his attention to the formation.

"Legionary Quintus Sertorius was the first man to scale the walls here today. His bravery embodies the fighting spirit that all of you displayed today. The wounds that he has received embody the wounds that these barbarians have given to our mothers and our wives for too long … but we can rest assured, they will be healed in time." A courier ran to Maximus's side and knelt down before him, holding up a military crown hastily constructed from the contents of the battlefield. "It is an ancient custom to honor the bravery of the man to first scale the walls of an enemy fortification with a crown and a promotion. I am hereby naming Quintus Sertorius a centurion of the Fourth Legion. He will wear the helmet of a comrade who gave his life for Rome today, and he will carry on their legacy of glory and sacrifice." He turned his attention back to me and extended his hand. "Congratulations, friend." With the help of Ax, I made my way back to formation.

"I truly wish that I could give you all crowns and promotions today, for I am sure that there is no man among you unworthy of our respect and praise. I cannot do that, but what I can do is confer another gift. We will be setting up camp here in Burdigala for two weeks, for rest and recuperation. Each man will be given a pass to do as he pleases, as long as he conducts himself with military discipline."

Maximus called the formation to attention, and we chanted Mars's name for some time, grateful for our lives and perhaps even more thankful for a few days of rest.

After the formation, I spoke briefly with Maximus, who was

overjoyed with his first taste of victory in the north. I pleaded permission to stay with Second Century.

"That close to them already, huh?" He smiled and told me he would see what he could do. I told him that if I couldn't remain with Second Century that I would rather remain a Mule with my men. He shook his head at my foolhardiness.

"I admire you, Sertorius. But Second Century already has a centurion—Gnaeus Tremellius Scrofa, if I'm not mistaken."

"Yes, but we both know that Centurion Scrofa is past due for the rank of first-spear centurion."

"I'll see what I can do," he said again.

It turned out that our first-spear had given his life in the Battle of Burdigala. Scrofa would take his place and I Scrofa's. It was fortunate for all involved, save the man who'd lost his life. But such is life in the Colors.

I was taken to a tent where I received attention from the medicus. He re-dressed my wounds, Lucius and Titus clutching my hands as I struggled against the medicus's needles. Arrea waited patiently for me outside.

Once I was patched up to standard, I was ushered to my new tent—propped up by my new "slave," Arrea. A centurion's tent is double the size of a Mule's and contains a real mattress rather than a cot. Arrea helped me into the bed and elevated my leg as the medicus had instructed her.

I rested my head and exhaled. I felt inextricably different than I had just a few hours before. I felt hungover. I felt like I was dying slowly; though the blood loss had been stayed, something more vital to my life ebbed from me.

When next I opened my eyes, Arrea was standing beside my bed, her hand on my head, analyzing my fever.

"Hello there." She didn't reply. I searched for something to say. "How do you know Latin?"

She took her time answering. "My father was a trader. We moved from village to village throughout Gaul, and sometimes ended up in Roman settlements. He would always tell us, proudly, that we were Roman citizens. But I think he was lying."

"How did you end up a slave, then?" As soon as the words left my mouth, I regretted them. "I'm sorry. It's the fever talking."

"My father had some problems." She stepped away and lowered her eyes. "Whenever we landed in a new town he would disappear for a few days and return with less than half his money, losing it gambling or on strong wine. We'd become used to it—even his violence and anger upon his return. But one day he left and never came back." She rubbed the tips of her fingers on the threads of her tunic. "My brother thought he'd simply run off and left us, but Mother believed he was killed for his gambling debts. For that reason, men came in the night and killed my brother, so that he couldn't seek revenge. And then ... they took me and my mother and prostituted us." She choked on her words.

"It takes great courage to recall a story like that. I am sorry I summoned up such memories."

She stepped to the bedside table and began fiddling with the medical supplies there. "It's no matter. Not a day goes by that I don't think about it. I've been a slave ever since. I was a little girl, no more than ten years old. And here I am, nearly ten years later ... all thanks to my father."

"And now you are free."

"No. I am your slave now," she replied quickly.

"You may call yourself that if you like, but I told you before that you are not my slave. I am a Stoic, and we do not believe in slavery. My father taught me that the man who owns a slave forgets that justice should rule the world. So you can come and go as you—"

"I will stay."

"Why?"

"Because you are the best man I've met since I became a slave. And I have nowhere to go." Suddenly I understood how very bad her captors must have been.

Arrea lifted her eyes and smiled at me. I couldn't help but admire her beauty. Her skin was soft and spotless, as fair as the snow of the Alps—although her face was lined with years of worry. She caught my eyes resting on the dimples in her cheeks and her smile vanished. She seemed anxious now, even scared.

"Is something wrong?" I asked.

"No …" Her voice was soft and reluctant. "You can have me tonight, if you'd like." She averted her eyes, looking at her feet.

"You don't have to do that, Arrea." She stood there for a long moment, as if she expected me to say something else. Finally, she turned and walked to the corner of the tent, where a small cot had been placed for her.

I tried to close my eyes and go to sleep. I had no desire to remain awake with my thoughts. But unfortunately, as many men of war know, that is easier said than done the night of your first battle.

I kept picturing his face. Not the first man I killed, not the once after that, but the young man I had dueled in the road.

A few times that night, his wide, dying eyes appeared clearly before me, jolting me with fear. As the fever began to take me, my strained thoughts became more fleshed out, more detailed. I suddenly found myself giving him a story: at one point, he was a carpenter by trade, then a shopkeeper, another time a hunter. I imagined his parents and the joy they'd experienced upon ushering a baby boy into the world. I imagined his first steps and the first word he spoke. I imagined the first sign of laughter in his eyes when his friends made a good joke. I saw the tears he cried when he learned that his grandfather had died.

Soon I believed that I knew the man intimately. I saw the face of a woman, clear as day, before me. The woman that loved him, the woman he loved. She kissed him goodbye before he left to fight the Romans, and the next time she would see his body, he would be cold, stiff, colorless.

The fever continued to grow, and I fell into a sleep-like haze, completely removed from the pain of my body. I found myself in the streets of Burdigala, propped up against the mud-thatched houses, the Man I Had Killed at my side. All of his wounds were still there, and fresh, but he appeared undisturbed. We talked almost like friends.

"Don't even bother trying to go to sleep," he said. "You're not going to be able to sleep for months." His words were in Latin, and his voice was piercingly familiar.

"But I need rest."

"And I wouldn't get caught alone, either. Because whenever you are, believe me, I'll be there with you. Every time you close your eyes, you're going to see mine." His voice was a forewarning prophecy, but he said it with concern. He seemed to care for me.

"But why you? I killed other men today—why won't *you* go away?"

"Because you could have lost. Because it could have been you." I looked down to find that I now bore his wounds. The same gladius was wedged in my gut, the same violent wound on the head. "Frightening, isn't it? Especially when you know that if you *had* died today, it wouldn't have been you to suffer. It would have been all the people that need you." I began to weep, and he comforted me.

"I don't know how to come back from this. I don't think I'll ever be the same." I could tell I'd upset him.

"Stop. If you are going to be this weak than it should have been you to die. Stop thinking about me. I'm just another dead Burdigalan. If it hadn't been you, someone else would have killed me. Did you think it was going to be easy to steal a man's life? And you stole a few Burdigalan lives today. But they don't matter now, because they're dead. Their corpses are nothing but a single tile in the larger mosaic of war's destruction. Stop thinking about dead Burdigalans when you can do something for the one that is still alive."

"What do you mean? Who?" I pleaded for an answer. I wanted to know.

"The girl. The girl! Take care of the damned girl." Then he died all over again, leaving his body the same as when I'd left it earlier that day.

I shot up in bed like a catapult let loose. I was drenched in sweat, my body burning hot and yet somehow cold as ice. In the corner, I saw the gently shaking body of Arrea. I grabbed my blanket and hobbled to her.

"You're freezing. Here." I wrapped it around her shoulders.

"You don't hav—"

"No, I don't, but you need it. You can have the bed if you want." She looked up at me, sleepy, but full of disbelief.

"You need to keep your leg elevated." She watched me with the strangest look in her eyes.

I returned to my bed and shimmied my way onto it. When I found a comfortable spot, I closed my eyes and tried to rest. Before long, I became aware of movement in the tent. I opened my eyes to find Arrea standing beside the bed, the blankets draped over her shoulders. She stared at me for some time, and I stared back. It seemed to me that neither of us knew what was happening.

She fell into me, tenderly. She wrapped the blankets around me and laid her head on my chest. I wrapped my arm around her and placed my hand on her shoulder. She nestled into me and fit like a glove.

Breath returned to my lungs. I was warm. A kind of warmth that doesn't come from a fever but from somewhere in the chest.

Thoughts of Reds, Mules, Nursia, the Senate, my injury … I forgot it all.

There was nothing but her.

She was the only thing real, tangible. The touch of her dainty hand on my arm, the smell of her hair. Every move she made echoed in my mind. I didn't know if it was permissible for a Roman conqueror and a Gallic slave to hold each other. I didn't know how long we lay there. My only judge of time was the swift beating of her heart against mine, the breaths that seemed to periodically slow and quicken. The only thing I did know was that I didn't want to let her go.

SCROLL XVIII

She never left me. For several days, she remained at my side. She fed me when I was too weak to do so myself. She tilted my head up so that I could drink. She held my hands in her own and taught me common Gallic phrases. "You are handsome when you speak my language," she would say and smile.

"You are beautiful all the time," I would reply, or so I remember—but I did dream a lot about her during those days.

At length, she nursed me back to health. My wounds wouldn't fully heal for some time, and I will always bear the scars, but I lived. Eventually the fever dissipated and my mind returned to me.

When I woke on the seventh day it delighted me to see her, and I said as much, my voice hoarse from so much sleep and so little talking.

"Why? Did you think I would go somewhere?" She cooled my forehead with a damp towel.

"There have been moments over the past week when I thought I'd only imagined you." She laughed at this.

"Perhaps you have." She warmed her hands on her tunic and placed them on my forehead. For the first time in days they didn't feel like ice on my burning face. "Your fever is leaving you. Your friends will be delighted."

"My friends? Have they been here to see me?"

"Oh yes. Quite often. You are a popular man, Sertorius. Many different Romans have come to visit you. One said he was your brother."

"Was there a blond man? Built like a bull?" I was thinking of Lucius. She nodded.

"That man has hardly left the tent." She brought me some wine, allowing me to drink independently for the first time in a while. "They say you are a centurion now. That you're an important man."

"Important is a relative term. Do you know what's happening in camp today? Perhaps I should go see my men."

"I have hardly left the tent, but I am sure they would be happy to see you up and walking … if you are able."

"Yes, yes. I think so. Will you help me don my gear?" She did. My helmet especially felt heavier than it had before the battle and the rest of my armor fit me awkwardly. I'd lost weight. "I'll be back soon," I said as I turned to leave.

"I will be here." She smiled. I felt myself do the same.

I made my way through camp, finding it unfamiliar, as things had changed over the course of the week. I nodded to the men I saw, and they all greeted me by name. For the first time, the Mules who passed by offered the traditional salute and I returned it.

"Stallion!" I heard shouting from across the field. It was Bear's voice, impossible to miss, and quickly echoed by the other men in my contubernium. They stood and rushed to greet me. Bear embraced me firmly, unwittingly causing my body to surge with pain, but I didn't care.

"Grumble, you owe me two days' ration. I told you he'd live," Terence said with a big grin as he took my hand. Grumble punched him in the arm and shook his head.

"I'm happy to see you," Basilus said, patting me on the shoulder.

"That woman taking care of you must be some sort of witch doctor. You looked like you were half in Hades." Ax gave his unique chuckle.

"It was the gods that did this. We've all been sacrificing for you, Stallion," Flamen said.

"I appreciate the support, friends. I'm doing just fine now."

"Ready to get back to the battlefield, huh?" Pilate asked.

"What in Gaia's earth are we doing, boys? Where is our military courtesy? This man is an officer now after all," Grumble said. They snapped to attention and saluted me. I halfheartedly returned it, laughing.

"Quit that! I won't have you men treating me like some crusty old tribune. I'm still one of you." They led me back to their cluster of tents, where we talked for several hours. They caught me up on the legion gossip and the recent blunders of various officers and legates. We talked of the Battle of Burdigala and forthcoming battles.

"Stallion, we should introduce you to someone," Ax said, pointing to a Mule sitting behind the men. He stood and saluted, his gaze diverted. He was barely older than a child.

"He is replacing you in the contubernium!" Bear added. "We call him 'Lefty,' because he marches like he has two left feet. He can't keep step."

"I can't imagine he is any worse than you when we first left Rome, Bear." I slapped him on the arm and stepped forward to shake the young man's hand. "It's nice to meet you, Lefty."

"My pleasure, sir." I could tell he was nervous, as new as they come.

"Here." I reached up for my helmet and unbuckled the chinstrap. "Take this." I handed it to him, and he received it as reluctantly as I gave it. "It will treat you well. Saved my life a time or two in Burdigala. I have a new helmet to wear now."

"One with a great big plume atop it," Grumble jested. "He's an important man now, after all."

As we continued on like this, I realized something about life in the Colors.

The men were afraid. Everyone was.

We were afraid of dying. We were afraid of killing. But perhaps more than anything, we were afraid to let anyone know. So we pushed our fears and our misgivings aside and instead told amusing anecdotes about our first conflict. Like you might expect, Basilus was the only one who didn't talk much. He laughed and nodded occasionally with the understanding of a veteran.

"What do we have here?" came a voice from behind me, interrupting a story. It was Centurion Scrofa, the newest first-spear centurion in the Fourth Legion. We all stood and saluted. He patted me on the shoulder and looked me up and down. "You look like a skeleton, Centurion." He laughed. "I'm happy to see you up and moving, though. We need healthy men."

"I'm happy to be here, Centurion. I'm ready to get back to the line." I'd intended to say that I was ready to be back with my men, but I believe he knew my meaning.

"Good. Well, I'm going to clue you in on something, men." He stepped into the center of our circle and nudged us closer. "I'm under orders to keep this information to myself until things become clearer, but I'll be damned if my old century doesn't know what's happening when some fat senator's son sits in his tent on all this information ..." His voice fell to a whisper. "The Reds are on the move. They've left Spain and are headed this way."

Silence.

Some men blinked away disbelief, others looked at their feet and tried to make sense of what we'd heard. We'd known of the Reds as this foreign menace for so long, that in truth they'd become myth to us. Somehow, it shocked us to hear that they were indeed real. And we were surprised at our own shock.

But it didn't take long for the excitement to begin. All of us gave different stamps of approval and motions of enthusiasm, some more obviously feigned than others.

"Think they heard about Burdigala and are returning for revenge?" Bear asked naïvely.

"The Reds don't give a damn about the Burdigalans. Or anyone else. They've simply had their entertainment in Spain, and now they need new women to rape and new cities to plunder. We'll see about that, though, won't we?" Scrofa said. We all nodded in agreement.

"I wanted you to know that real battle is ahead. The Reds will make these Gauls look like little boys with wooden swords. Isn't that right, Basilus?" Bass nodded with closed eyes. "So prepare yourselves accordingly. But don't worry. We're ready." He held up his fist. "Mars and Bellona keep you." We returned it, and he stepped off to warn the others.

I shared a skin of wine with the men. Now, no one said a word about the Reds, or about the Battle of Burdigala, or of future battles. We still laughed and told tales, but there was an ominous presence in the air. Everyone was thinking about the Reds, and everyone knew it.

As I entered my tent, I stopped to admire Arrea. She was sitting on a stool by my bed, humming softly and stitching up the tattered tunic I'd worn during battle. She looked up and met my eyes before returning to her work.

"Were they happy to see you?" Her voice was sweeter than honey-water.

"What? Oh, yes. They certainly were." I stripped off my cuirass and plopped down on the bed. Arrea paused from her work and looked me up and down.

"What is wrong?" she asked after a while. "There is something in your eyes."

"Not a thing."

She said nothing in reply, but waited patiently until I added, "The Reds are moving toward us."

Her brows furrowed inquisitively. "Who?"

"The Cimbri and Teutones and their army of allies. They've left Spain and it looks like they're ready to fight Rome again."

"I see." She finally set my tunic aside and sat down on the bed beside me. "Let me look at your wound." Delicately, she removed the dressing and began to dab the dried blood and pus from it.

"Arrea?"

"Hmm?"

"Why are you still here?" I asked. I didn't know exactly what I meant, or what I was about to say.

"What do you mean?" She sounded almost offended.

"Why are you still here? With me? You finally have a chance at freedom, and yet you remain here, dressing my wounds and stitching my clothes. Why?"

She continued to work diligently, carefully. "Quintus, I've told you. I have nowhere to go."

"Of course you do. You can go anywhere!" It occurred to me then that her servitude bothered me immensely. This girl was no slave.

"Quintus ..."

"You can marry, you can have children!" Finally her composure broke. She pulled away from me and hid her face.

"I cannot have children." Her lips trembled.

"Why?" I asked, perhaps more sheepish than I'd been just a moment ago.

"I am barren. My first master impregnated me, and when he found out, he beat me until I lost the child... ." She covered her eyes with her hands, the blood from my leg dressing her forehead. "After he sold me, my next master attempted to impregnate me, since he'd failed to do so with his own wife. But he was unable to." She finally looked up at me, with wet, glistening eyes. "I am a barren woman who has known nothing but slavery and servitude, Quintus. I don't know how to do anything but avert my eyes and wash a man's feet. No man would have me."

I reached for her hand and held it. I wanted to tell her that any man would want her. Barren, freed slave—nothing could tarnished her. I wanted to tell her that I would want her. But I couldn't.

"Arrea, if you stay here ... if you stay here, and the Cimbri defeat the Romans, as they have before, they will sack our baggage train and our camp, and they will take you. You will be enslaved by cruel men again."

Finally she turned to me, her tears gone. Her eyes bore more strength than mine ever had. "Then defeat them."

I pulled her in close, and she climbed into the bed beside me. I wrapped my arms around her. For some time, she ran her fingers over every scar along my neck and arms, inspecting me delicately. "I am staying." And that was that. She was more sure of staying in Gaul that day than I was, and in the days to come I would truly need her reassurance.

SCROLL XVIV

Titus and Lucius came to see me in my tent the next day. None of us could hide our delight. Titus pretended he always knew I would be fine, while Lucius didn't was jubilant.

"You should have seen your face. You had no color," Lucius said. "Let me see your wound." I pulled up my tunic and revealed it to him, pointing out my lesser wounds as well. His reaction was indiscernible.

"You look jealous!" I laughed and slapped his back.

"I feel uncomfortable sitting on a horse while the men risk their necks." Though I had joked, he did not.

"Ha! I'll trade places with you anytime."

"I have trouble believing that. The man who volunteers to scale the walls could hardly be so careful with his own safety," Titus scoffed, though perhaps with a touch of pride.

"I'm assuming you've both heard the news?" I asked. Their eyes widened, and they exchanged a perplexed look.

"Yes, but we didn't know *you'd* heard it," said Titus.

"Don't worry, I'll keep my mouth shut."

"We're not concerned about that. We're thinking of your health. You don't need to worry about those Reds. We'll take care of them."

At first I nodded, until I realized what Lucius meant. "Wait, what? *Who* will take care of them?"

"*We* will. I know you'll want to be here for the fight, but Rome will be victorious," Lucius said, eyeing me levelly.

"What? Of course I'll be here! I'm not going anywhere." I couldn't believe what I was hearing. Leaving hadn't entered my mind. I'd just been made a centurion. The gods had spared my life, so I could continue fighting for Rome.

"Quintus." Titus's voice was stern, no give. "There will be other battles, and you can certainly earn glory when that time comes, but we need you to be healthy first."

I shook my head. "Titus, I am healthy!" Behind us, Arrea laughed.

"Look at your damn leg, little brother. You're useless right now."

"No, you look at the progress I've already shown! I'm already up and walking, right? By the time the Reds get here, I'll be in perfect shape."

"And I will sacrifice to Mars and Bellona that you are. But there is no reason for you to stay here and risk your life. Maximus has already informed me that you have been authorized to seek a medical discharge. There is no reason to not take that and go home," Titus said.

"I can think of several reasons, big brother. I should leave why? The risk?"

He gritted his teeth. "It's a big risk."

"Of course it is. But we're here to fight the Reds, aren't we? You knew that when you joined, and I knew it when I joined. We didn't come to fight bandit tribes and rebel villages."

"And what if we both die? What then?"

So that's what this was about. My heart leaped. Titus was not worried about my injuries, so much as he had realized the gravity of our situation and he wanted me home safe. I think Lucius, too, had been so frightened by my near escape that he couldn't bear the thought of me facing another.

"That was always a possibility, was it not?"

"And what will happen to our home? What will happen to Mother if both of us die?" Though Titus's voice was stern and his posture strong, I'd never seen him so vulnerable. Perhaps for the first time I was seeing him afraid.

"I could also ask what will happen to our home if I return now with my tail tucked between my legs? How am I to earn a living for them, huh? What of my future wife and children—what of *your* wife and child? I'll have to take care of them all by myself if you're gone. And how can I do that now? With no patrons and no job?"

"What about Marius?" Lucius asked.

"Perhaps I could rely on him. But old favors are quickly forgotten. If I am out of the legion, he has nothing left to gain from me. There is no going back now, friends. There is just as much risk associated with leaving as there is with staying. So I am staying. I appreciate your concern for me, truly, but I would ask that you not mention it again."

"And what of your slave?" Titus motioned to Arrea. I turned to her. If not for her determination to stay, perhaps I wouldn't have been so sure of myself either.

"She is not my slave, she is my shield-bearer." She tried to hide her grin. Lucius laughed, and Titus grunted.

"No matter what you call her, what will happen to her if our camp is raided?"

"Damn it, Titus! You just said Rome would be victorious. We haven't lost the damned battle yet, so stop acting as if we have!" My temper flared, though I'm sure the irony of my argument struck Arrea like a blow. Titus nodded his head and said nothing more about it.

The flap of my tent opened.

"Permission to enter, Centurion?" came an unfamiliar voice.

"Yes, come in," I said, and a man who was unknown to me entered and saluted.

"General Mallius Maximus is requesting your presence.... I mean, he is requesting Prefect Sertorius and Contubernales Hirtuleius. He said you were also welcome to come, Centurion."

"When does he need us?" Titus asked.

"Presently. Come in full kit." The soldier saluted and turned on his heel to leave. We followed him.

As we entered Maximus's tent, the gathering of officers looked diligently over a map and paid us no mind.

"Thank you for coming, gentlemen. We're still waiting on the Eighth's legate," Maximus said, distracted. "Oh, it's good to see you, Quintus." I'd never seen him so visibly stressed, even during the bloodshed of the elections. He clenched his jaw, shuffled his feet, and cracked his knuckles. The other men around him echoed his posture. He gestured to his slave. "Give them some wine."

"Centurion, why are you here?" the legate of one of the other legions asked me.

"He is here on my bidding. He is an old friend," Maximus said before I could reply. "You look good with a centurion's helmet, Quintus Sertorius." He gave a forced smile.

"I thought only first-spear centurions were being informed?" a prefect asked.

"That is true. But if I have asked this man here, then that should be enough for you, Prefect," Maximus said with irritation. He knocked back the remainder of his wine and requested more, much as I'd seen Marius do when worried.

"Quintus, have you heard what is about to happen?" Maximus asked as all eyes turned on me. I saluted and gazed past them.

"I have heard only whispers, sir," I replied.

"The Reds are on the move. We haven't encountered their force at large, but our scouts have seen their scouts. And the size of their scouting party is really more like a small army, if that tells you anything about their numbers. They are leaving violence and destruction in their wake."

"The Cimbri and Teutones are bloodthirsty animals. They need little reason to kill," a legate spoke up.

"Even so, they kill to send a message, and it is a message I intend to take seriously. They bring violence, and they will receive that which they seek to give."

"Agreed, sir," the legate replied.

"Quintus, do you think the men are ready? Are they prepared to fight?"

"And he means a real fight. Not simply killing peasant Gauls," the same legate added, before receiving a disdainful look from Maximus. I stumbled over my words, unsure what to say.

"The men—especially the newer recruits—have had a lot thrust at them very suddenly. So many pitched battles at the beginning of the campaign is unprecedented."

"Unprecedented?" A grizzled old prefect approached me. "Unprecedented? You coward! What do you think the men of Scipio's legion did when he sailed for Spain to fight Hannibal's allies? Do you think they sat on their asses until they damn well felt like fighting? The rank and file don't get to decide when they fight! They will be told when and where, and they will follow orders honorably or face the consequences! What do you think—" Maximus waved him into silence.

"Excuse me, Prefect. May I continue?" I asked, waiting for his temper to cool.

"I asked him to tell me how the men feel, and he is simply responding to my question. Continue, Centurion."

"The men don't need any more fights like Burdigala. We won an overwhelming victory there, and victories tend to inspire confidence. While the men are confident they can destroy villages of Gauls, they are less confident that they can fight the Reds. They've heard too many myths and legends. They need to fight the Reds soon, or they'll lose faith in themselves entirely."

"There are no myths and legends, only facts," the old prefect said.

"No, I agree with the centurion. So if battle begins tomorrow, they will be ready?" he asked again.

"As ready as they'll ever be, sir. I believe they will face the enemy with courage and dignity. But I cannot be certain they will be victorious."

"I don't believe there is any way for any of us to be certain of that, friend." Maximus shook his head and sighed. He returned to his map. "One hundred miles. One hundred damned miles southwest. They could be upon us in days." He brought his thumb to his mouth and bit the nail. "But I do not intend to meet them here. We would be surrounded and butchered. We will have to leave Burdigala and find a location with strategic advantage. Prefect Sertorius, ensure that a scouting party from the Fourth Legion leaves at first light to begin the search. Understood?" Titus nodded. "It is still my intention to talk with the Reds before we endure a pitched battle. If we can prevent bloodshed, we will. If not, then we will be in a position of strength." The officers in the room shifted uncomfortably—some clearly disagreed.

"And how will a display of weakness place us in a position of strength?" the old prefect asked, neglecting to call Maximus by his proper title.

"Amnesty is not weakness, Prefect. And you'd do well to remember that." He looked up from the table to address us. "I don't want any of you thinking I am afraid of bloodshed. I am not afraid of the Reds or their allies, and I am prepared to fight them presently. But the Mediterranean is large enough for both of us, if they are willing to lay down their arms." Some of the officers shook their heads, and Maximus replied more forcefully, "Gentlemen, do you not see that by meeting with the Reds, we give them a choice? There is nothing more detrimental to an army's morale than a choice. As of right now, the Cimbri know that they cannot settle here without facing Roman retribution. They must conquer or be conquered, kill or be killed. They are stranded and far away from whatever corner of Hades they came from. If they know there is even a *chance* at peace—after so many years of fighting—their men will continue on with less enthusiasm. Our men, however, defend their own homes. They have no alternative but to conquer or be conquered, kill or be killed." Everyone fell silent. "I will meet with the Cimbri, even if I have to do so alone, to talk of their *surrender.* And nothing else. If they refuse, then they shall die."

A man entered the tent and saluted. He was clad in ceremonial armor, with a freshly pressed and cleaned tunic, a firm purple plume atop his helm. He stood to attention with the laxity of someone who was accustomed to meeting with officers.

"Can I help you?" Maximus asked, irritated.

"I have been sent to speak with Consul Gnaeus Mallius Maximus," the man replied.

"I am he."

"I am an envoy, sent by the Senate and populous of Rome, to inform you that your consular colleague and friend Quintus Servilius Caepio will be joining you here in the north at the head of two legions. Rome received word that the Cimbri and Teutones are on the move, and duly voted for Consul Caepio to receive a special commission as your joint commander." I looked to Titus, and his eyes said it all. Knots materialized in my gut, and I know he felt it, too. Maximus exhaled deeply and shook his head.

"That petulant child always gets his way, doesn't he?" Maximus looked to me.

The envoy stepped forward and extended a sealed scroll. Maximus took it and opened it with his dagger. After he finished reading, he exploded with anger, slamming his fist on the table and sending a cup of wine to the dirt. The veins in his neck bulged and his face turned scarlet. I had never once seen a shred of such emotion in the stoic Maximus.

"These are my men, damn it! *My men!*" he shouted, then gritted his teeth. He lowered his head and fell silent as he realized the envoy could not be the target of his fury. In a quieter, more melancholy tone, he replied, "The Senate has passed a measure giving the Fourth Legion to Caepio's command, to balance out the force. There is nothing I can do." My knees began to shake and I felt they might buckle. I struggled to hold on to my cup of wine. I looked to Titus, but his face was blank and he stared at the ground, his mind seeming to pore over the endless possibilities of what this meant for our futures.

"When will the consul be here?" Lucius found the gumption to ask.

"Tomorrow," the envoy said cheerfully. "I myself left just shortly before his army did." Maximus beat the table again. The officers all kept their eyes down. "If you'll excuse me, I will excuse myself. May Fortuna guide you against the Cimbri."

Finally Titus looked up at me. We locked eyes, and he shook his head.

"To Hades with Fortuna!" Maximus kicked a box of parchment and threw his cup of wine at the tent entrance just folding back into place after the envoy's exit.

Lucius grabbed my forearm and said, "So it begins."

SCROLL XX

Gaia seems to be intrinsically in tune with the events of man. On this day it was, as it has been during many other such days, gray and dark. The air held a bitter chill, and the sun remained hidden behind a vast expanse of angry clouds.

For hours, the Fourth stood in a silent formation, just before the walls of Burdigala. No empty chatter, no whispered jokes about the officers. The only sound was the whip of the cohort flags in the sporadic bursts of winds. The Burdigalans themselves—those that still lived—watched intently and with curious anticipation. They didn't need to speak our language to understand something was amiss.

I'm not sure how long we stood there—certainly it was several hours—before we heard the distant rumble of a marching army. As Consul Quintus Caepio and his legions neared, the earth began to shake beneath our feet. Trumpets and drums rang out in glorious fashion.

At length, Titus and the legate of the Fourth stepped forward and received word of Caepio's approach. Once they came within view, the command was given to open the gates.

"Forward, march!" Centurion Scrofa's voice rang as we stepped out from Burdigala and back into the wilderness. The feeling in my gut was the same as when we marched on the city. We were going to meet our comrades—a reinforcing army that greatly increased our chances of victory in the north—and yet somehow it felt as if we approached a hostile force. Though Titus and I had our own reasons for this feeling, the entire Fourth moved like a funeral procession.

When we finally reached Caepio's force, his soldiers parted to allow us entry. We stood in formation as they broke for lunch. They spread out and separated, gathering in their individual cohorts, centuries, and contubernium. We stood there, at attention, while they fed themselves, laughing and sharing stories as we had in Burdigala.

It began to rain—the kind of rainfall that scalds the skin. Each drop felt like frozen knives against the bare flesh of our forearms, but nevertheless, we were left to stand there for a great length of time. I interpreted this as a statement.

As they dined, I spotted my old mentor Quintus striding through the camp. He took command of the legion with a halfhearted salute and looked us over. He wiped the breadcrumbs from his hands onto his tunic and picked at the food in his teeth.

When Caepio used to tell stories of how he'd once been a conquering general, I always found it hard to imagine him in armor. Nor could I picture in him the commanding aura that men like Marius were famous for. But here he stood now, in a breastplate and helm so finely crafted that it made Maximus's look like a Mule's kit. Though his vain patrician gait was still apparent, he did not look like an imposter in his armor.

"So this is the Fourth Legion?" he asked and nodded. His voice was so familiar to my ears and instantly reminded me of every experience I'd had in Gnaeus's home. "I applaud and salute the efforts of my consular colleague in preparing you men for what lies ahead. You certainly look the part." He clasped his hands behind his back and strutted before the formation, analyzing each face.

To my relief, he didn't seem to spot me.

"But let us get one thing out of the way: you are my legion now. You are my men. We will do things my way, not your former commander's, and you will obey my orders to the letter or you will be punished accordingly. I call on you to remember that my colleague has never before commanded an army without the watchful eye of his father-in-law. He seems to have done an adequate job, though I'm sure this has been a trial-and-error command for him thus far." Some of Caepio's officers laughed. "I, on the other hand, have conquered an enemy. I know what it is like to wear a laurel of victory and enter Rome's gates as a conqueror, as an imperator. If you men fulfill your duties and perform them admirably, perhaps you will be with me when I enter Rome triumphant for the second time." He continued to analyze the men; perhaps he searched for me. Titus stood at the front of the formation with the legate, just paces from Caepio, but they never met eyes. "I am about to release you to your centurions and to lunch. Eat quickly, for we are leaving this godforsaken corner of Gaul before nightfall. Dismissed." This time, Terence and Grumble had no colorful quips, nothing about the Colors or spit-shining gear. Ax and Bear gave us no cheerful anecdotes. Flamen said nothing of the gods. We were all silent for some time.

"All right men, start lining up for grub," I said to them, not knowing what other orders to impart.

"Centurion Sertorius?" I heard a voice from the distance.

"Moving!" I shouted, as taught, in the direction of the voice. It belonged to one of Caepio's tribunes. I stopped and saluted. He didn't care to return it.

"The general requests your presence," he said, "now." I failed to hide my dismay, but nodded to Basilus to assume control of the century, and I set off to find the man I had vowed to destroy.

It didn't take long to find him. Even against the darkened sky, Caepio's armor glistened. Titus and I stood at attention beside each other, as Caepio conversed with a Gallic tribal elder. I couldn't hear what they said, but the man seemed to enjoy divulging whatever information he gave.

The Gaul wore fur robes and a ring on every finger, but even from where I stood I could smell his stench. He smelled like grease and bear fat. His teeth were rotten, his hair matted.

A man approached us: Lucius Reginus. Apparently Quintus had found a way to bring his companion with him. I spied the tribune's crest on his breastplate.

"The consul has been anxious to speak with you both." The distaste was prevalent in Reginus's voice. "When he addresses you, do not utter a word unless you are directed to do so." His lip curled, as if we were a cheap wine he desired to spit out. "Remain at attention until the consul is ready to speak with you." And that is what we did. Quintus Caepio continued to converse for some time with the Gaul, a translator standing by.

Before long, another man arrived before us. He removed his helmet and handed it to his aide. He turned and greeted me with a halfcocked grin. I couldn't place him at first, but eventually recognized Sextus Caesar.

"If it isn't Marius's old friend!" he said, patting my shoulder abrasively.

"Sir." I nodded, but avoided eye contact.

"Don't remember me?"

"I do."

"Just don't like me, then?" He scoffed.

"So it was you?"

"Yes, it was I." He bowed as if at the end of a play. "I betrayed Marius and almost had your little friend killed."

"Marius is your brother-in-law. How could you betray him?" Titus, beside me, looked bewildered.

Sextus shrugged. "I saw an opportunity and I took it. My brother married into a senatorial family, my brother-in-law rules the world, and yet I was left with nothing. So, I decided to forge my own path."

"And what did Caepio promise you?"

"Now, now." He wagged his finger as if scolding children. "You best call him by his title these days. He brought me here, didn't he?" He stepped closer and leaned in as if telling me a secret. "Caepio needed a senator outside of his party to propose the bill that appointed him special commander here in the north. As a most gracious thank you, I was made legate, under the divine auspices of our great consul."

"How could you do that?" I demanded, unable to hide my disgust.

He smiled and shrugged again. "It wasn't very difficult. This is Rome, after all, not Plato's Republic." He came so close to me that I could smell his breath. "It's a shame those scoundrels didn't finish the job, isn't it? Then maybe I could have been consul." He patted my face and stepped away. I did all I could to restrain myself.

"Marius will kill you if he finds out."

"Then I must silence any little rats who might tell him." He pretended to turn and lunge at me before bellowing and walking away.

I thought I'd escaped Roman politics when I left for the north. But it had followed me. Its reach was inescapable.

After some time, Caepio waved off the Gallic man. He then spoke with Reginus and some other officers before he finally turned to us.

"Well," he chuckled and looked us up and down, "the gods truly do have a sense of humor." He moved in front of us with the arrogance I imagined he had on the day of his Triumph. He took his time before continuing, clearly basking in what he believed to be his final victory over us. "Now your lives are in my hands. I have the legal authority to do with you as I wish. I can have you flogged. I can have you demoted.…." He stopped and looked at my rank. "Really? A centurion? I thought Marius and his puppy dog would have taken better care of you." He shook his head and smiled triumphantly. "I have the legal right to kill you, if I so desire." He savored the sweetness of every word.

"You have the legal right, but not the moral right," Titus spoke up. "Sir." He remained at attention and kept his eyes forward. "The gods would bring death and dishonor to you and your house."

Caepio's face distorted. "Your brother made similar threats to me and my family before he left our care. And besides, haven't the gods brought you here, so that you may receive the punishment that I see fit?"

"Your political maneuverings brought us here. Along with the entire Fourth Legion," I said. This time Caepio did not reply.

"I have the right to kill you, but I do not intend to. Despite the indecency you have shown me and my family—even after all the generosity we showed to the both of you—I will show you clemency still. I need able-bodied men, even if they are treacherous, cowardly, and disloyal." I bit my tongue. If I'd lashed out, Caepio surely wouldn't have hesitated to change his mind. "We will be in battle within three days. That man just informed me of the largest treasury in Gaul, so we will be attacking Tolosa to capture it."

"But, Consul, we've never had any quarrel with Tolosa," Titus said. We were prisoners, as sure as if irons had been strapped to our ankles.

"I don't care." Caepio shook his head. "They have gold and we need it to fund our campaign." He approached me, so close I could hear the whistle of his nose as he breathed. "You will be ready for battle and your legion will be in first order of march."

"Consul, Quintus is not well. He isn't ready for battle," Titus interjected, pleading.

"Again, I do not care. If you are unwell, I will have you stripped of rank, discharged from the army, and sent back to whatever pigspawn village you people hail from. And believe me, I would like nothing more than to send you packing with your tail between your legs." I met his venomous eyes.

"I am fine. I'm prepared for movement and for battle."

"Just as well." He shrugged. "Perhaps the Gauls will finish what they started and sever your leg clean off." He nodded to my wound. "Tell your men to be ready. First and Second Century, Fourth Legion will be the first to enter Tolosa's walls." I saluted, despite the disgust I felt in doing so. We turned to leave. "And make your peace with the gods now. Who knows if you will have time to do so later?"

SCROLL XXI

This march was different. Everything about it was different. Something in the air, maybe. For the first time I stood out from the century, beside my contubernium, as a centurion. We didn't talk much. It didn't seem like there was much that needed to be said; we already knew how everyone felt.

I'll admit the march was hard. I struggled just to keep the pace count, to keep my legs moving in rhythm. Ax, who was closest to me, nudged me once and asked how I was doing. I nodded and continued without saying anything more. I wanted to fall out and travel at a slower pace with the other injured soldiers at the back of the formation. But I had signed myself up to go on, and therefore I was determined to do so without complaining or wavering.

When we'd marched under Maximus, he'd treated us to his presence occasionally. He would lead his horse to the front of the line and work his way back, speaking with the Mules and the centurions, inspiring us and ensuring that morale was high.

We enjoyed no such pleasantries under Caepio.

He didn't even travel on horse. Perhaps it was too cold for him, or perhaps the strain of horseback was too much for him to bear. He was carried in a litter, toward the back of the formation and heavily guarded. Sextus Caesar would occasionally ride up beside us on his giant steed, but would only wink at me before gallivanting off to find other Mules to taunt.

Perhaps this was Caepio's greatest flaw. That he did not expose himself to Gaul. He did not see what we saw. For, like I said, this march was different. Why? Because the Reds had been there. Their scouting force seemed to have arrived at every point along our journey but disappeared like ghosts, leaving no evidence of their presence except for the carnage and destruction they left in their wake.

The first time we saw it was on patrol. While marching under Caepio, it seemed that every guard duty, patrol, and mess duty was given to the Fourth.

"How come it always falls to us to do these damn things?" Grumble asked, echoing our irritation. These details always came at the end of a long day's march, so we still had to walk around Gaul in full kit while the rest of the men relaxed.

"Because we're still Maximus's legion to Caepio and our lives are expendable." Though I never mentioned it, I was always suspicious that Caepio had made certain that most of these tasks trickled down to my century in particular.

The patrols were certainly a nuisance, but I didn't mind them. It was nice to get away with just my men. It made me feel like a real centurion. And it gave us some time to move without keeping in step and to enjoy the wind on our faces. We usually spent the time talking about the other legions or listening to Terence's impressions of Sextus Caesar and General Caepio.

While we entertained ourselves in this way, paying only minimal attention to our surroundings, one of the men in my century yelled for me.

"Centurion, there is a billow of smoke coming from over there." He pointed across the distance. A light gray smoke was indeed pouring into the sky behind a grassy knoll.

"Good eye, soldier. Let's move." I turned the men about and we double-timed to the hill. As the hundred of us reached it, we saw before us a small Roman garrison, all its buildings burned and its soldiers slaughtered.

"Gods help us," some of us said.

"Everything down there looks halfway to Hades," Terence said. "No sense in going closer."

I shook my head. "Our orders are to clear the area and report any activity. I think this constitutes as activity, don't you?" I patted him on the shoulder and led the men down the hill.

Even from a distance, the smell warned us to come no further. Rotting or roasting flesh, burning foundations, loosened bowels.

I gave the order. "Spread out by contubernium."

Everywhere we looked, the ground was covered with bodies of dead Romans. The tops of the aged pines surrounding the small camp shook with the ascending—perhaps lingering—souls.

We searched and searched but found not a single enemy among the bodies. It was as if a violent spirit of the gods had come down and extinguished these lives in a single, violent motion.

"How is this possible?" someone asked.

"It's the Cimbri," replied another.

"It can't be the Cimbri. We would have known if they were here."

"That is where you are wrong," Basilus said. "It is their scouting party. They move in great numbers but are as silent as ghosts. No Gallic tribe could have done this."

Though they continued to debate, I couldn't take my focus away from the bodies before me. Many of them had had their stomachs opened and their entrails spread out like grotesque works of art. The mangled, headless corpses of others were nailed to trees or hoisted in the air with pikes.

"There is no one here, Centurion. Let's head back," one of the Mules said.

"We have to bury them," Bear said with resolve.

"We don't have the time. Or the space. There are too many," Pilate replied, but not without sympathy.

"The gods will be angry with us if we don't," Flamen insisted.

"Yeah, well, I think the gods will be angrier with the Reds. And that's all that matters," Grumble said, sighing.

I decided to gather the bodies and place them together.

It is surprising how heavy a dead body can be. These men had been lost to the world for some time, and they were bloated, stiff, and cold. It was almost as if they struggled against us to stay on the earth where they'd been slain.

"Place a coin in their mouths for the ferryman," I instructed, and some of the men hastened to gather denarii from their belts, while others shook their heads at the waste of good coin. "If you feel you've been cheated, see me after we return. I will compensate you. But while you are here, show some damned respect."

When all the bodies were gathered, we covered them with oil and burned them. It is Roman custom to mix the ashes with wine after cremation, and some of the men fell to arguing about it.

"That's a waste."

"It is the proper thing to do."

"All of you be quiet," I said firmly, but in a hushed tone. "Let us show our respect with silence now. We have plenty of *that* to spare."

The chatter was replaced by the crackling of the fires. For some time we watched, unsure how those lifeless things could have ever really lived at all. Our eyes became strained, both from the brightness of the flames and the horror of what we witnessed.

Upon returning to camp, we reported all that we had seen but said nothing of it to each other. I don't believe I've ever mentioned it since. I could give no real response to such atrocity. "All for the glory of Rome" seemed to fall short in the face of such meaningless slaughter.

The further we marched, the more such sights we encountered. Far from seeing the Cimbri scouts, we saw only the destruction they left. We kept our eyes forward, away from the carnage, trying to focus on the cadence and the movements of our feet.

But we all saw it.

We now understood the kind of enemy we were up against.

But before that, we had to survive Tolosa. Before we could fight the Reds, we had to "fund our campaign."

The morning of the battle, the military tribunes woke us early, shouting that we had better be in proper form. There would be an inspection in a few hours, and the tribunes had noticed that some of us hadn't been shaving regularly.

Still half-asleep, we wandered between our tents, or else attempted to shave with our daggers and the water from our wineskins.

I looked at Terence and noticed the hilarity lighting up his face. Before we knew it, he tilted his head back and let a bellow roll from deep in his chest. We all grinned and waited impatiently to hear what was so funny, and I found myself chuckling beforehand.

"The-these Tribunes! Do they—do they not know hair keeps growing when you're dead?" He hunched over and clutched his belly in his laughter, while men from other tents gathered to join the fun. "They want us to die as dignified, clean-faced men, so we can rot in the ground as hairy beasts!" But by this time, all of the joy had evaporated from his voice. He looked down, his lips quivering. His breathing became heavy and he blinked rapidly. We all watched uncomfortably and shuffled closer to him.

No one offered any comfort. We had none to give. It would have made our fear real; it would have drawn it to the surface. So, instead we only stepped closer, as a silent form of empathy, because we were all scared. We were all scared.

I can still remember that sound. It was deafening. Each time our battering ram smashed against Tolosa's gates, the sound echoing in our helmets, we would lose our hearing, and somehow even our vision was affected.

Disoriented. That was our whole experience. Being disoriented.

Most soldiers experience a siege like this, but only few know what it is like to be the first in line, just behind the siege unit.

"Steady, men!" I tried to shout above the tumult, but I'm not sure a single Mule heard me. Our shields were joined and hoisted above us, trying to ward off the javelins, arrows, and stones hurled at us from the barricade.

A booming sound canceled out all others. The gates came

crashing down and orders were given to advance. We moved slowly, methodically, inside the foreign city, in the tightest defensive positions we had trained for. Still, the training was not enough to fully prepare us.

I fell in line with my men, my old contubernium closest to me. One might assume it feels safe behind that wall of shields, but we were no more protected than the Tolosans behind their ramparts. Arrows and javelins began to pierce the shields and rip the flesh of my men. Crazed Tolosans flung themselves into us, doing whatever they could to open up our ranks. Men pounced on top of the formation and stabbed through whatever holes they could find.

Screams began to lift up into the morning air. We were so disoriented it was impossible to know if we were among those poor wailing souls. In our desperation, men began to bunch closer together. "Get your intervals, men!" I shouted, an order that only some heeded.

We pushed forward. We stumbled over the limp bodies of the comrades who fell before us and tried to keep our balance.

We found ourselves in an open corridor, just behind the gates, and the orders were given for the centuries to spread out. Centurion whistles blew and flags waved with a variety of different orders, but it was so difficult to discern what we were supposed to do, what we *could* do. Even as a centurion, I found myself lost in the madness.

Then it happened. I remember it clearly. Through a narrow gap in our defenses came whistling a javelin, and it struck one of the men to my right. Someone in my original contubernium. We tried to keep our eyes fixed forward and to our flanks, where the enemy assailed us. We tried to keep our positions and continue on with the mission. But we couldn't help looking over our shoulders to see the victim.

"Who was it? Who was it!" a cry came from one of the men.

"It's Terence!" came a harried grunt.

"No, it's Bear!" The breath left my lungs and my heart beat so hard that my chest swelled beneath my armor.

"Push forward! Repel them!" I tried to shout. But my voice wavered and my tone was weak. It must have been the most pitiful command ever issued by a Roman centurion.

A fresh wave of assailants met us, angry and violent. Clubs smashed against my shield and sent shockwaves down my arm and spine. I felt that my wrist might snap. I tried to plant my feet, but my ankles threatened to lock and give way beneath me.

And so we pushed on. We shoved our swords past our shields at whatever was before us, and shoved harder when met with resistance. If I killed in that battle, I'll never know. In that frenzy it is impossible to keep up with anything—no time to pause or reflect, no stolen glances of dying faces that could haunt me in my dreams.

So this was how I experienced Tolosa. I don't know what the history books will tell you, and I don't really care. For me and my men, it was mayhem. Just bloodshed. Our only thoughts were of survival and our comrade who had fallen from the javelin.

As the Tolosans fled back to the inner parts of the city for a final defense, we broke ranks and ran to our fallen friend. I shouldn't have allowed it, but there was nothing I could do. My entire contubernium had to know who among us was lost. My men couldn't march a single step without knowing, nor could I.

We searched for some time, frantically, and it was a difficult task in that sea of corpses, Roman and otherwise. Finally we spotted him. He didn't really look like anyone we knew, but we were certain. It was Bear. We gathered around him.

"Bear, Bear!" we shouted as he raised a fist.

"I'm fine, I'm fine," he said over and over again, but we could see dark blood pooling in the corners of his lips. We searched for the wound and at first found nothing. Foolish relief rushed over us for a split second, until we saw that his shield was propped up over his torso. Slowly, Pilate leaned forward and pulled back the shield, revealing the broken end of a javelin wedged into Bear's stomach, blood and tissue spilling out around it. "Wait, is it bad? Is it bad?" he asked, squirming.

His teeth began to chatter as if he were freezing. Blood spilled over his chin like a broken fountain with each breath. We tried to restrain him, as gently as we could, but he kept trying to feel of the wound and the javelin.

"Bear, stop! Stop!" We knew he couldn't remove the spear. We didn't want to see what would happen. Finally, we forced him to lie back.

"Oh gods, am I going to die?" he asked, his wet eyes frantically searching for hope in each one of us.

"No, no, Bear! We're going to get you to a medicus and they're going to patch you right up. You'll be back in the ranks within a few weeks." Ax pulled Bear's face toward him and nodded comfortingly.

"You'll be just fine, pal," Grumble said, taking hold of one of his hands.

"We aren't going to let anything happen to you." My voice shook. Flamen knelt behind us and prayed. Terence tried to hide the tears on his face.

Bear wasn't convinced. He shook violently and a groan came from deep in his chest.

"Bear, Bear ..." Basilus stepped forward and took one of his hands between both his own. "Look at me.... Look at me...." he said, his voice calm and soft.

"Okay," Bear managed.

"You are going to die." Bear seemed to soften at first, but eventually he began to weep. Our hearts broke.

"What? I can't die. I can't...."

"No, Bear, look at me. Look in my eyes. It's okay." He pulled Bear's hand to his chest. "It's all right. You are going to die, but you aren't going to die alone. We're here with you." We all stepped to him and placed a hand somewhere on him, one by one.

"I ... I ca— I can't ..."

"Shh, it's okay. Tell me, who do you love the most?" Bear thought about it for a moment, a soft breath lifting up from his chest.

"My mama.... My mama...."

"Think of her. Remember what your mother looks like. Let go of everything you don't want to take with you. Think of better times. Think of your home now." Bear looked up at the sky. His legs squirmed beneath our fingers, but he was calm. He convulsed a few times, and his breaths became forced and infrequent. "Just let go. Relax your limbs. Feel the warmth in your fingers and toes? Do you see all those nice colors?"

Bear nodded. He kept his eyes fixed above him on the sky, until he tried to say something. He whispered. His lips moved with the last thing he wanted to tell us. He fixed his eyes on Basilus. And he just ... stopped. Nothing changed, but we knew. Basilus lowered his head and closed Bear's eyes with the palm of his hand.

"Oh ... gods." Terence moaned from beside me. Ax leaned back and clutched his face, rocking slowly back and forth.

"Shit ..." Grumble said, biting one of his knuckles and closing his eyes.

"Until Elysium, brother," added Flamen.

"Hadn't even been with a damned woman," Pilate managed to say.

"He was ... the best," Ax added. I wiped a tear from my eye and pulled a coin from my belt. I slid it between his lips, a token for the ferryman to see him safely into the afterlife.

"We'll miss you, kid," Basilus said, patting Bear's chest. We all wept.

Around us, the Mules were going mad, looting and burning, like wild dogs over scraps of meat. We heard shouts that the gold had been found and that the Tolosan treasury made King Midas look like a proletarian. The city was ours to take and do with as we liked, but we all sat there beside Bear, not knowing how to walk away or say goodbye.

I wasn't there to see it. I wasn't there, but Titus was. He said the look on Caepio's face when he first saw the temple's gold revealed a glee that sprang from deep in his heart. He suddenly seemed less confrontational, less affected by the world or its people's doings. It was as if Quintus Caepio had already won the war.

I'm asked from time to time whether or not I managed to see that infamous gold, but in truth I did not. What I did see was the train of wagons that carried it off. It seemed to stretch back for miles. Titus asked Caepio why he was sending it back to Rome, if the money was for the campaign. The consul replied that he couldn't fund the campaign with money in Gaul, but Rome's coffers would have to do the job. The answer was never quite satisfactory to those who lost friends in that battle.

A strange thing happens to you when a peer dies. I'd watched as men took their last breaths. I had seen my father go and old Manius Hirtuleius after that. But that was different. Why? Because they were older, they had run their course. Perhaps we who were left to mourn did not think so, but it appeared that the gods deemed it to be true. They were old, and old men die. But a young man? A man even younger than myself—not six years from being a child? That was a different feeling entirely. I would say that none of us were ever really the same again.

We didn't speak of it, but I think we began to understand that peculiar look in Basilus's eyes. In an instant, we became acutely aware of our own mortality, realizing it could have been us, and that our deaths could be just around the corner. Youth was no longer an adequate reason for life to be sustained.

Life seemed absurd, random, fragile. We could have died and the war would have gone on as if we'd never been there. It was like watching a gambler roll a die, waiting to see what might come—or in our case, who Pluto would call to the underworld next. For the first time in my life, I wondered if the gods were truly guiding us, or if it was all simply luck in the end.

After we burned the bodies of our men, we returned to camp. When I saw Arrea, I tried to speak, but could find no words. My eyes were wet and my throat dry. I knelt at her feet and placed my head in her lap. She tried to comfort me.

"Everything is okay now. You are safe. You are safe now." Her fingers were soft and delicate as she ran them through my hair; she tried to calm me in the same way we had tried to calm Bear.

I wanted to tell her everything that had happened and all the things I now understood about war. About life. About death. But I couldn't. I just said again and again that it was awful. She seemed to understand.

She continued to hold me as she went about examining my wounds, which had reopened during the conflict and were bleeding again. She patched me up and dabbed a cool cloth against my head, squeezing my fingers until the trembling began to slow. She helped—she truly did—but I'm not sure that tremble has ever really gone away, even to this day.

You experience war differently from this perspective, being on the front lines and holding a gladius.

It was a great victory! I'm sure all the newsreaders were shouting in Rome. I'm certain that all the crowds would gasp in awe that a city as large as Tolosa was taken with so few casualties. But they didn't understand how much we had really lost. They didn't know those men. They didn't know Bear.

We left Tolosa three days later. Back out into the wilderness.

This further cemented the grief in our hearts.

Caepio had his gold, but we had nothing to show for our experience, save fresh scars and holes in our ranks. We received word within a week that Maximus had left Burdigala as well, leaving behind a small garrison to keep our new settlement from rebelling against us. Both forces would soon be in Cisalpine Gaul, not a day's march from one another. But we wouldn't meet. We wouldn't see them again until battle with the Reds was imminent.

SCROLL XXII

Events slowed down. Our hearts did not. News reached us every day of the Cimbri advance. We received frequent false reports that the Reds were on our doorstep, but all our intelligence confirmed that our enemy was getting closer. We marched at a slower pace, in a hurry to get nowhere, waiting only to see our enemies' plans unravel. We moved south, passing within view of our deconstructed camp outside Narbo where I'd been reunited with Titus.

We continued to move, but Caepio had no intention of hurrying. He had his prize. It wasn't the money. How could a man like Caepio ever care for riches? He'd never wanted for anything in his life. He had no need to horde up a fortune for himself. Rather, he had won himself *glory*. He knew that people would cheer when his vast sums of stolen gold arrived in Rome and allowed the city to feast, to believe that more prosperous times were at hand. He had his victory. There was a glint in his eye. And he didn't feel the need to subjugate my brother or me any longer; he mostly ignored us, allowing us to live in his ranks as long as we weren't insubordinate.

But fate has a habit of changing things just when men feel assured of destiny's outcome. The fickle nature of the gods is the subject of both comic and tragic plays alike.

We had made our camp just west of the Gallic town Arelate. Having made nearly a full circle through Gaul, we'd returned to the more familiar side of the country. Caepio seemed to have run out of places to march us, so we set up camp, and this time didn't deconstruct it the next day.

We listened to the reports of our scouts—both of the Reds' advance and the movements of our allies under Maximus. We were all tense. The tightness in the shoulders, the perpetual headaches. We could hear the noise of the war rumbling somewhere in our futures, and waiting for it was exhausting. I was always on the verge of vomiting. I lost my appetite and the will to shine my gear to perfection. We simply waited.

After a week went by, Caepio ordered all of the centurions to a briefing led by himself, Sextus Caesar and a few other legates, and a few prefects. We already knew the sort of thing we would hear: prepare your men, prepare yourselves, war is at hand … but we all attended as instructed and did what we could to sift through the repetitive information for any real intelligence.

It was here that the rumbling began. It started with the opening of the gates, distant Mules shouting. The galloping of a lone horse. Most of the Centurions, myself included, craned our necks to catch sight of the commotion. Caepio and the others tried to ignore it and continue the briefing.

The lone horseman cut through our ranks, straight for Caepio. I caught just a glimpse of him behind the helmets of my comrades. The rider was covered in dust from a hard journey; he was sunburned and crossed with minor wounds. He was Roman but bore no shield or helmet. I couldn't even distinguish his rank.

A prefect stepped forward and demanded to know what was happening. The soldier replied in a hushed voice, and the prefect stepped grimly aside, allowing the Roman to address Caepio.

"What on Gaia's earth is the meaning of this?" Caepio demanded.

"General Caepio, the gold has been captured." The man held his arms akimbo and tried to catch his breath, forgetting all military bearing.

Caepio cleared his throat and looked back in disbelief. "What?"

"Our century was attacked en route to Rome. All our men were butchered and the wagons seized. I have no idea what became of it." My heart dropped. There was silence among the small formation and the Mules gathering around us.

Popular rumor suggests that Caepio ordered the hijacking himself and had cut a deal with some rebel tribe to stow away a portion of the riches for his own use. But I can say from firsthand experience that if that were true, then Caepio was the most brilliant actor of his time.

I have never, to this day, seen a proud man brought so low. The voice that had always been so confident, quavered now. His eyes darted back and forth, and his lips trembled. His legs seemed to buckle and he fell into Tribune Reginus, who steadied him.

"No." Only the utter silence of the camp made Caepio audible. And then, just as we believed the consul might collapse, rage passed over his eyes. "And what have you to say for yourself? How did you survive?" The man began to explain, but Caepio screamed, "Arrest him! Have him tried for treason! Desertion!" His fury rang out around the camp. As the soldier was apprehended, Caepio cursed the man with his left hand. Reginus and another tribune tried to restrain him, and he struggled against them but eventually gave up. As he went slack, so too did the grip on his arms. He grabbed his helm from his aide and without another word walked slowly from the formation.

Now it was Caepio's turn to wait, and he did so … constantly. He was like a shade in Hades watching for his opportunity to return to earth. Whenever Caepio addressed the men or gave orders, he seemed distracted, despondent. He was on edge, but never fully aware. On the few occasions he addressed my brother or me, he seemed to have forgotten who we were altogether. We were treated, like many others I assume, with apathy. A general lack of concern. The stubble of his beard grew, and the bags under his eyes turned gray. He was never the same again. And I can say with assurance that if that gold had reached Rome, what happened next would have never come to pass.

A week or so went by without any instructions from Caepio. We were left without orders, as idle as a log in still waters. So I waited all day and lay awake all night.

Every night I would hold Arrea in my arms and stare off, thinking about the Reds, about Nursia, about Bear. I would watch her occasionally, as she nestled up to me in a deep slumber. She made me smile. I would rub my fingers over the skin of her shoulder, and it sent warmth up my arms to my heart. She had come down with a cold, and I found myself laughing whenever she snored. Such a beautiful creature omitting such a noise was enough to break me from my contemplation. I would hold her closer still and try to rest before my thoughts returned to me, and I'd lie patiently until morning light and another formation.

It was during one of these nights that word finally arrived of the Cimbri location. From what I understand, no one took it seriously at first—given that we'd already received so many false reports. But at some point during the night, Caepio's scouts verified the situation: the Cimbri were indeed within just a few miles, setting up camp just outside of Arausio.

I learned of this when Ax entered my tent before first light.

"Stallion! Wake up!" he hissed. Fortunately I was not really asleep.

"What is it? What's wrong?" I stirred, sensing that something different must be happening. I began to hear Mules rumbling outside the tent, receiving the same news as I.

"The Reds are finally here. It's almost time. We've been put on standby." I assumed he must have been on guard duty, because he was already in full kit.

"I'll be right out." Though I hurried, I stole a moment to kiss Arrea on the cheek.

The legions were suddenly alive. I could see in the darkness that the men were already oiling their shields and helmets. The nervous chatter had begun, the trembling hands, the tapping feet.

"Stallion," my men addressed me. I asked how they were feeling and made sure they had everything they needed.

There was a briefing at this time, for the higher officers. Centurions like myself were not invited, but when it was concluded Titus sought me out.

"Brother," he said, shaking my hand. His tone was serious, filled with anticipation.

"So this is it?" I asked. My men gathered to listen.

"This is it. They're really here. I just left the consul's tent. The battle could begin at any time."

"What was the final decision? What are we going to do right *now*?" I was desperate for something definite. Titus took his time replying.

"Caepio was invigorated when he heard the news, like a spirit entered him.... He was mad, even. He rambled about how the gods had brought the Reds to us. He said they had placed themselves directly between our forces and Maximus's. He believed they've guaranteed their own destructions. We would have been marching out to meet them presently if we hadn't been able to dissuade him. We managed to get him to send word to Maximus first. A dispatch has already been sent, and as soon as we have communication between the two forces, battle could begin."

"Today even?"

"Yes. Today." He grabbed my shoulder and looked me in the eyes. "Are you ready? Are all of you men ready?"

"Yes, sir!"

"To Mars then. I need to be getting back to Caepio." Titus gave me an uncharacteristic hug. "I'll see you again before everything starts. That's my word."

As soon as he left, I spun on my heels and ran without restraint for my tent. There was only one thing on my mind.

"Arrea. Arrea, sweet girl, you have to wake up," I cried as I barged in, and she burst from her sleep.

"What? What is it? Is everything all right?" she demanded to know. I was already gathering up her few possessions and slamming them haphazardly into one of my bags.

"You have to leave. The Cimbri are in the area. They are here and battle is upon us."

"Quintus!" She strode toward me and tried to impede my progress. "We've already discussed this! I am not leaving you!"

"I will not be dissuaded this time, Arrea," I said in a soft voice, fixed on the task at hand.

"I told you that I am not leaving!"

I dropped the bag and turned to her. I grabbed her by the elbows, tenderly I hope, and pulled her into me.

"Arrea! I don't need you here to die with me! Because I am *not* going to die!" I was breathing heavy. "I am not going to die. But I need to know that you are safe. And I will come for you." Before she could respond, I pulled her in close and kissed her. I held her there for this one moment, this moment that seemed to last forever, but still not long enough. The smell of her hair, the taste of her breath. It was something to fight for. When I pulled away I grabbed a scroll with my centurion's seal on it. The contents were unimportant. "Go to Arelate. Wait for me there, and take this scroll with you. If anyone attempts to harm you, let them know that a Roman centurion will find them and bring with him all the wrath of the Furies."

I handed her the bag and paused to hold her soft hands. Her dark curls fell over her shoulders in a waterfall. In that thin, simple gown, she was the most beautiful thing I had ever seen. Her hands trembled but her eyes were brave. I had never been so in love. "Go!" I said again and she finally turned, holding on to me until distance separated us.

As she saddled the bag and departed, the bugles of war sounded in the distance. A full assembly.

SCROLL XXIII

I can only imagine the look on Caepio's face when his scouts returned from Maximus's camp with the news that Maximus was in the middle of negotiations with the Cimbri elders. I bet he flew into a rage, cursing and howling. He probably called his colleague a coward and a traitor. He most assuredly shouted that Maximus was trying to take all the glory for himself. By the end of his fit, he would have attempted to say that the fool was walking into a trap, that he would get himself and all his men killed.

Caepio always did like to think of himself as a hero. He'd lost his chance for glory when the Tolosan gold was absconded with, and yet here he had a second opportunity. He could save Maximus from the "trap" set for him and become the savior of Rome in the process. So he ordered all his legions to form up, and we set out without hesitation.

The journey was not long, but as things tend to go in moments like these, a lot happened in a short time.

Lucius Hirtuleius

I simply waited in the background. There was a gentleman's agreement that only officers would be present at the meeting, so Maximus had decided a few contubernales like myself should be with him as glorified bodyguards.

I can't tell you how tense the negotiations were. It was impossible for us to look at the Cimbri elders without imagining the blood of our countrymen on their hands, and perhaps they felt the same way about us. Both parties feigned cordiality—rather poorly in my opinion—but tried to smile and display amicability.

The Cimbri and Teutone leaders were unlike any men I had ever seen. They all had striking blue eyes, long beards, and thick manes of fire-red hair. All of them wore mismatched gold armor, each telling a story of personal bravery—as the pieces had obviously been collected from fallen enemies. One of them wore gauntlets that looked awfully Roman. The shortest among them was larger than our tallest, and I remember thinking that if their men resembled their leaders at all, then Rome was in trouble. There were five of them, if I recall correctly. Four of them claimed to be Cimbri chiefs, the other the king of the Teutones. The four chiefs all interacted like equals, but they did defer most important comments to one man in particular, who introduced himself as Boiorix. He did most of the questioning and answering, although he spoke sparingly.

They seemed removed, unaffected. Their decision to show up without so much as a single bodyguard was the greatest display of arrogance I had ever seen, but there were other ways too that they revealed their lack of fear. Maximus tried to speak of peace, of abstaining from war and more needless deaths, and yet they seemed unmoved.

"Are you translating me correctly? I don't think he is understanding me," Maximus asked their translator. The more Maximus talked, the more unconcerned the others appeared, and indeed, we began to wonder why they had bothered to come. The only ready answer was the way in which they passed around our wine, as if they were already celebrating our defeat. They seemed to prefer it to the ale they'd brought with them; in an act of kindness, we partook of what they had brought, and I can attest to its putrid nature.

It seemed to me that negotiations were hopeless. I believe we had all come to the same conclusion and were about to depart peacefully but to prepare for war, when we heard bugles in the distance. The Cimbri leaders glared at us.

"What is that?" Boiorix asked through the translator.

"I don't know. Truly, I don't know," Maximus said, turning to us to find nothing but blank stares. Word arrived. Riders from both parties informed us that a Roman force had arrived in full array on the other side of the Cimbri camp. Both parties drew their swords and stepped up to protect their most important members, all of us no doubt calculating what might happen with their men against ours.

"Have you done this?" Boiorix asked from behind his men.

"No. I had nothing to do with this," Maximus replied honestly, sympathy and shame apparent on his face. Our parties watched each other for a moment, before seeming to decide that we had reached an impasse.

"We will let you live for now, then. You had better start running. I will be coming for your head as soon I destroy your men," Boiorix said as he sheathed his weapon and turned to depart with no further concern to the threat we posed. They left for their camp, confident of their final victory. We stayed in ours, not quite as certain.

SCROLL XXIV

The Cimbri army had lined up in full array prior to our arrival. They'd received word of our advance and were clearly anxious to meet us. We marched in silence, the Fourth Legion on the right flank of the formation. Our instructions were to remain silent, to appear as ghosts approaching the enemy. No war chants, no battle cries, no enraging speeches. The Cimbri, on the other hand, beat their chests with their fists, a rhythmic thud that seemed to pull us toward them like a powerful cosmic force.

Their forces began to split apart and a Cimbri woman proceeded to the front of the ranks. She was draped in all black and wore large feathers in a tangled mess of hair. Her eyes were covered in dark soot. She turned to the army and began to lead a chant. Though we didn't understand the Cimbri language, the words haunted us. Her piercing cries echoed throughout the valley, followed by the earth-shattering response of the men.

A man was led to her. A prisoner. To my eyes he appeared to be Roman, bearing the scarlet tunic of a soldier, but he also wore a beard, which may have been a result of captivity. The woman turned to our force and spat, fire and malice in her eyes as she hoisted both a staff and a dagger into the sky. The Cimbri chanted louder still, gnashing their teeth and stomping their feet. She turned to the prisoner and cut his throat so deep that his head nearly ripped off. When he hit the dirt, she promptly mounted him, and labored to cut him from sternum to groin, pulling back his rib cage and revealing the entrails. She clutched the intestines in her trembling hands and held them in the air, ignoring the copious amounts of blood that fell freely upon her face. The Cimbri ignited in a rage and began a charge toward us.

Most of us threw up, but eventually controlled our stomachs so that we could steady ourselves before their assault.

"Launch pila!" The order was given.

"Throw your pila, men!" I echoed, stumbling to do so myself. The first ranks let loose a volley of the spears, followed by those of the men behind us. Several Reds crumpled to the dirt, but the rest remained undeterred, moving faster still.

"Shields, shields!" I shouted. The men moved closer together and the front line linked their shields. We felt less safe now than at Tolosa or Burdigala. These men were huge, and our shields seemed little more than wooden discs before their might. Our allied cavalry wheeled around from beside us, exposing our flanks but assaulting the enemy nearest us. And the tumult began, a sound that echoes in my head even to this day.

Just as we had volleyed our pila at them, they catapulted themselves into our line. With no concern for their own lives, they cast themselves onto our swords, shimmying to the hilt so they could slaughter the man who gripped it. Others brought their great swords down on the shields of the first rank, easily smashing through some and breaking the arms of others. The men cried out and terror ensued. We tried to set our feet and gain our balance, but I could feel the ranks slowly moving backward. They were like the force of a flood let loose, and we were pushed back in its current.

"Steady, steady!" I shouted. I turned to see the fear in their eyes. I'm sure I wore the same expression. I saw Ax's face covered in the blood of a fallen foe, his eyes wild. We had all lost our senses.

The right flank, where I was stationed, began to find its footing, but the left and center were faltering and falling back. We heard foreign war horns in the distance. Another full force, the Teutones, arrived and assaulted the left flank, trapping us completely and blocking any means of retreat. It is often said that a battle is won before it is ever fought, and Caepio had done nothing to secure our victory. We had not scouted the enemy camp and so had walked into a trap.

The left and center pushed back further still, and we were forced to wheel about with them, finding ourselves pinned by two forces and the swift Rhone River at our backs.

They advanced more furiously still. Our men were already exhausted from the march and the short battle. I could see from their sluggish sword thrusts that my comrades were weak, and I had difficulty finding power myself. I tried to maintain proper form and my composure, but the shoulder of my sword arm was losing strength, the joint was tight and weak.

To my left, Terence hit the dirt. He crumpled over himself, but I couldn't see what caused it.

"Grumble, secure him!" I shouted. From the first rank, Grumble moved forward and pulled our friend from the fray.

A piercing whistle shot through the morning air. I looked for it, only spotting the arrow at the last second before it struck Ax in the sternum. My comrade dropped his shield and grabbed the arrow. He gritted his teeth and trembled with anger. He let out a roar to match that of the Cimbri, and broke off the arrow where it entered him. He picked up the sword of a fallen soldier beside him and rushed further into the fray, wielding both.

"Ax! Ax! Get back in line!" I struggled against an assailant, hollering his name. "Ax!"

Before I knew what had happened, I hit the dirt, lost of all my senses. For a moment, I was at peace. *This is what Bear felt*, I thought. Then, one by one, my senses returned to me. First it was the noise, the booming chants and blood being spilled, the thud of bodies on the ground. I had no idea what had happened. My hands instinctively moved to my face, but I could feel nothing. Everything was numb.

Suddenly I was hoisted into the air. I felt my soul was ascending into the afterlife.

"The centurion! The centurion has fallen!" was the shout.

Suddenly the noise of the frontline drifted slightly away and the sound of an angry river entered my ears.

"What? What happened?" My voice was thinner than a whisper and whoever had saved me was no longer present.

I felt my face again, suddenly noticing the bloody mess of flesh that now covered my eye and the hard foreign element lodged within. A slinger's stone had taken the place of my left eye. I struggled to roll over to empty my stomach on the earth.

It's all right, I thought. *I'm still alive. I can keep fighting.* But I couldn't move. The adrenaline could no longer make up for the pain. I felt like my head had split in half and one side was twice the size of the other. I tried to stand but fell back over. I tried to pick up my sword but had no grip.

I managed to steal a glance at the men, and they were faltering. Everywhere I could see men I knew being hacked to pieces. I spotted a man running toward me. I squinted my only good eye to make him out, but I wasn't certain he was real. Finally, when he reached me, I could see that it was Flamen. He put his hands on my shoulders, and my body, in shock, struggled violently against him.

"Stallion, Stallion! It's me. It's me! The line is broken, the men are in full rout. Caepio has fled."

"Damned coward!" my voice, hoarse and weak, rose from me.

"I'm going to get you out of here, come on!" He began to lift me.

"What about the others? Please! What about Bass? Pilate?"

"Come on, we have to go." He lifted me onto his shoulders. Suddenly, I felt his body stiffen and we both hit the dirt. I scrambled to my knees.

A spear was lodged in his back. He was already dead. All around me, a haze of men were casting off their armor and running to the river.

Everyone alive was fleeing. But there was one man I knew would never retreat without orders. Titus. The thought of his name sent strength to my limbs and I found my way to my feet. I had to find him. No matter what, I had to find him.

SCROLL XXV

Lucius Hirtuleius

The Reds wasted no time in attacking us. As soon as their leaders returned to them, they began to move. By the time Maximus had formed us up, the Cimbri had surrounded our camp. They began to assault the walls, launching torches over the barricade. We could hear the wooden walls splintering around us.

Maximus himself began a chant.

"Jupiter!"

"Optimus!" We shouted as loud as we could, trying to summon up courage in our own hearts.

"Jupiter!"

"*Maximus!*" We grew louder as the Reds' assault continued.

The walls crumbled far to my left and again at the gates. Then again somewhere behind me. The Cimbri began pouring in like a violent flood, clogging up the entryways they had made. The orders were given for us to stay in formation, but as the Cimbri hurried to surround us on all sides, the line broke and a brawl ensued. There was nothing conventional about this combat. We fought on their terms, hand to hand, man against man, sword against sword.

There was no bird's eye view for me. I could see nothing but the man before me. I couldn't tell what was happening or who was winning, but I knew in my gut that we were fighting a losing battle. The Cimbri were too violent, too anxious to spill Roman blood. Our trembling men could barely hold their shields to meet the assault. I felt, correctly, that our men were being butchered.

But they fought valiantly. They were afraid, yes—terrified, even. But they fought for their homes, for their lives. That was the first time I had witnessed courage in its truest form. Mule, centurion, tribune, consul ... they fought wildly, with urgency and desire, for their own survival and that of their comrades. I still carry the image of a man standing face to face against a horde of Cimbri and meeting them still. When he fell, he took none of them with him, but he had defeated his own fear. This and other sights like it admonish me today. Courage: to stand and fight when others run, to do what you know you must even when you would rather do otherwise.

Maximus himself fought without a horse, in the ranks of his men. I couldn't spot him during the conflict, but he was there, being cut up with the rest of the men. Finally, his officers compelled him to leave with the Eagle, the symbol of Rome's eternal glory. When the battle was truly lost, they cried out that they wouldn't let the Reds steal another consul from Rome. But knowing Maximus, he was doubtlessly angry with himself to have left the field of battle.

After he had taken to his horse, he spotted me.

"Hirtuleius!" he shouted, his party moving toward me. "Come on, we have to go! The line is broken!" Blood spattered his face. "I won't let our Eagle be taken by these barbarian bastards!"

"I can't, Consul. I have to stay."

"What?" He shook his head. "We have to go—now! Get on the damned horse! Rome doesn't need any more martyrs today—she needs men who can continue the fight!"

"I can't leave." I thought of my friend. I thought of what his mother would say if I lived and he didn't. How could I return to Nursia and address the woman who had taken my little brother in when he had nowhere else to go, and tell her that I had left her son to die? "These bastards killed my father. I'll be damned if I let them kill my friend, too."

"Hirtuleius, he is in another camp! You'll never find him—alive or dead! You will *both* die!" I thought of all the men I had watched go to the afterlife. Courage.

"The gods will decide that," I said, the melee continuing all around me. Maximus shook his head. I thought I saw jealousy in his gaze. He wanted to stay, too, but he did what was right for Rome.

"Then kill one more Red for me." We saluted one another, and he and his party raced off.

SCROLL XXVI

I'm still not sure how I found him. I stumbled around for some time, the Reds ignoring me. Maybe they thought me already a corpse. I could barely see and couldn't make out any faces, but I heard his voice.

"Fight me! Kill me, you cowards!" I heard his voice. I knew it was his. It could only be his. Fresh strength rushed through me as I angled my neck this way and that, finally spotting him on the ground, trying to prop himself up.

"Titus!" I shouted and ran to him. Both his legs were missing at the knees, savagely hewn off and lying near him.

He flailed violently, lashing the ground with his fists. "They won't kill me!" He shouted, "Finish what you started, *cowards!*"

"Titus! Titus, it's me, it's your brother!" When he finally looked at me, he cringed and began to weep.

"Little brother ... little brother ... your eye." He reached up and put a bloody hand to my cheek.

"Come on, I'm going to get you out of here," I said.

Suddenly he straightened. His composure seemed to return to him. The noble strength of my father flooded his eyes. "No. Fate has made her choice. This is my resting place."

"Brother!"

"Look at me. Look at me. I'm finished. Drained of what sustains me." He looked at his bloodied stumps and closed his eyes. "You have to live, brother. You *have* to. Mother needs you. Volesa needs you ... my boy needs you."

"But I need *you*." I grabbed his hand between both of my own.

"I know you do ... but I will be with you. Just like Father is with us." I began to cry. "I need you to do something, brother."

"What do you need?"

"I need you to tell my wife and son how much I love them. I need you to tell Mother how thankful I am for how she raised me ... I need you to go to them and tell them that I died well. That I died a Roman ... that I died bravely."

"Please ..." I lowered my head, trying to find something more to say.

Still clutching his hand, I looked to the river that had turned scarlet, almost the color of our flags. The limp bodies of the Romans who'd attempted escape had risen to the surface in warning to those who might consider fleeing over those waters. But men still swam between them, fighting the current. My feet went numb as I considered that path. The Rhone was far more violent and swift than the river that had nearly killed me as a child. But that way held a chance. A small chance.

"I'm going to get you out of here." I bent over and put his arms over my shoulders and strained to lift him. I almost made it to my feet before he began struggling against me.

"Brother, no! Leave me. This is where I die."

"But I can get you to Mother!"

"Quintus ... this is where I die." Tears welled up in his eyes. "With my men. I will die with my men."

I felt my heartbeat slow as I accepted his wishes, the truth of his situation. "Do you need me to do it?"

"No. By my hand." He reached for his sword and pulled it to his chest. He gave me a nod and clasped me by my neck. "Go. Go!" he pleaded.

"I love you, Titus." I struggled to release his hand.

"I love you too, little brother."

Finally I stood. I turned to the river. I walked toward it, my heart racing now.

I felt I might throw up again, but had nothing left to give. The memory of drowning returned to me. I remembered what it felt like when the river nearly dragged me to my death. Here, the Rhone was swift, and it taunted me, threatened me with every fear I'd ever known.

But that river made me a promise. It promised me life. It promised that my mother would have at least one son return to her. It promised that my brother's name would live on, that Gavius would have someone to provide for him and care for him. It promised that I would return to Arrea.

I pulled off my helmet and cut the breastplate from my chest. Before I knew what I did, one foot moved in front of the other. This was it, my greatest test. Courage the only thing that could sustain me now. As I reached the riverbank, I paused, placed a few toes over the precipice and looked down at the rushing current. I turned one last time, saluted my brother, all the men who had died that day. Without another thought, I turned and plunged into the sharp, cold river, thinking only of home.

AFTERWARD

He found me in a pile of brush. I'd swum against the current for some time before I finally lost my strength and slipped under. The gods must have been looking out for me that day and caused my limp body to wash up against the riverbank. But I can't give all the credit to the gods. My friend Lucius would have searched to the ends of the earth until he found me. He carried me back to land and pumped the water from my lungs.

I don't remember this, but he has told me the story many times. I woke and looked at him with what he claims was the strangest expression he had ever seen.

"I knew you would come," I said to him as he hoisted me up and moved me to the shade of a few trees. He wrapped me in his cloak.

"What are we going to do, Quintus? Where can we go now?" he pleaded. "You need help. Look at your eye." I have the hazy memory of his tear-stained face in this moment.

"Arrea is in Arelate. She can help me … she can help us," I said to him. I must have passed out again shortly thereafter, for I remember almost nothing of our journey to Arelate.

Lucius carried me the entire way.

When we arrived, the sound of Arrea's voice was enough to rouse me from my stupor. I stood and went to her. I'd never been so relieved in all my life. I pulled her in close and wept on her neck.

"I told you I would come back."

The two of them helped me to a cot in Arrea's rented hut and ensured that I was comfortable. A doctor arrived soon after and sedated me well. When he was sure I was unconscious, he performed the surgery necessary to remove the stone from my eye.

I didn't wake for several days. When I did, Arrea was resting on the bed beside me, running her fingers through my hair. At first, I didn't say anything, deciding to enjoy the feeling of life for the first time in a long time.

"Hello." My voice was hoarse, but she gasped when she heard me. She didn't reply but wrapped her arms around my neck.

"Quintus!" Lucius came shouting into the room. "You're awake!"

"Alive, more like. It feels like I've spent the past few weeks traveling the River Styx."

"You might have been if it wasn't for your friend." Arrea nodded to Lucius.

"You shouldn't joke about that, Quintus! You were probably closer than you think."

"I thank you for my life, brother." He took my hand between his own and shook his head.

We talked of the battle. I told them about Ax and Flamen, how they fell, and about my last moments with Titus. They mourned with me, and they comforted me.

Despite how it may seem, the occasion wasn't all sad. There was still life. We were still breathing, and there is always hope in that. Titus would live on through me, just as I would carry on the memory of all my brothers who fell for Rome and the Fourth Legion.

After a while, we tried to make other sorts of conversation. Lucius and Arrea formulated new nicknames for the "one-eyed" Sertorius and we laughed heartily. When silence came over us again, Arrea suddenly remembered that she had received several letters for me and went into the other room to collect them.

"Lucius, tell me. How are the men? Did anyone survive? What about Maximus?" I asked hurriedly.

"Rumor has it that Caepio and Maximus both made it back to Rome. Some are pushing for them to be put on trial for treason." I tried to find something to say, but couldn't find the right words.

"There is a camp nearby where some of the men are rallying. Last I heard, there were no more than a handful, but more are showing up daily."

"Any of mine? Any of the men in my contubernium? My century?"

He lowered his head. "I'm sorry, friend."

"Here you go," Arrea said, returning and handing me a stack of more letters than I'd received during the entire campaign. "One of the couriers said he has been looking for you since you were with Maximus."

I took my time opening them, one by one, and spilling over the words again and again. Many were from my mother, others from Volesa, and even one that Gavius had tried to write all by himself.

Most of them contained nothing exceptional, as if catching up after a few weeks of absence. They informed me of the training of our horses and how the crops were growing this year.

Then I received a special letter. My mother informed me that Marius's grain had indeed arrived—several wagons of it. The people had all wept with joy and collectively thanked the gods for their blessings. Color and life seemed to return to Nursia, she said.

I tried to stifle my joyful tears as I passed the letter on to Lucius and Arrea.

"I guess it was all worth it then," I said as Lucius gave a slight nod.

"You have one more," Arrea said, pointing to the only scroll I had missed.

Formal and neat, it bore a stamp I knew well. I hurried to rip it open.

Centurion Quintus Sertorius,

I heard about the battle. It's a damned shame. Also heard you're alive. I'll be needing your services again. We're going to hunt those bastards down. Every last one of them. I'll see you soon.

Imperator Gaius Marius

I read it several times. My heart raced though my breath was slow and controlled.

"Looks like we aren't done yet." I handed the scroll to Lucius. He placed a hand on my knee and nodded.

"Looks like it."

Like and follow us on Twitter, Facebook, Instagram, and Pinterest @vbdavisii, or visit my website at vincentbdavis.com for the latest news and updates on Part Two of The Sertorius Scrolls, "The Noise of War".

ACKNOWLEDGMENTS

My desire has always been to make this an accurate and thoroughly researched novel on the Late Roman Republic, and I have taken painstaking efforts to ensure this is the case. That being said, I am sure there are errors within these pages that I have missed. Where no errors exist, I have many people to thank, their works and their legacies.

The most fundamental piece of history in my research has been my ever-faithful companion, the Nobel-prize-winning *History of Rome* by Theodor Mommsen. It is usually taboo to refer to a modern source before the primary sources, but Mommsen was able to distill those ancient historians in a way that remains unrivaled. Secondly, I must thank the late historian Philip Spann for his *Quintus Sertorius and the legacy of Sulla*. No historian has given Quintus Sertorius such a thorough analysis, and without his works, this book would have been impossible.

My copies of Plutarch, Livy, Polybius, and Sallust have been opened and reopened during the several years I worked on this story. I am certain their spines will continue to crack as I dig deeper. Plutarch in particular has been of immeasurable importance to me, especially because his *Lives* compelled me to begin writing about antiquity in the first place.

I should also mention *Caius Marius* by P. A. Kildahl, *Sulla the Fortunate: Roman General and Dictator* by G. P. Baker, *Sulla: The Last Republican* by Arthur Keaveney, and *The Gracchi, Marius, and Sulla* by A. H. Beesley. The impact these works have had on my understanding of Ancient Rome and its most powerful men will become increasingly apparent as this story continues.

Other resources I've used are T. Robert S. Broughton's *The Magistrates of the Roman Republic, Volume I*; *A Day in the Life of an Ancient Roman: Daily Life, Mysteries, and Curiosities* by Alberto Angela; and Andrew Lintott's *The Constitution of the Roman Republic*. Needless to say, there have been numerous others I've skimmed over the years. In my glossary, I've used the *Oxford Classical Dictionary, Second Edition*, where applicable.

Finally, I want to thank those closest to me, who have made this journey not only bearable, but enjoyable. I'd like to first acknowledge my mother, Jayme, my father, Vince, my sister, Courtney, and her husband, Myles. I must also mention my grandmothers, all my uncles, aunts, and cousins. I cannot possibly thank all of them without mentioning my late grandfathers, Buddy Rowlette, Donald Davis, and Jimmie Hutchison, to whom this book is dedicated. Without their leadership and legacy, I would not be half the man I am today, and I wouldn't have had the fortitude and patience to finish this project.

Next, I must thank some of my closest friends, Conor, Perry, Jack, and Izzi. Your loyalty and friendship has been a constant source of joy and strength in my life. I'd like to give a special thank you to Conor, who was (and I'm sure will continue to be) my first line of defense when I write something horrible, and the first person to clap me on the back when I do something well. Perry was also an amazing resource for me on the idea development and implementation, and there are flavors of his suggestions all throughout the text. That being said, all of you have been instrumental to my career and have always listened to me ramble on about Rome and about story ideas. I am deeply grateful for each of you. To anyone else who has stood by me all these years (you know who you are), I love and appreciate you more than words can express.

I should also thank Bynum, Columbia, Bassat, McCann, Leitzke, Gilreath, all the "Joes" of the 489th—in particular, Armetta,

Krueger, Wright, Melancon, and Fisher. All of these men have been a pleasure to serve with and have shown me what it means to be a "legionary" more than any history book could. I have been blessed to work under some of the best NCOs in the Army, but SFC Leavell in particular has been an exemplary leader. He, and others like him, will continue to be a source of inspiration as I write about grizzled centurions.

I'd like to thank all of my teachers and professors. Mrs. Brading, my high school Latin teacher, added fuel to the fire of my love for antiquity, and her instruction will continue to pay dividends in my work.

I must also thank all those who had a hand in this book. Firstly, I must thank my editors, Sheryl and Michael. You must have the patience of saints to work with all of my flaws. I hope that the finished product will make you proud, as this story is as much a result of your work as it is mine. I'd like to also thank my designer, Richard, whose work will certainly bring many of my readers here in the first place.

And finally—*finally*—I would like to thank you, the reader. As cliché as it may sound, a book is only as good as its readers. Your willingness to take a risk on a first-time author means more to me than any book deals or royalties ever could. I hope that you've enjoyed the story as much as I have and will stick around for Book 2 (The Noise of War), set for release in Q4 2017. Thanks again!

Vincent B. Davis II
02/14/2017

GLOSSARY

- *Ab urbe condita*—Roman phrase and dating system "*from the founding of the city.*" *The Ancient Romans believed Rome was founded in 753 BC, and therefore this year is AUC 1. As such, 107–106 BC would correspond to 647–648 AUC.*

- *Aedile*—*Magistrates who were tasked with maintaining and improving the city's infrastructure. There were four, elected annually: two plebeian aediles and two curule aediles.*

- *Agnomen*—*A form of nickname given to men for traits or accomplishments unique to them. Many conquering generals received agnomen to designate the nation they had conquered, such as Africanus, Macedonicus, and Numidicus.*

- *Amicus (f. Amica)*—*Latin for friend.*

- *Asclepius*—*The Greek god of medicine. There was a temple to Asclepius overlooking the Tiber River, and this is where Rabirius and many other wounded veterans congregate.*

- *Augur*—*A priest and official who interpreted the will of the gods by studying the flight of birds.*

- *Auxiliary*—*Legionaries without citizenship. At this time, most auxiliaries were of Italian origin, but later encompassed many different cultures.*

- *Ave*—*Latin for hail, or hello.*

- *Bellona*—*The Roman goddess of war and the consort of Mars (see also* **Mars**)*. She was also a favored patron goddess of the Roman legion.*

- *Bona Dea*—"*Good goddess." The term was occasionally used as an exclamation.*

- *Boni*—Literally "good men." They were a political party prevalent in the Late Roman Republic. They desired to restrict the power of the popular assembly and the tribune of the plebs, while extending the power of the Senate. The title "Optimates" was more common at the time, but these aristocrats often referred to themselves favorably as the boni. They were natural enemies of the populares.

- *Centurion*—An officer in the Roman legion. By the time Marius's reforms were ushered in, there were six in every cohort, one for every century. They typically led eighty to one hundred men. The most senior centurion in the legion was the "primus pilus," or first-spear centurion.

- *Century*—Roman tactical unit made of eighty to one hundred men.

- *Client*—A man who pledged himself to a patron (see also **patron**) in return for protection or favors.

- *Cocina*—Kitchen.

- *Cohort*—Roman tactical unit made of six centuries (see also **century**), or 480–600 men. The introduction of the cohort as the standard tactical unit of the legion is attributed to Marius's reforms.

- *Collegium(a)*—Any association or body of men with something in common. Some functioned as guilds or social clubs, others were criminal in nature.

- *Consul*—The highest magistrate in the Roman Republic. Two were elected annually to a one-year term. The required age for entry was forty, although exceptions were occasionally (and hesitantly) made.

- *Contubernalis(es)*—A military cadet assigned to the commander specifically. They were generally considered officers, but held little authority.

- *Contubernium*—The smallest unit in the Roman legion. It was led by the decanus (see also **decanus**).

- *Decanus*—"Chief of ten," he was in a position of authority over his contubernium, a group of eight to ten men who shared his tent.

- *Dignitas*—A word that represents a Roman man's reputation and his entitlement to respect. Dignitas correlated with personal achievements and honor.

- *Dis Pater—The Roman god of death. He was often associated with fertility, wealth, and prosperity. His name was often shortened to Dis. He was nearly synonymous with the Roman god Pluto or the Greek god Hades.*

- *Dominus(a)—Latin for "master." A term most often used by slaves when interacting with their owner, but it could also be used to convey reverence or submission by others.*

- *Domus- the type of home owned by the upper class and the wealthy in Ancient Rome.*

- *Equestrian—Sometimes considered the lesser of the two aristocratic classes (see also* **patrician***) and other times considered the higher of the two lower-class citizens (see also* **plebeian***). Those in the equestrian order had to maintain a certain amount of wealth or property, or otherwise would be removed from the class.*

- *Evocati—An honorary term given to soldiers who served out their terms and volunteered to serve again. Evocati were generally spared a large portion of common military duties.*

- *Faex—Latin for "shit."*

- *Falernian wine—The most renowned and sought-after wine in Rome at this time.*

- *Field of Mars—"Campus martius" in Latin. This was where armies trained and waited to deploy or to enter the city limits for a Triumph.*

- *Flamen Dialis—Priest of Jupiter Optimus Maximus.*

- *Forum—The teeming heart of Ancient Rome. There were many different forums, in various cities, but most commonly the Forum refers to the center of the city itself, where most political, public, and religious dealings took place.*

- *Gerrae—"Nonsense!" An exclamation.*

- *Gladius(i)—The standard short-sword used in the Roman legion.*

- *Gracchi—Tiberius and Gaius Gracchus were brothers who held the rank of tribune of the plebs at various times throughout the second century BC. They were political revolutionaries whose attempts at reforms eventually led to their murder (or in one case, forced* suicide). *Tiberius and Gaius were still fresh in the minds of Romans in Sertorius's day. The boni feared that another politician might rise in their image, and the populares were searching for Gracchi to rally around.*

— *Hastati—Common frontline soldiers in the Roman legion. As a result of the Marian Reforms, by Sertorius's times, the term hastati was being phased out and would soon be obsolete.*

— *Imperator—A Roman commander with imperium (see also **imperium**). Typically, the commander would have to be given imperium by his men.*

— *Impluvium—A cistern or tank in the atrium of the domus that collects rainfall water from a hole in the ceiling above.*

— *Insula(e)—Apartment complexes. They varied in size and accommodations, but generally became less desirable the higher up the insula one went.*

— *Jupiter—The Roman king of the gods. He was the god of the sky and thunder. All political and military activity was sanctioned by Jupiter. He was often referred to as Jupiter Capitolinus for his role in leading the Roman state, or Jupiter Optimus Maximus (literally, "the best and greatest").*

— *Jupiter's Stone—A stone on which oaths were sworn.*

— *Kalends—The first day of the Ancient Roman month.*

— *Legate—The senior-most officer in the Roman legion. A legate generally was in command of one legion and answered only to the general.*

— *Mars—The Roman god of war. He was the favored patron of many legionaries and commanders.*

— *Medicus—The field doctor for injured legionaries.*

— *Military tribune—Senior officer of the Roman legions. They were, in theory, elected by the popular assembly, and there were six assigned to every legion. By late second century BC, however, it was not uncommon to see military tribunes appointed directly by the commander.*

- *October Horse—A festival that took place on October 15th. An animal was sacrificed to Mars, which designated the end of the agricultural and military campaigning season.*

- *Optimates—(see **boni**).*

- *Patron—A person who offers protection and favors to his clients (see also **clients**), in favor of services of varying degrees.*

- *Peristylum—An open courtyard containing a garden within the Roman domus.*

- *Pilum(a)—The throwing javelin used by the Roman legion. Gaius Marius changed the design of the pilum in his reforms. Each legionary carried two, and typically launched them at the enemy to begin a conflict.*

- *Plebeian—Lower-born Roman citizens, commoners. Plebeians were born into their social class, so the term designated both wealth and ancestry. They typically had fewer assets and less land than equestrians, but more than the proletariat. Some, like the Metelli, were able to ascend to nobility and wealth despite their plebeian roots. These were known as "noble plebeians" and were not restricted from any power in the Roman political system.*

- *Pontifex Maximus—The highest priest in the College of Pontiffs. By Sertorius's time, the position had been highly politicized.*

- *Pontiff—A priest and member of the College of Pontiffs.*

- *Popular assembly—A legislative assembly that allowed plebeians to elect magistrates, try judicial cases, and pass laws.*

- *Praetor—The second-most senior magistrate in the Roman Republic. There were typically six elected annually, but some have speculated that there were eight elected annually by this time.*

- *Prefect—A high ranking military official in the Roman legion.*

- *Princeps Senatus—"Father of the Senate," or the first among fellow senators. It was an informal position, but came with immense respect and prestige.*

- *Proconsul—A Roman magistrate who had previously been a consul. Often, when a consul was in the midst of a military campaign at the* end of his term, the Senate would appoint him as proconsul for the remainder of the war.

— *Publicani*—Those responsible for collective public revenue. They made their fortunes through this process. By Sertorius's time, the Senate and censors carefully scrutinized their activities, making it difficult for them to amass the wealth they intended.

— *Quaestor*—An elected public official and the junior-most member of the political course of offices. They served various purposes but often supervised the state treasury and performed audits. Quaestors were also used in the military and managed the finances of the legions on campaign.

— *Res Publica*—"Republic," the sacred word that encompassed everything Rome was at the time. More than just a political system, res publica represented Rome's authority and power. The Republic was founded in 509 BC, when Lucius Brutus and his fellow patriots overthrew the kings.

— *Rex sacrorum*—A senatorial priesthood, the "king of the sacred." Unlike the Pontifex Maximus, the rex sacrorum was barred from military and political life. In theory, he held the religious responsibility that was once reserved for the kings, while the consuls performed the military and political functions.

— *Rostra*—A speaking platform in the Forum made of the ships of conquered foes.

— *Salve*—Latin for hail, or hello.

— *Saturnalia*—A festival held on December 17 in honor the Roman deity Saturn.

— *Scutum(a)*—Standard shield issued to Roman legionaries.

— *Taberna(e)*—Could be translated as "tavern," but tabernae served several different functions in Ancient Rome. They served as hostels for travelers, occasionally operated as brothels, and offered a place for people to congregate and enjoy food and wine.

— *Tablinum*—A form of study or office for the head of a household. This is where he would generally greet his clients at his morning levy.

- *Tecombre*—The military order to break from the testudo formation and revert to their previous formation.

- *Testudo*—The "tortoise" formation. The command was used to provide additional protection by linking their scuta together.

- *Toga virilis*—Literally "toga of manhood." It was a plain white toga worn by adult male citizens who were not magistrates. The donning of the toga virilis represented the coming of age of a young Roman male.

- *Tribe*—Political grouping of Roman citizens. By Sertorius's time, there were thirty-six tribes, thirty-two of which were rural, four of which were urban.

- *Tribune of plebs*—Elected magistrates who were designed to represent the interests of the people.

- *Triclinium*—The dining room, which often had three couches set up in the shape of a U.

- *Triumph*—A parade and festival given to celebrate a victorious general and his accomplishments. He must first be hailed as imperator by his legions and then petition the Senate to grant him the Triumph.

- *Via(e)*—"Road," typically a major path large enough to travel on horseback or by carriage.

- *Zeno*—The founder of Stoic philosophy. Sertorius was a devoted reader of Zeno's works.